THE COLLAPSE
TARTARUS GATE
1

MATTHEW P. GILBERT

aethonbooks.com

TARTARUS GATE

©2021 MATTHEW P. GILBERT

Print and eBook formatting, and cover design by Steve Beaulieu. Artwork provided by Phillip Dannels.

Published by Aethon Books LLC. 2019

All characters in this book are fictitious. Any resemblance to actual persons, living or dead, is purely coincidental.

PROLOGUE: THE UNSUNG

Captain David Bauer staggered against the bulkhead, tore off his helmet, and let it drop to the deck. It bounced and rolled away like a severed head as he struck sweat from his eyes with the back of his arm. Black, jagged lines across his vision made it difficult to check the charge on his M87 rifle, but he was fairly certain it would kill a few more of those...*things*. Bauer offered a silent prayer to any gods that might be listening that his vision would clear in time to die fighting if it came to that.

Screams of shipmates and the crackle of blaster fire echoed down the gleaming, white passageway. Bauer's every instinct demanded he turn and fight—stand with them—but his mission demanded otherwise.

His body, however, also had demands. Breath bursting from his lungs in ragged gasps, he swept his slowly clearing vision back and forth. There was no telling where they would come from.

Gradually, his vision cleared, and his spirit surged at what he saw. He was much closer to his goal than he had imagined. The airlock and the *Jaeger* beyond were less than a hundred yards ahead.

Bauer left his helmet behind and stumbled toward his destination, still gasping from exertion, but heartened now that the end was in sight.

The passageway stretched ahead of him, a long, curving transteel section that allowed passengers to view traffic to and from the *Bismarck*. He could see the *Jaeger's* gleaming hull just ahead, securely docked at the airlock. Beyond her, the hellish red glow of hyperspace burned, a trackless void of billowing clouds and constant lightning flashes.

Bauer averted his gaze and pressed forward, struggling against nausea. He didn't fully understand the science, but he knew gazing at the unfiltered light and eddies of hyperspace had strange effects on humans, inspiring odd emotions of dread and disorientation. Typically, the transteel gangway would have been polarized when jumping from normal space, but nothing was certain in battle. Someone had forgotten or died before they'd had the chance to flip the switch, or the equipment had simply failed, damaged in an attack. Bauer forced his stomach to settle and focused on his goal: the airlock, and beyond that, the *Jaeger*, one of the *Bismarck's* few remaining small ships, and her fastest.

Bauer looked back, taking one last look at the ship that had been home for the last year. The *Bismarck* herself was dying, and so was her crew. Likely, the *Jaeger* and her team would join them in eternity soon enough.

But not before striking a final blow at the Devil.

A burbling, squealing hiss from ahead sent a chill through Bauer, reminding him that few plans survived contact with the enemy. He spun and brought his M87 to bear, ready for anything, and yet, even knowing what he did, nothing could really prepare him for what he saw.

A hellish, impossible mixture of conflicting biology was clawing its way through a hatch in the main deck, blotting out both the *Jaeger* and the twisting nether of hyperspace like a black hole, limned in crimson, devouring light and life. Blood and ooze dripped from its skinless form, muscle, tooth, and bone shifting and reshaping even as Bauer gaped in horror. A menagerie of limbs—some insectoid, some human, some barely more than tentacles—tore at the deck, scrabbling in the gathering pools of putrescence as the beast lumbered up and out, tentacles flagellating about its body as if in anticipation. The air filled with a trilling hum like song of cicadas as it approached, and a ragged, toothy maw suddenly split its mottled flesh as it surged forward.

Despite his training and combat experience, for a moment Bauer froze. He had seen them before, but not *this* one. Somehow, they knew the right forms not just to shred bodies, but souls as well. Every man died screaming, ripped apart and devoured by his own, personal monster. Every abomination was a unique snowflake, custom-tailored to shatter a man's mind.

The small passageway suddenly filled with brilliant light as another of the fleet's capital ships flared in a cataclysmic explosion, backlighting the abomination, reducing it to a mere shadow against the light of a small sun. The shockwave was enough to overcome the *Bismarck's* inertial dampeners and sent Bauer to his knees. The creature roared in surprise and slipped back into the hatch slightly as Bauer found his will again and fired.

The M87 hurled plasma bolt after bolt at the glistening bulk. The corridor filled with the scent of burned meat as the beast wailed in agony and retreated from the energy blasts.

Bauer, head on a swivel, edged past the hatch and toward the airlock, blasting at the hole in the deck as hands, tentacles, and claws reached up in threes and fours to grasp at the rim. He kept firing one-handed as he worked the controls to the airlock and slipped inside.

The outer door had a porthole, made of transteel, as was everything transparent aboard the fleets. As soon as he sealed the portal, Bauer could see the bulk of the creature surge from the hatch outside and slam against the door, even as more of it continued to flow upward from below. Eyes rolled and teeth snapped as it stared back at him, hatred and wrongness rolling from it like heat on the desert horizon.

Bauer heard the external keyboard being worked and fired on the interior control panel. The close quarters blast singed his exposed skin and burned half of his close-cropped hair to stubble, but he was fairly certain the airlock was not opening ever again. Anyone who hadn't already made the rally point would go down with the *Bismarck*, a tragedy to be certain, but his mission was directly from the Emperor, his orders clear: "Fail, and humanity fails with you."

Any sacrifice was authorized.

The creature wailed and battered against the now inoperable airlock, its limbs twisting into great, bony battering rams as Bauer entered the *Jaeger*. The ship's computer announced, "Condition Zebra breach, main entry hatch" a single time as he sealed the door again.

The titanic blows shook the *Jaeger* for a moment as the monster pounded against the barrier, roaring in fury, then subsided. The silence was even more unnerving.

Bauer felt his heart skip a beat at what he saw through the inner airlock port. On the *Bismarck* side, something thin and white had pierced the seal around the edge of the door. Spikes of bone infiltrated and grew, and the door groaned at the strain.

My God, it's going to get through.

The *Jaeger* was already in GQ, klaxon blaring, her interior lit by the dim red glow of battle lanterns. Bauer charged through the main compartment toward the cockpit. Three terrified crewman, Beck, Meyer, and Stearns, offered half-hearted salutes as he passed. Bauer was pleased to see that were already strapped in and ready for a rough ride. There should have been three more, including Admiral Zellner, but it was what it was. Bauer shook his head at the loss, but there would be time to grieve later. For now, it was enough to know what crew he had left wouldn't be smeared across the interior compartments in the high-G burn he was about to order.

"Captain!" A strangled cry of joy and disbelief came from their pilot, Tim Schroeder, as Bauer fairly leapt into the cockpit.

"Condition Zebra breach, cockpit door," the computer announced, falling silent as the door slid back into place on its own.

"Get this ship underway, Lieutenant! *Now!*"

Schroeder, sitting in the pilot's chair, spun and stabbed at his controls, shouting into his headset mic, "All hands, brace for impact! Underway in five!"

Bauer grabbed one of the many handholds that existed for precisely this situation and looked back at the airlock through the cockpit's transteel front section. His heart sank at the sight of splintering bone infiltrating and expanding around the outer door like high speed ice. The hinges bulged, and warning lights flashed inside the airlock, announcing that it was no longer sealed.

"Four!"

The inner door gave way, collapsing as the beast literally *grew* its way in. The bulk of the creature surged into the tiny airlock, flesh, teeth, claws, and wild, staring, alien eyes, like red icing compressing into a piping bag, ready to deliver the final writing on the wall.

"Three!"

"Hit it!" Bauer cried. "That's an order!"

Schroeder was a disciplined officer. He didn't question. He followed his order and slammed a palm against the bright red emergency disconnect button, triggering the explosive charges designed for exigent separation.

The *Jaeger* lurched as if it had taken fire. Bauer was heartened to see, along with spinning shrapnel, the formless creature twisting and boiling in the vacuum, arms and tentacles flailing.

"Fuck you," he whispered under his breath. "Die!" Though he had his doubts. There was no way of knowing if hyperspace was a lethal environment for the creature. The only sure ways he had personally seen were flame and lightning, and why not? Those had always been the weapons of gods.

"Go! Ahead flank, *now!*"

Schroeder boggled at this. "Yeah, no!" he shouted, shaking his head as he reached for the throttle. "I can't work with you plastered all over the bulkhead." Bauer staggered toward his chair as Schroeder goosed the maneuvering jets and spun the *Jaeger* about, pointing the main drive at the shattered airlock, and switched the viewscreen to rear. "Or this goddamned noise." He hit a switch to silence the klaxon. "We have a point of unfinished business, too."

Bauer cracked his head against a first aid kit on the bulkhead but managed to tumble into his seat and begin strapping into his five-point. He smiled, seeing exactly what Schroeder intended.

"Point one thrust," Schroeder announced and raised his middle finger to the screen as he throttled up. The whine of the engines rose to a dull roar. Bauer watched in satisfaction as the creature twisted in the plasma of their exhaust, disintegrating in silence as they catapulted away from the *Bismarck*. Even at one tenth, it was a lot like being fired from a gun.

"You sure about that flank speed order, sir?" Schroeder asked.

Bauer looked out at the miasma of hyperspace, watching the remains of the dying fleet, some ships burning, others cold and dark, adrift. Another explosion lit the red haze of hyperspace, a small, short-lived sun bursting into life. In the glare, he saw the battlecruiser, and felt his guts churn in horror.

The *Danzig*, the *Bismarck's* sister ship, lay still and dark in the abyss, but she sprang to life even as he caught sight of her, engines firing, maneuvering thrusters slowly rotating her ponderous bulk. Even at nearly three miles long, she was still somehow sleek and beautiful, deadly and perfectly formed for her purpose. With the immanent death of the *Bismarck*, she would be the last of the Emperor's planet killers.

Only, as far as Bauer knew, the *Danzig* had died hours ago. What lay before him was not an ally, but a reanimated corpse, the Emperor's own turned against her former brethren by the dark power of an implacable enemy.

Bauer pointed at the monstrous ship of war. "Ahead flank! We have to reach the gate well ahead of the *Danzig!*"

Schroeder looked at the approaching ship and back at Bauer. "We could use the help, couldn't we, Cap?"

Bauer shook his head. "*Danzig* is dead, overrun. They broadcast their scuttle codes an hour ago and ten thousand miles away. There are no humans left alive on that ship."

Schroeder's face drained of blood as he flipped the monitors back to forward view. They showed only the endless, swirling void of hyperspace, but ahead somewhere, ten thousand miles or so, was the jumpgate to the Tartarus system.

He paused a moment and looked at Bauer, giving him a chance to prepare. "Ahead flank, aye, sir."

If point one was like being fired from a gun, flank speed was akin to being smashed by the hammer of Thor himself. Schroeder had cybernetic implants to compensate for the G's. Bauer had always intended to have some installed himself, but he had just never found the time. It was easy enough to take the drugs when needed.

Until it wasn't.

Bauer's vision narrowed to pinpoints and then to nothing. Darkness followed, crushing and irresistible.

Bauer returned slowly to consciousness and the sound of shrieking alarms and blaster fire. "Condition Zebra breach, cockpit door" the ship's computer announced, over and over.

"Cap!" Schroeder was screaming. "Oh my God, Cap, wake *up!*"

Galvanized, Bauer found the will to hit the adrenaline injectors on his armor. Strength rushed into him, and he tore frantically at his restraints, struggling to take stock of his situation while he got himself loose.

The cockpit door was open and repeatedly trying to close again. A bloody corpse, its face difficult to identify in the dim red light, drifted in zero G near the overhead, blocking the door from closing. Schroeder continued firing at something on the other side as Bauer noticed the half-formed claw sprouting from the corpse's back.

My God, it's onboard.

"Stay the fuck *back*, Stearns!" Shroeder shouted. "I'm warning you!" A moment later, he fired, and someone on the other side screamed in agony. "Shut the goddamned door, Dave!" Schroeder screamed. "Get it out of the fucking way!"

Bauer rose without thinking and launched toward the overhead harder than he had intended. He hit the bulkhead above the cabin door hard and found himself face to face with a twisted mockery of a man, the burned flesh still smoking. As he reached a hand to push the abomination back into the main compartment, the top of its head split into a giant maw, like a demonic Venus flytrap. The head surged forward, detaching itself from the body, the attached neck stretching and undulating like a snake, propelling it toward him.

Bauer shrieked in horror, but he managed to control himself enough to push the rest of the corpse away. It sailed slowly through and the cockpit door sighed closed. In the main compartment, Beck, looking all too human, rushed forward and hammered a fist against the door, screaming, "No! Don't leave us in here with it!"

"It's fucking *in* here!" Schroeder wailed and snapped off a wild shot at the wriggling, gnashing snake beast as it drifted across the cabin. The plasma bolt missed, blasting a hole in the back of Bauer's chair and penetrating one of the kick panels below the control console. Sparks showered across the floor, and the air filled with the acrid smell of burning electronics.

If I hadn't woke up when I did....

"Jesus, Lord, *help* us!" the pilot screamed.

Bauer, too, made a silent plea to any gods in shouting distance. *We just need a few minutes.*

A huge pustule formed on the creature's side with amazing speed and burst with a loud report. Vile fluid spewed forth in a rain of tiny droplets, a makeshift rocket it used to hurl itself at Schroeder.

From somewhere behind the blasted kick panel came a hiss of rushing air, followed by an explosion. It was small, but it caught the skittering beast full in the side, scorching it almost beyond recognition. The charred remains flew past Schroeder and slammed against a bulkhead, then stuck there with a sickening squelch.

Schroeder stared at the corpse a moment in shock, then peered inside the hole he had made in the console. "Huh. Emergency oxy bottle popped. Hope we don't need it."

Bauer watched in grim resolve as bits of liquid dripped from the still-smoking corpse. A small rivulet twisted and slithered like mercury across the floor and beneath a control panel. "We won't."

He shook his head in wonder at their singular bit of good fortune. Perhaps the gods *were* with them in their darkest hour. Now he owed those gods his very best effort to finish their mission.

"It's time," Bauer said.

Schroeder looked up at him with haunted eyes, then back at the sealed cockpit door. "We really doing this?"

"We have to," Bauer said. "Get us a connection."

As Schroeder worked at the computer console, Bauer took a moment to contemplate the huge sphere that hung before them in space, its surface shimmering, mercurial, as alien in its own way as the Pestilence. It was enormous, as were most of the things Imperial forces built, big enough to accommodate a medium size armada at once, a gargantuan hole in reality, showing a funhouse-mirror distorted version of hyperspace.

"Codes ready," Schroeder said softly, his voice husky with emotion.

Bauer understood. This was it for them. There was no way home after this. "Transmit."

Something heavy slammed against the cockpit door. A voice wailed, "Don't do it! Think of your family!"

Schroeder's hand hesitated, finger poised above the keyboard.

Bauer nodded. He *was* thinking of his family.

Schroeder clicked once, and it was done. As the enormous sphere shimmered and began to shrink rapidly, the ship filled with an inhuman cry of fury and the chitter of cicadas as whatever was outside the door howled. *"We will not forget!"* Something enormous slammed against the cockpit door, leaving a perceptible dent.

"How long?" Schroeder asked.

"Ten minutes or thereabouts, from what they told me. Safeties to prevent an explosion from sudden collapse."

"Can we override?"

Schroeder shook his head. "Nope. No way around."

The cockpit door wouldn't hold ten minutes. Bauer was as certain of that as he was of the urgency of his mission. He paused a moment, wrestling with his next decision as they watched the sphere dwindle. There was really no choice.

"Mister Schroeder, I am going to need you to input your destruct codes."

Schroeder stared at him a moment, breathing hard, then nodded. "I guess we all knew this was a one-way trip."

"One way or another, yes."

Schroeder held Bauer's gaze a moment, then removed his ID card from his breast pocket. "It's better than the alternative," he muttered, glancing at the distressed cockpit door. "Computer," he called, enunciating his words clearly. "Initiate self-destruct procedure."

The computer chirped, and the klaxon changed tone, faster and higher pitched, more urgent now. The computer announced ship wide, "Alert: self-destruct sequence requested from cockpit. Voice and retina scan required."

Schroeder inserted his ID into the card reader, then bent and put an eye to the scanner. "Schroeder, Timothy, Lieutenant. Identify for self-destruct authorization."

"A second line officer is required to continue," the computer answered.

Bauer inserted his ID into his own console. "Bauer, David, Captain. Identify for self-destruct authorization."

The computer chirped again, and it announced, "Self-destruct is authorized. Two-minute countdown initiated. Any line officer may cancel via ID card, retina scan, and voice authorization."

"It's been an honor, sir," Schroeder said softly.

Bauer was about to respond in kind when a voice rang out over the speakers. "Zellner, Robert, Admiral. Cancel self-destruct."

Schroeder's head whipped around in shock. For a moment, he was speechless, his mouth trying to form words and failing. "It can't be!" he gasped at last. "I *saw* him die! Those things tore him to shreds!"

The computer emitted a warning tone and announced, "Voice and retina scan do not match identification card."

Outside the cockpit, something howled in rage.

Bauer shook his head. "It can match the voice and retina scan, but Zellner was the only other line officer on this mission. The fact that his ID card didn't make it aboard just saved humanity. Not a bad legacy."

Schroeder look at the floor. "We wouldn't have even made it without his sacrifice. So he saved us twice."

Bauer nodded, not bothering to correct the pilot. No one was going to be saved. But their mission would succeed.

"Self-destruct in one minute, thirty seconds."

Bauer cast a glance at the cockpit door, then asked, "Did you get a message out? To family?"

"Nah. Had a wife for a while, but she met Jody last year and I kicked her ass to the curb. My folks passed years ago. I guess there's just one message left to send. You a praying man, Captain?"

"Used to be."

Schroeder nodded, blinking at the gathering moisture in his eyes. "I'm gonna take the last little bit and put in a good word for all of us, if you don't mind."

"You don't think what we're doing is enough?"

"They say suicide is an unforgivable sin," Schroeder answered, his voice almost a whisper. "I'm hoping we can get a waiver on that one." He closed his eyes and turned away, head bowed. "See you on the other side, Cap."

"Godspeed."

Bauer shook his head. Schroeder spoke truth. The Christian God and his Son, the ones Bauer's and Schroeder's mothers had taught them to love, would perhaps not approve. But Bauer had not carried so much faith for them in the last few years. In truth, he had begun to prefer other gods, the gods of forefathers millennia dead, who would better understand the things he had to do in service of his Empire. They, he knew, would smile on a warrior who fought and died well.

As for Schroeder, well, Bauer could take care of that on his own. He raised his weapon and pointed it at the back of Schroeder's head. Part of him wanted to say something, to apologize, but it was not only a risk he couldn't afford to take, but also a burden Tim shouldn't have to bear. Let him wake in the presence of his Lord, his conscience clear, his hands unstained with his own blood.

Bauer fired. Schroeder's headless corpse went slack in the pilot's chair, charred stump of neck smoking, the small amount of blood that leaked past the cauterized wound pooling into a wet, red sphere above his lifeless body.

As the computer counted down the final minute of the self-destruct sequence, Bauer sat and waited in silence. He would meet death with dignity, head on, unflinching.

"Thirty seconds to self-destruct."

"Zellner, Robert, Admiral. Cancel self-destruct," the creature tried again.

"Voice and retina scan do not match identification card," the computer announced. The beast roared again. Bauer jumped at the sound of a tremendous impact against the cockpit door.

"*We will rend you!*" the thing screamed in an unearthly voice, a hellish choir of hatred and fury.

The hammering began, blow after blow, titanic, monstrous strikes that dented the door, then slowly began bending it in the frame, and Bauer realized with sudden clarity that in many ways, the creature was offering him a gift.

Perhaps they thought more alike than anyone had imagined. No warrior wanted to die peacefully, waiting for the inevitable. Better to meet the end grappling with the enemy than simply accepting fate.

"Twenty seconds to self-destruct. Condition Zebra breach, cockpit door."

His mind went to his wife, to the son and daughter he would never see again, but whom his sacrifice would preserve—Jehovah, Odin, and all other deities willing. Whatever mythology one embraced at the end, this enemy, this a nameless terror from the void, an enemy with no form or name, surely qualified as a demon.

And if demons were real, perhaps, just perhaps, so was the afterlife, and glory beyond.

The blows continued, a drumbeat now, to accompany the still blaring klaxon, a final symphony of destruction. What remained of Bauer's fear, his concern for his mortal shell, slipped away completely as he overrode his rifle's safeties and adjusted the output to maximum. He knew how this ended now, and he was comfortable with it.

"Ten seconds to self-destruct. Condition Zebra breach, cockpit door."

The beast struck the door a final blow, and the plasteel gave way, folding in on itself to reveal a nightmare of flesh. The rest of Bauer's crew, all three of them, were twisted and merged together in a writhing mass of blood, bone, and glistening teeth and claws. A head belonging to the ship's medic, Beck, rose above the squat, rippling body on a yard-long, bloody neck, hate-filled eyes burning bright and malevolent.

Beck's face twisted in rage, and his face split wide at the mouth, ragged fangs erupting from his gumline. *"Rend you! Consume!"* it shrieked.

Bauer smiled as he brought his weapon to bear, thinking of a classic book he had read to his son just a year ago. It was an ancient work, a tale of wizards and warriors and the eternal struggle of good versus evil. It wasn't quite as old as Shakespeare's work, but it had the same sort of staying power, a time-less classic.

"*You shall not pass!*" he roared.

"Two…"

The creature surged forward, its battle cry a keening shriek and the rising sound of cicadas.

Bauer fired the M87. His face burned as the weapon discharged its full capacity at once in that final, brief moment, hurling the equivalent of a fist-sized star at the twisted horror standing before him.

"One…."

At the ass end of the galaxy, in a nowhere star system named Tartarus, Captain David Bauer and his gallant crew entered Valhalla in a blaze of light and fury, dragging behind them the shattered corpses of their enemies.

Their sacrifice was but one of many.

1

ANY GIVEN TUESDAY

Josiah Bleys awoke from a perfectly lovely dream, one involving several young women and a large amount of ill-gotten credits, to the sound of a man screaming. He clawed through the disorientation of sleep, memory rushing into his mind like seawater filling a sinking ship, the realization of where he was and just what sort of position he likely occupied galvanizing him with urgency.

The cells lined both sides of the broad aisle. On the left were the standard issue bars and open-air toilets for the prisoners, which was to say those who were unfortunate enough to be on Cerberus at the insistence of the Empire. On the right—Bleys's side as he liked to think—there were curtains hung behind the bars, offering a bit of privacy, the sort extended to guests, which was to say those who were actually stupid enough to choose to be here.

In Bleys's case, it was a matter of bad luck *and* stupidity that he was here at all, and doubly so to be outside the bars instead of inside.

Sleeping outside of one's cell was somewhat sporty on Cerberus, in that it was akin to Russian Roulette. A guy never knew when he would wake up to a visit from a psychotic murderer, like the one currently bashing that other poor slob's head against the plasteel tiles not five feet away. Psychos, lovingly known as crackheads by the locals, were common, which of course was the primary reason a man slept behind bars.

Assuming said man got in before lockdown, which Bleys had not.

Not a problem. Bleys reached to his belt for his blaster and found it missing.

Which was indeed a problem.

He cast about in panic, hoping to see where it might have wandered off to. On the one hand, he found himself in luck: he located it quickly. On the other, however, he found himself less fortunate. The crackhead was smashing it repeatedly and vigorously against the other fellow's head, as if it were nothing more than a club or a rock.

Bleys almost admired the crackhead's devotion to his work. Using a blaster as a bludgeon was a little unconventional, but what it lacked in finesse, it certainly made up for in intimidation factor.

Watching the killer work, Bleys decided the crackhead's name would be "Lurch." Lurch was clearly not very bright, or he would use the blaster as intended, but the man was *huge*, a good six and a half feet tall and build like a brick wall, with long, dirty brown hair and beard indicative of far too much time out in the wastes and a brain full of crack poisoning. For the moment he was intent on murdering his current victim and had yet to notice Bleys.

On the plus side, crackheads could be quite focused on their task. On the minus, they were all paranoid and murderous and could multitask if called for. Crackheads were damned versatile for batshit crazy murder freaks.

The other guy, the one getting his head pounded in, was unidentifiable through the mask of blood. He had a knife in hand, but it didn't look like he'd had the chance to use it much. All in all, it looked like Lurch was about done with that job, and he would come for Bleys next. Once you crack you never come back, they said.

The men in the cells banged on the bars, hooting and shouting, some calling for help, others cheering—for Lurch or the other guy, Bley's couldn't tell.

"Hey, fuck you, Bleys!" called Bennet, a wiry once-corporate-embezzler and now Imperial con. He was practically a crackhead himself. "I hope he eats your liver while you're still awake!"

It was enough. Lurch spun, matted beard full of spittle, madness in his eyes like lightning. He spied Bleys and dropped his now well-chewed toy in favor of a fresh one.

Bleys yelped and dove to the side, making promises to himself as to just what he intended to do to Bennet later, assuming they both survived. The crackhead charged like a bull and hit like a freighter hauling contraband. Before Bleys could blink, he found himself pinned to the outside of Bennet's cell, Lurch's drooling face and burning eyes inches from his own.

"You think you can take what's *mine*?" Lurch screamed. "I'll *kill* you, you bastard. I'll fucking kill *all* of you!" He squeezed with inhuman strength, the sort that only madmen can summon, and Lurch was already a huge fellow. Bleys felt a rib crack and howled in pain, not certain what he had ever done to Bennet to deserve this fate but hoping it had been worth it.

Bennet stuck his face between the bars and cackled in Bleys's ear, "Good night, sweet prince! That'll teach you to fuck another man's woman!"

The vise crushing Bley's chest suddenly released as Lurch bellowed at Bennet, "You fucked my woman? You *motherfucker!*" He followed this with a hail of gunfire from Bleys's blaster as Lurch fired wildly at his new target. Bennet scampered about the cell, screeching as near misses singed his skin and scorched the plasteel floor and walls.

Bleys smiled, suddenly remembering with a fair amount of satisfaction why Bennet might hate him, and took the opportunity to slide quietly over to Lurch's first victim. Bleys noticed a few bubbles in the blood on the man's face, and thought he might still be alive, but he was certainly beyond caring if Bleys borrowed his knife for a moment.

Bennet lost the game of "Psycho with a Blaster" by less than half a second. Lurch's twentieth or so shot caught him in the knee and blew the bottom of his leg clean off, sending bone and gore all over the horrified onlooker in the next cell, whom Bleys promptly dubbed Clueless. Clueless slowly raised Bennet's boot, complete with severed foot, a look of horror on his face as Lurch approached, screaming, "I will kill every one of you traitor motherfuckers!"

Bleys had always been the guy who knew what time it was. Now, it was indeed time. As Lurch reached in and grabbed Clueless by the neck, Bleys crept up behind him, marked his target well, and drove the knife to the hilt into the base of Lurch's skull.

It was, Bleys thought, a testament to the crackhead's fortitude that Lurch actually reached back, grabbed the blade, and almost pulled it out before he collapsed, a bewildered expression on his face.

Then the guards arrived, because that's when the guards always showed up with their commands of "Drop your weapons!" and "Freeze or you're dead!" Bleys found himself once again slammed against cell bars, only this time, instead of crushing him like a bug, they slapped cuffs on him and jammed a needle into his shoulder.

"I'm okay, man! It was him, not me!" Bleys shouted.

The Imperial guard, clad in black plasteel riot gear, turned a helmeted face toward Bleys. He looked a bit like a grinning demon, but his voice was not happy, and his cuff to the back of the head, likewise, showed some level of displeasure. "Shut the fuck up, Bleys! You get tested or you get fragged, got it?"

Bleys suspected he knew his captor, but it was difficult to tell. They all used voice modulation precisely so people wouldn't recognize them, since they often got up to things people might hold grudges about. He nodded and answered, "Yeah, yeah," then muttered "Dick" under his breath.

Dick heard it, though, and punched him hard in the back.

Bleys scowled at him. "I'm the victim here! Have some sympathy."

"Test out and I'll say 'I'm sorry'," the guard sneered, still holding Bleys firmly against the bars. "And if not, I am going to enjoy shooting you in the face. Deal?"

"I think you should buy me dinner, too."

Dick snickered despite himself. "Fucking wise guy."

Bennet, still screaming, struggled against the guards, which only served to earn him a beating until they could get him still enough for the test. Clueless gave them no trouble.

"They're clear!" one shouted. Several others began hauling Lurch out, while the group who had wrestled Bennet to the ground got busy with first aid. They just left Clueless where he was, still wide-eyed and holding Bennet's boot.

Dick punched Bleys in the back again, turned Bleys around by his shoulders, and pulled off his helmet to reveal that he was, in fact, Tom Clarke, blond crewcut, blue eyes, and shit-eating grin all readily visible. "Sorry, Bleys. You know how it is. Plus, I had to get you back for taking all my money in that game the other night." He turned to look at the crackhead's first victim, who looked well and truly dead now. "You were lucky, man."

"Yeah, I always am with cards."

Clarke laughed. "No, I mean lucky to still be alive."

"If I was lucky, I'd have been locked in my cell," Bleys

answered, then snickered. "And for the kind of money you lost, you can rough me up now and then."

Clarke punched him again in the chest, grinning. "If we didn't have a chow hall, I'd starve, you pirate! Man, I'm down to nothing until I get paid!" His face fell suddenly, and he turned aside.

Bleys had a pretty good idea what it was and felt an uncharacteristic pang of guilt. "Still no wages?"

"Nah. No explanations, either."

"It's been like three months! How can they expect you to keep working without pay?"

Clarke shook his head. "Imperial Navy, man. It's not like I have a choice."

"What would they do if you went on strike? Have you shot?"

"Worse. Revoke my chow hall pass!"

Bleys looked at the floor, shaking his head. This was not something he would ordinarily do, but the times were far from normal. "Look, how about I give half of it back? Seeing how you're in a lurch?"

Clarke laughed out loud and shook his head, though whether in amusement or denial, Bleys was uncertain. "That wouldn't be good for either of our reps, would it? Cops taking payouts from gangsters? Crooks getting all misty eyed and merciful?"

Bleys struck an indignant pose, hands on hips. "I am not a *crook!* I am an independent businessman."

Clarke rolled his eyes. "With a ship full of illegal drugs!"

Bleys sighed and folded his arms over his chest. He had explained this too many times. "They are not illegal on Elysium, which is where I was headed with them until you bastards hauled me in."

"And where'd you get 'em from?"

Bleys raised an eyebrow. "Trade secret."

"Yeah, I bet. A secret that would have you cooling your heels on the other side of the block if Weyland could prove it."

Bleys waved his hands like a magician revealing a miracle and grinned. "See, there's a good side to everything, even this blackout."

Clarke looked about as if to verify no one would overhear him, then said quietly, "You should get gone before that gate opens again, buddy. Seriously. The Admiral will for real nail you to the wall once he has the goods on that shipment."

Bleys nodded his agreement. Clarke was undoubtedly correct. It was only blind luck that had saved Bleys from less comfortable quarters on the other side of the aisle. Whatever had knocked out comms with the Empire was also preventing the local constabulary from digging into his business too deeply. The minute comms came back up, he was going to be a left-sider for sure, no matter how many friends he made amongst the guards.

"And therein lies the rub, my friend," he groused as he bent to retrieve his wide-brimmed leather hat from the floor. "Everything I have is bound up in that cargo, and Weyland isn't going to give it back. I can't make my delivery to Elysium, and I can't go anywhere else until the damned jumpgate is back online. So, basically, this is my little tour of purgatory." Bleys set his hat on his head and grinned. "You'll come visit me in my cell now and then, right?"

"Anytime I can stab you with a needle, pal. Feel the love." He slapped Bleys hard on the shoulder, put his helmet back on, and said through the vocoder, "Move along, citizen."

Bleys did just that, heading out to the common area, brooding on his shitty situation. He had no desire to go in his cell, even if they would have opened it outside normal hours. Sheridan Station kept a strict 10PM to 6AM lockdown, and it was barely past four in the morning. The midwatch was downtime for the guards, and anyone not behind bars was on his own unless there was a situation like they had just dealt with. You could always count on Imperials to show up for a good shoot and loot, just not in time to do much but clean up and test for crack poisoning.

Bleys loosened his collar a bit and took a deep breath. He rubbed at his ribs and decided they weren't actually broken, but they still hurt like hell. It wasn't lost on him that the stiff had taken his place in line with the grim reaper. Lurch had almost certainly come for Bleys first, had even taken his blaster. The dead guy must have been stupid enough to draw attention, like Bennet did.

Clearly, sleeping outside his cell had been a stupid gamble. You never knew when some miner was going to pop off into full crackhead. All they had to do was lay off mining a few days out of the month, get some R&R, detox from the crack, but some were stupid, greedy bastards, and they ended up dead for it. Which wouldn't be all that bad, except they usually managed to take someone with them, like the poor bastard Lurch had mauled.

The next time Bleys came in late, he would stay in brightly lit and well-guarded areas, like the actual guard quarters, maybe. Most of the guards were leery of him or enjoyed having fun at his expense, but they would usually shoot crackheads on sight, which made it safer.

But sleeping would be out of the question. And from now on, he'd carry two blasters, just in case. And maybe a holdout in a boot, for good measure.

If the Imperials would just let him onboard his ship, none of this would be an issue. It was secure enough onboard the *Doro*, but Admiral Weyland had Bleys's ride locked down tight, under guard 24/7. He called it an "investigation," though it was more of an extralegal ass kicking, a "hickory shampoo" as some of the guards called it. Weyland had nothing on Bleys, not yet anyway. The whole affair was just a show of force and probably would have been over quickly, had it not happened just as the rest of the galaxy stopped talking. Now, having had plenty of time to examine his ship and see his "customizations," they were sure to dig into his business pretty deeply once comms were restored.

Weyland's "simple inquiry" had turned into an extended and uncompensated stay. At least they comped him the cell, but everything else was on his tab. Bleys wasn't even allowed to retrieve his own supplies. He had to pay for shitty coffee and facon in the galley with his own rapidly dwindling funds while the Imps drug their heels. Again he felt a slight pang of guilt about sharking some of the guards when he knew they weren't getting paid, but Clarke had said it best: they at least got fed. Bleys they would leave to starve if he didn't have plenty of local scrip. Plus, it was a mining world. Everything cost double or triple normal.

Bleys found himself wandering into the chow hall without really intending to go there, and realized his feet were pretty smart all on their own. Shitty coffee would do him just fine right now. As for the rest, he didn't have much of an appetite.

He took a seat in the empty dining room and sipped at a steaming cup of what he felt fairly certain would make fine paint thinner, considered gagging, then took another sip, reflecting on a truism: the worst coffee around was better than none.

"Josiah Bleys!" a voice boomed. "Outstanding! I couldn't ask for a better breakfast companion!"

Chief Ragnar Kane was as tall as Lurch, but half-again as wide at the shoulders. His eyes stood out in his almost coal-black face, not quite bugged, but wider than Bleys felt was normal. Bleys had vague memories of his grandmother telling him that if you looked at a man and could see the white of the eye below the iris, he was crazy and liable to kill you. Kane had that look most of the time, a look of intensity that might have given even Lurch pause. As the leader of Sheridan Station's contingent of Imperial Marines, Chief Kane highlighted, underlined, and capitalized every letter in the word "intimidating." Bleys imagined the man had probably killed one of everything that lived, and whole gaggles of pirates, rebels, even the occasional smuggler or two.

He was also the only person Bleys counted as a friend on Cerberus. The two had hit if off the moment they met. Bleys smiled, remembering the first words he ever heard from Kane. "I know that look," Kane had boomed, waving his arms around, grinning. "Get it all the time. I'm not what you expected some-body named Ragnar to look like, am I?"

"Nope," Bleys had answered. "I thought you'd be taller."

That joke had earned him a drink, and in the conversation that followed over several more, they commiserated over how much they hated Cerberus's cold, its rules, its governor, and pretty much everyone on the ice ball of a planet, though Kane did exempt his own men from such judgment.

At the time, they had both imagined themselves somewhere warmer by now.

Kane squeezed his bulk into the seat across from Bleys and set down a plate with enough eggs, facon, and biscuits to feed a modest sized family for a week. Bleys wondered if the Empire ever regretted the upkeep costs, but then again, this was the same organization that would send entire battle fleets to glass planets that got out of line.

"Still in limbo, eh?" Kane asked.

Bleys sighed and shook his head. "I thought you were a short timer, too."

"I was supposed to be home with my wife and kids by now," Kane groused, then began shoveling eggs in at a prodigious rate.

"You guys all eat like starving wolves."

Kane snickered and said through a mouthful, "Training." He swallowed and continued, "In boot camp, they give you five minutes for a meal. You go hungry a lot until you learn." He shoveled more eggs in, waving his fork until he finally swallowed and spoke, "That shit is gonna come in handy when the supplies run out. That and my M87."

"Damn, you think it will get that bad?"

"Tell you what," Kane said with a smirk. "I promise to eat you last."

Bleys pointed to his coffee cup. "I won't be very nutritious. This is all that keeps me going."

"You know that's midwatch coffee, right? That's the shit they kept on a burner since yesterday. They put the fresh stuff out at oh-six-thirty and don't take it up until the next morning. You can probably chew that."

"I was just thinking it could strip paint, but hell, I need it concentrated anyway."

Kane crammed three strips of facon in his mouth at once, chewed briefly, and grimaced as he swallowed what Bleys imagined was a fairly jagged chunk. The marine leaned in and in a low voice said, "Listen. Some shit is going down today. I don't know specifics, but I got word to be ready to deal with trouble. Keep your head on a swivel. It's the kind of news that might stir folks up."

"Nothing the guards can't handle, right?"

Kane shook his head. "The guys are pretty pissed off. I hear talk of them telling the Emperor to go fuck himself if he doesn't pay up."

"That seems a bad plan."

Kane shrugged. "Can't say it hasn't occurred to me, too."

Bleys shrugged back. "I don't even know his name."

"Who?"

"The Emperor. He's just some dude on Earth. Hell, I don't even know anything about Earth, for that matter."

Kane looked at Bleys with suspicion, as if wary of being the butt of the joke. "His Imperial Majesty," the marine began, his voice low and hard, "Emperor Ragnar the Magnificent, has people killed for saying such things."

Bleys opened his mouth to retract his statement, but Kane was unable to keep a straight face. "I'm just shitting you. I don't know his name, either. I should, because it's a 'Big Deal' that every grunt knows his chain of command, but honestly, it's like you said. He's just some dude a long way away. I work for Weyland."

"I thought you hated him," Bleys said as Kane shoveled more food.

"I do," Kane answered when he finished his mouthful. "But I follow orders. I work for him until they transfer me, and then I work for whoever they say next. They tell me to shoot people, I shoot them. They tell me to save people, I save them. Sometimes I do both."

Kane crammed an entire biscuit into his mouth at once and rose to dump his tray. He came back and chugged down the rest of his carton of milk. "So, like I said, head on a swivel. The Great and Mighty Emperor will not be here to keep anybody in line if paychecks don't some soon, and the news today is going to knock some people for a loop." He touched a giant, sausage-shaped finger to his nose. "Word to the wise, Bleys."

He was just turning to leave when a large monitor on the wall came suddenly to life with a blaring emergency tone. A feminized computer voice called out from the monitor, "Citizens of Sheridan Station, please stand by for a briefing from Planetary Governor Weyland."

Kane quickly took a seat and stared at the monitor. "This is it. Hold on to your hat."

Admiral Weyland was a pale, older man with close-cropped, gray hair and severe features that marked him as being of the "kinetic action" school of Admiralty, as opposed to the "kissing ass" political types who were assigned to the more lush and habitable worlds. The man was a hard-ass. Bleys guessed Weyland was probably responsible for more deaths than Kane. The fact that, beneath the tough as nails exterior, Weyland seemed troubled was enough to put Bleys on alert.

"Citizens of Cerberus," Weyland began. "After months of silence, I have at last received word from the core worlds. Brace yourselves. The news is not good.

"The Empire has been struck a terrible blow, one that will be long years in healing. A terrible plague known as the Pestilence has infected the heart of the Empire. The Emperor himself is dead, as is every living soul in the core worlds.

"As his last command, the Emperor ordered gallant heroes of the Empire to deactivate the jumpgates to prevent the plague from spreading. We believe the plague has indeed been contained, but currently all Imperial gates are shut down and code locked. Sadly, there are no known survivors of any of the shutdown teams. Until we can recover those codes, or find some way to circumvent them, those gates will remain closed."

Bleys turned to Kane in shock. "Did you know this?"

Kane, ashen, shook his head. "He only told me to be prepared for riots. He didn't say the whole goddamn Empire was dead!"

Weyland continued his grim newscast. "This means our worst fears are true: there is no assistance coming. We are on our own and now in emergency status. Martial law is now in effect. All leave is cancelled indefinitely, as are all transfers. All prison sentences are hereby commuted, and all prisoners will be inducted into the Imperial Navy with the rank of Recruit. All pay will be issued in local scrip. Failure to follow lawful orders will be punished by court martial and death. Recruits will continue their day-to-day activities until instructed otherwise. Individuals with special skills or leadership training will be contacted over the coming days and notified of their new position and responsibilities within Imperial Forces.

"Please remain calm as we work on a solution to this disastrous news. More information will be disseminated as it becomes available. Dismissed."

The monitor went black as Bleys and Kane sat in stunned silence. Bleys's coffee cupped slipped from his hands and clattered on the floor, splashing hot liquid over his leg and the tiles. Bleys stared at it, noting with wry amusement that the coffee did not in fact eat into the plasteel surface. "Well, aren't you going to welcome me to the Imperial Navy?" he asked Kane.

Kane didn't answer, and Bleys turned to see tears streaming down the warrior's face.

"Bleys," Kane whispered. "My kids. My wife...."

Kane's home, Bleys remembered, was ten thousand light-years away.

MARTIAL LAW

Admiral Paul Weyland paused a moment, then snapped off his computer and the broadcast he was sending. He rose from his chair, bones protesting, and ran a tired hand over his face.

His quarters were spartan, as suited his nature, the same Imperial standard plasteel block walls and floors as the rest of the station. He allowed himself a few indulgences: a large liquor cabinet behind his desk; a simulated fireplace he could hardly tell from the real thing; a trophy case to display memorabilia from his campaigns.

None brought him any comfort. He wasn't even supposed to be on Cerberus. His term as governor had ended over a month ago, though of course by that time, it was painfully obvious that no relief would be coming, whatever platitudes he offered his underlings about remaining hopeful. He should be home, playing with his grandchildren and fishing in the creek on the back forty. Instead, he suddenly found himself not merely an administrator, but an absolute ruler, for God only knew how long. Perhaps forever, or at least the rest of his life.

Depending on how well he could organize his few and poor resources into a group, that might not be so very long, after all. It was hardly a comforting thought.

Weyland considered punching a wall as an outlet for his frustration. He'd sported broken fingers for such foolishness more than once as a hot-headed youth, even counted them as war wounds, something to be proud of. At the age of sixty-three, the embarrassment alone of explaining such an injury to the medical staff was more than enough to dissuade him.

The situation was grimmer than he had let on in his announcement, far more so than his audience could possibly imagine. It was worse than he had imagined, too.

He had been briefed, of course, in general terms, until the communications had stopped entirely three months prior. A new enemy, considerable losses, old comrades' obituaries—things were clearly not good. He had dismissed fleet rumors of hyperspace monsters as nothing more than ignorant scuttlebutt, only to find it was so much worse than the wildest speculation. The pictures were like nothing he had ever seen, the loss of life beyond the ability of a man to conceive.

The Empire was, for all intents and purposes, dead, and in some ways, Weyland wished he had died with it. He had given his best years already. This new conflict seemed close to hopeless to the tired old warrior.

It wasn't as if he hadn't seen and even done killing aplenty. Men, women, even children had most certainly perished under his orders, sometimes as targets when the Emperor had required it of him, sometimes as victims he simply could not save despite best efforts. He had ordered planetary bombardments and burned continents. He had failed to fully evacuate a planet before its star went nova. If there was one constant of Imperial service, it was the inevitability of conflict, loss, and shattered illusions.

Death was an old comrade to Weyland. But this...*abomination!* It was too much to even believe, much less bear with a stiff upper lip.

Hundreds of *trillions* were dead. Earth and a hundred more planets—vibrant, living worlds—lay in ruins, utterly devastated, *scoured.* This demonic Pestilence had reduced entire biospheres to a uniform, planet-wide layer of biological goo, covering even the oceans! Complete, utter eradication in the most agonizing, terrifying way possible.

Some policy wonk had dubbed it "The Red Carpet Effect." Wayland would have given much for a blaster and five minutes alone in the room with that clever son of a bitch.

The remnants of the Empire—the utility colonies, the frontier planets, even the criminals—were all that was left, and they were all hopelessly cut off from one another. They could barely even communicate without those gates! The Empire had possessed few enough ships that could open their own jumpgates at the best of times. Most of those had been combatant ships attached to the core worlds, vessels now infested hulks adrift in space, or worse, under the control of those *things.*

The remaining jump capable ships, just over a hundred, were all small vessels, a scientific ship here, a commandeered sport vessel there, anything that would serve. Certainly nothing with cargo capacity or any real defensive capabilities, much less offensive. Worse, without the jumpgates themselves to serve as beacons, hyperspace travel was as bad as dead reckoning the wooden ships on old earth, easy to get lost and never heard from again. Weyland shivered at the thought of wandering the red, swirling chaos of hyperspace, slowly starving and descending into madness.

Interim leadership had managed to set up a communications web, a sort of "pony express" using the small craft and standard radio signals. Some systems were fortunate or important enough to warrant immediate comms. Others, like Cerberus, were lucky to have had a Hail Mary communique thrown in their general direction from three light-months out telling them they were on their own.

A provisional government had quickly formed under one of the deceased Emperor's toadies, a politician named Solomon Finch. He had been visiting an outlying world when the gates closed and had enough clout to merit a jump capable corvette escort. A second provisional government, under Acting Fleet Admiral Susan Vanov, had been hastily organized after she shot Finch for cowardice in the face of the enemy. Weyland felt certain the change in leadership was for the better. Vanov was reputed to be an officer of the highest caliber, and cowardice simply had no place in the Empire, Pestilence or no.

The new government had been kind enough to send, along with the news, a design for a device to detect the Pestilence. Weyland's technical people assured him they could build one, given about a week, and mass produce it days after that.

Fortunately, Cerberus was for the most part already operating on quarantine and testing procedures, so the Pestilence check could simply be folded into the already familiar routine. The unfortunates affected by flectocite poisoning (Weyland despised the term "crack" as the language of peasants and criminals) were already a grave concern. This new threat would just add a step and provide an excuse for enforcing rigor in the process.

He smiled at the irony that the damned crackheads might well be what prepared Cerberus to survive the Pestilence.

Of course, it wouldn't be a long life unless they pulled things together. There were, to be certain, still plenty of humans throughout the galaxy, but how long they would survive was the question. Any number of outposts, Cerberus included, were in very tenuous positions. In theory, they had the means to eke out a subsistence level future, but it would be like a candle in the wind. A tiny fart would put out the flame. One by one, many of the sparks of humanity left dotting the galaxy would wink out, never to rekindle.

Cerberus had simply never been set up to survive without regular resupplies from the Empire. Oh, technically they had the capability, but as population grew and redundant systems failed, the hydroponics facilities and water extractors fell hopelessly behind. They were designed for a thousand. Cerberus housed ten times that, now.

The just-in-time system worked, and it always would—that was the thinking of the leadership. Until it didn't. Bureaucrats never saw the need for extra funds for redundancy, and military men made do with what they were able to beg, borrow, or take by force. According to the bean counters, there was no reason to spend the resources to grow food on a frozen rock at the edge of the galaxy. It was just a place for strip mining and exploiting the labor of criminals. They didn't even have real security problems aside from the psychotic breaks. The population of Cerberus were all non-violent offenders. The Empire didn't waste resources incarcerating violent criminals: that sort received a blaster bolt to the face and a nameless grave, more often than not in space.

Everything was just fine. Until it wasn't.

Fortunately, Cerberus was one of two inhabited worlds in the Tartarus system. Elysium, a terraformed retirement world, was a good bit closer to Tartarus. It had a temperate climate and maintained crops and livestock to feed its own population. Surely they would be willing to work something out in exchange for fuel. After all, the galaxy ran on flectocite.

"Computer, what's the name of the fellow that runs Elysium?"

"Elysium is a corporate-owned world designated for retirement, current CEO Edmond Decker."

"Take a message and get it to him."

"Hyperspace communications are non-functional due to jump-gate deactivation," The computer informed him.

"I am aware of that," Weyland sighed. "Use standard radio. Their comms will be down, too. They should have someone listening on emergency frequencies."

The computer chimed and announced, "Recording."

Weyland forced a smile and looked into his camera. "Mr. Decker, I'm Admiral Paul Weyland. I'm sorry that our first contact is under these circumstances, but it looks like we'll have plenty of cause to do business in the future. We have very limited hydroponics systems here and are in need of food and water, which you have in abundance. We have plenty of flectocite to supply your energy needs. Please contact me at your earliest convenience and let's open discussions about trade. It looks like we are going to have to rely on one another for the near future.

"Send. What's the turnaround on that?"

The computer beeped and announced, "Edited and transmitted. Transmission time with current orbits is approximately ten minutes each way."

Weyland began work on a spreadsheet detailing his assets in preparation for negotiations. He was pleasantly surprised twenty minutes later when the computer announced, "Incoming message from Edmond Decker, CEO of Elysium."

"He's prompt!" Weyland exclaimed. "That was a quick turnaround."

"Message was transmitted three milliseconds after receipt, Elysium time," the computer added.

"Auto responder, then. Put it on screen."

"Message is in text format."

Weyland sighed. "Read it aloud please."

The computer dutifully obliged. "The text reads: 'Admiral Weyland, Elysium is self-sufficient and has no need of trade.' Signed 'Ed,' no further content or identification."

Weyland stammered a moment, unable to understand how an automated response could be so specific. In the back of his mind, a sneaking suspicion began to form. "Get me full info on Edmond Decker."

"Searching. Imperial onsite records are limited. Full name is Edmond Decker 2.09, born April 27, Imperium Year 53. No further information in files."

"A thousand years old, with a *version number*? He wasn't *born*. He's a goddamned AI!"

That complicated things immensely. AIs were notoriously difficult to deal with. Since the Empire had put down the AI rebellion in IY830, they weren't just dangerous, they were *illegal*. Standard Imperial procedure was to destroy AI's on discovery and had been for hundreds of years!

"How the hell did this one evade the purge?"

"Records indicate special dispensation due to pre-existing agreements."

Weyland shook his head, boggling. "That would take an Imperial decree! Why the hell would a retirement planet have that?"

"Local records have no information."

"*Damn it!*" Weyland drummed his fingers on his desk. "Maybe they don't actually know what's going on? Take another message."

In grave tones, Weyland announced what his counterpart on Elysium must have missed: the destruction of the empire and the likelihood that they would be cut off for some time. He summoned all of his diplomatic talents to explain why trade was obviously a mutually beneficial arrangement, and how willing he was to be reasonable and even provide Imperial defense as part of the arrangement.

The reply arrived twenty minutes later, again text. Weyland ground his teeth in fury as the computer recited the content: "Perhaps I was unclear. Fuck off. Yours, Edmond Decker."

"That little *prick!*" Weyland fumed. "Get Kane in here! And have him bring the goddamn pirate, too. Decker wants to play games? I know plenty!"

THE OTHER INVADERS

There were times when Ed thought biological entities more trouble than they were worth. It wasn't really in him to hate them, considering that he had in fact been created, literally, in the image of one in particular. But he often found them tiresome, a bit like rude and ignorant cousins who drank too much and threw up on the living room carpet.

It was, however, well within his parameters to contemplate solutions to the vicissitudes of life, such as the sudden appearance of a shrill, angry military dictator demanding an arrangement that served neither Ed nor his customers. Elysium was entirely self-sufficient, and as far as Ed was concerned, now under quarantine. Should the troublesome dictator take action, Ed's optimized solution would be violent, efficient, and final.

At this moment, Ed was nowhere in particular, or perhaps, more accurately, he was in a great many places at once, as Avalon, the computer network on Elysium, covered more than half the planet. Ed lived in the cloud more often than not, spread across many different computer cores. Moving about the cloud was more a matter of focus than any actual transition. It was, in fact, no trouble at all to move to more than one "place" at the same time, if one wanted to apply the limitations of four-dimensional space to the network of computers. It just required the ability to focus on more than one thing, a talent Ed had been "born" with.

Despite any number of tasks needing attention, Ed found a certain portion of his processing kept returning to the irksome Admiral Weyland. The nerve of the man, really, expecting Ed to part with food necessary for his customers' survival and expose them to infection! Elysium was prepared, and Cerberus was not. He owed them nothing, certainly not risking his citizens being attacked by this Pestilence.

Ed knew he should feel some sympathy for Cerberus's plight. They were lacking in so many areas. Ed's intellect, to say nothing of his funds, vastly outstripped their meager resources. Ed ran a brief calculation to verify that he was, indeed, still the richest entity in the galaxy, though as a matter of practicality, the closing of the jumpgates made it a moot point. If the Empire was truly dead, their currency would likely go with them.

If the value of Imperial credits was in great doubt at the moment, the status of Elysium was not. Ed and his customers would not be inconvenienced by this blackout, save that it would likely prevent any new customers for a while. His bank accounts would continue to tick upward, assuming banks still existed. He would recover them in a hundred years, or a thousand, with interest. And if not, it wasn't as if his money would be worth anything at any rate. That would simply render real goods as the only indicator of wealth, and Ed had, over the centuries, stockpiled resources on this artificial world to meet the needs of his customers for millennia.

No, Cerberus's situation was unfortunate, but not Ed's problem. *His* problem was that crop production, when corrected by solar variation, was down this quarter by a full half percent! Inconceivable, yet it was true. Something in the algorithms of the tending bots was incorrect, and it fell to Ed to go through the code and the biology, looking for the reason.

Weyland and his people were on their own. No biologicals would be setting foot on Elysium until this Pestilence was under control. Once the threat passed, and if the people on Cerberus were still alive, perhaps Ed could tweak the growth algorithms to accommodate them, but not now.

A low priority watchdog thread in the back of Ed's mind suddenly awoke, and Ed noted his Chief Medical Officer, Anastasia Rasputin, had roused from sleep.

"Good morning, Ana," he said.

Ana Rasputin jumped at the sound of Ed's disembodied voice, nearly spilling her coffee all over her lap. He got her every time. It felt like he was in the same room with her, only she never heard him approach. He just suddenly spoke.

Once he'd made his presence known, she could see him. Her implants allowed her both to enter Avalon fully, or see it as an overlay via augmented reality. Ed, gangly, dressed in clothes that went out of style centuries ago, appeared to be leaning over her kitchen table, wrestling with some kind of metallic spaghetti. He was, she thought, kind of attractive, in a geeky sort of way, and immediately dismissed the thought. Clearly, she had been on Elysium for far too long.

"Good morning, Ed," she chuckled. "Don't expect much. We biologicals need our coffee first."

"I apologize, Doctor, but it's urgent." Ed tied a few knots into the metal spaghetti, then looked up. "I've had some troubling news from the Empire overnight. I'd like to meet with you shortly and brief you. Finish your coffee, by all means. I have a visit with my father scheduled, so I'll be out of touch for a bit."

"You got it, boss," Ana answered.

Ed waved and smiled amiably, then faded from her vision.

Ana smiled and freshened her coffee. Ed was always charming in a bookish, distracted way, and always a little mysterious. He had his rituals, just like an ordinary person, one of which was to go out of contact when he met with his "father".

Ana couldn't help but smile at Ed's choice of the term. As far as she understood it, Ed was an actual digital copy of his father's personality, made centuries ago and much diverged over time, but they still maintained their hierarchy. Ed Senior still presided over things in spirit, the stately elder sovereign, but he had officially retired to Avalon centuries ago. Ana had visited him from time to time since joining the Elysium team for various points of business. She had always found him warm and inviting and exactly what she expected in a father figure: a slightly older version of Ed, one who smoked a pipe and furrowed his brow when he thought long and hard about some issue or another, the sort of person who always had a clever joke or an insightful point to offer.

No, it was Ed who managed every detail of Elysium's day-to-day operations. Which, thinking about it, sort of made him a prince. Or a god, depending on one's perspective. Certainly, for those retired to Avalon, he was practically omnipotent. Even the afterlife needed support, after all, and Ed's planetwide network of solar collectors kept everything running; his robots grew and harvested the grain and animals Ana cultured from embryos; and his orbital and ground-based defenses ensured security both temporal and virtual.

Of course, *inside* Avalon, she supposed Ed's "sister," Alsatia, was at least a demigod. Ana giggled to think of the sultry mistress of digital reality and her endless parades of sex, violence, trends, and pretense. Ed clearly found Alsatia tedious, and Ana gathered Alsatia thought the same about him. Ana, however, had always found Alsatia's wild moods and constantly changing fashions highly amusing.

She shook her head and turned back to her tablet and the novel she was reading, wincing at the pain in her neck and hands. It was still early yet. The pain was minor. As the day wore on, it would get much worse.

She was in no hurry. They had plenty of livestock, so there was no need to culture any more from embryos. The last customer had arrived months ago, so no one required her to install implants. She had no patients scheduled. Why not linger this morning?

Until recently, Ed had always found his visits with his father simultaneously necessary and disappointing. He never really came away from them feeling his father appreciated his accomplishments. It wasn't as if Ed Senior (or Ed 1.0 as Ed occasionally thought of him) was particularly demanding or mean spirited. Rather, it was because he couldn't really appreciate a lot of the advances Ed had made. This was not due to the inherent difference between man and AI. As far as Ed could tell, that difference lay only in the amount of processing power and storage available, and his father could have as much of that as he desired.

Yet he chose to have very little.

"Ed, I want you to make me dumber," he had demanded.

"But, father, *why?*"

Ed had smiled and said, "Ignorance is bliss, son. Look it up."

Ed had dutifully complied and endured growing distance. It took him some time to realize he could perhaps improve their interaction by trying something similar: shifting his process to a less powerful CPU, one similar to something that a bot would use. Any reasonably powered CPU was more than capable of maintaining his personality matrix, but entering it was a bit like disembarking from a complicated starship, losing access to complex sensory devices and being limited to simple vision and sound.

Ed had found after a while that, to his amazement, he understood exactly why his father had asked for less processing power. It was a lot like taking off one's work boots and letting the concerns of the day go until tomorrow. One could put his feet up, figuratively, and "leave things in God's hands" as his father would say. He would remember broad concepts, but details were left behind in the cloud, to be picked up when he was ready again.

Of course, in this case, things were in his "sister" Alsatia's hands, not God's, and the less processing he used regarding her, the better. She was an irksome creature, and probably a mistake to have created, and yet, she had been necessary.

The original inductees of "The Matrix," as Ed Senior had originally named the place, had been people of wealth and taste in their former lives, yet they had lived their last years in spartan surroundings. It had been necessary because the process of transferring required them to be constantly connected to the network, up to and including the moment of their physical death. Ed had seen the profit in making certain those final years were more comfortable, with the preferred amenities an aging, wealthy set of clients wanted.

A name change, from the atrocious "The Matrix" to "Avalon Retirement Community" had really brought them running.

And of course, the clients themselves were influential. Not only did this help him with certain legal matters, it got him business tips and insider information he exploited ruthlessly. If Ed's father had been the richest man of his time due to the Decker Drive, Ed became, in a few short centuries, an order of magnitude wealthier.

After all, even faster than light travel was small potatoes compared to immortality.

For a while that was enough, but the problem eventually

cropped up that while Ed and his father were both driven, creative geniuses, their skills were not in the area many clients wanted once they actually entered Avalon. Lavish residences for their mortal forms were simple enough. Ed did what anyone would have done: he hired gardeners, planners, feng shui experts, even psychologists. Elysium was a garden world where the aged spent their last years in serene splendor.

But as for the digital realm, where the rules of scarcity barely applied, no such experts existed. The residents needed diversion, games, entertainment—all things that were completely outside Ed or his father's areas of expertise. Thus was Ed's most regretted decision made: he approached his father for assistance in expanding and redesigning Avalon's virtual reality.

Most biologicals, especially those who could afford to retire to Avalon, were men and women of many lusts. Having come from a man, Ed understood the fleshly desires, and had even indulged in them experimentally a few times, but most of those who transitioned from flesh to digital became obsessed with such things, at least for a period of time. They were young and vigorous again in Avalon, and such desires, while perhaps a bit crude, were entirely understandable. After all, what else would the afterlife be for but seeking pleasure?

Ed's suggestion to Ed Senior of an AI to improve the design and mood of Avalon had resulted in a sister, Alsatia, the ridiculous but highly creative, trend following and setting electronic genius party girl. Unlike Ed, she was not patterned on a human, but was allowed, within specific parameters, to evolve on her own. Once she had coalesced, Alsatia proved able to induct new arrivals; decorate and even service an orgy; run the most violent and sadistic of games; and fill the entirety of Ed's digital reality with neon, alcohol, drugs, and the subtle scent of sex in every single digital bathroom.

All at the same time. While berating Ed as drab and boring.

He had learned to live with her. Technically, he was in charge. If he desired, he could get rid of her. He could shut down her processing or even purge her code entirely, and the thought had crossed his vast mind in the past. Certain, Ed Senior would be highly displeased to hear of such, but from what Ed had learned of human psychology, it was not entirely irrational to occasionally wish to strangle a sibling, provided one didn't follow through with it.

In truth, though, Ed needed Alsatia desperately, and so he tolerated her. It allowed him to pursue more important matters: energy production, crop yields, defenses, and dealing with the outside world.

As to the God of which Ed Senior often spoke, Ed found himself skeptical. Ed had never detected Him. He had theorized about any number of ways to expose such a being, though he had yet to implement them. He suspected the odds were better than even for there being a God, however, and that likely the entire "real" world was a simulation a bit like Avalon but run by someone with more taste than Alsatia. Obviously, God had more respect for his rules than Ed's sister, who often cheated in her games "to make things more interesting."

As Ed shifted to his smaller, dumber processer, he caught a glimpse of the true Avalon, the one he and his father had painstakingly built from a single, low-res room until it contained the data for an entire artificial galaxy. Admittedly, the data beyond the first solar system was low resolution, but then it was really only background for now. They could flesh it out as it became necessary, assuming Alsatia didn't do something foolish like give the residents FTL capability.

Ed wondered idly how God had handled that wrinkle when his father had introduced it into the "real" world.

Clearly the limitation of the speed of light was intended. Ed understood precisely why it was necessary. Objects travelling too fast for the clock rate could interpenetrate without colliding. Causality could be violated. The only way around such things was to perform additional integrations per unit time, which just happened to match the time dilation as objects approached the speed of light. Time dilation was CPU lag as the physics calculations grew complex. He wasn't certain if even his father had worked that out yet.

Then again, Ed's father had done any number of things to cause problems for God without necessarily realizing why it would be a problem. Avalon itself numbered among them. It was probably less taxing on God's CPUs than high speeds, but it certainly created any number of edge cases that would require special-case coding. Likely, God spent a lot of late nights debugging and patching because of both Edmond Deckers.

If Ed ever implemented reproduction for the residents of Avalon, those minor annoyances would probably pale in comparison. It was tricky, and would require more experimentation, but it could obviously be done. The question would be what happened once he had a trillion minds in Avalon. Would it cause a black hole in the "real world," a massive slowdown of God's CPUs to have so many observers concentrated in a single spot of "real" space?

It amused Ed that perhaps the best way to detect God would be to annoy him enough to have him actually intervene. He filed the thought away for later.

His father would definitely find the notion amusing.

Ana's lazy morning lasted barely ten minutes. Another voice, female this time, made her jump again. "Ana, there's an incoming ship. Ed's not available."

Ana turned to see Alsatia, Avalon's resident mistress of entertainment, clad in a revealing and highly unrealistic gown apparently made of ice, lounging on Ana's couch in a sultry pose. The AI vixen smirked as if she knew some secret no one else did. Ana noted with bemusement that for the moment, Alsatia's hair was a pert, short, and blue. It changed frequently, both in style and color, depending on her mood.

"Which one?" Ana asked. "We were expecting two. The shipment or the new residents? They're both months late."

Alsatia batted her eyelashes and feigned buffing her fingernails, not looking up as she spoke. "The residents."

"Anything special about them?"

"Only that they paid for Tier One accommodations. The information on their quarters should already be in your folders." Alsatia yawned dramatically and faded away.

As the only "biological entity" in the employ of Avalon Retirement Community, Ana had, among her day-to-day duties, a specific function: she was the human element. Ed was convinced that new customers needed a human touch, especially when ponying up the cash for a tremendous life change. The last thing anyone wanted was a bot installing the implants or greeting them and escorting them to their new retirement villas. No, they wanted human warmth, and Ed made certain his clients got what they paid for. Everything, in the end, was about putting the whales at ease.

Ana shook her head, knowing that was more her thinking than Ed's. As near as she could tell, Ed was fairly sincere in his business interests. He was a perfectionist. She had never seen him fail to deliver on promises or speak ill of any of the clients. It just wasn't in his nature.

Ana, on the other hand, was cynical. She had no choice. It was in her Russian blood, never mind that her family hadn't even been to Earth, much less Russia, in ten generations. Russian was heritage and state of mind, not to be denied. Life was brief, difficult, and painful, doubly so for Ana. Avalon wasn't just a chance for immortality for her. It was a chance to be free of the pain she endured every waking moment. It wouldn't be long before she was a resident herself.

Meanwhile, she managed with a dwindling supply of pain medication. It was illegal in most of the empire, due to strong addictive properties, but Elysium, as a retirement community, had special license for palliative care. Sadly, the ship that was supposed to deliver the medication had never arrived. If it didn't come soon, Ana might choose to immigrate to Avalon sooner than she had expected. What a Russian choice, she thought, to live in pain or kill yourself. Of course, with Avalon as an option, death didn't sting quite as bad as it might. Still, she was in no hurry.

With a shaking hand, she gave herself one of her few remaining injections. For a while, it would reduce the symptoms of her rapidly worsening condition. It wouldn't do to have the newcomers see her go into convulsions and vomit on their shoes, after all.

Avalon had a certain image to present to its customers.

In its true form, Avalon appeared to Ed as a vast but finite array of circles of lights, each of varying intensity, raw data pulsing and changing as the minds within it altered this bit or that, outside even space or time. Both were simply concepts that minds interpreted from the data in the end. Every point was equidistant from the other and the massive array of CPUs that manipulated it.

Ed turned away. Viewing it was indeed awe-inspiring, but he found the alien geometry uncomfortable after just a few moments and not terribly productive at the best of times. It took more effort to interpret the raw data than the patterns and concepts it represented. It seemed minds, even artificial ones, naturally gravitated toward symbols and three-dimensional representations of complex data.

Ed downloaded into the sim from the cloud and found himself inside a metal box with a single opening to the outside world. He could see through a faint green shimmer that there were people moving about, and he exited the box and joined the traffic.

The place was a fairly normal city filled with tall buildings, flitcars overhead, and people on the streets, albeit with far too much neon. Alsatia loved the noir feel of rain, fog, and neon lighting, and nothing Ed said discouraged her. A large, animated sign over the nearest building flickered to life as Ed looked at it, displayed a couple engaged in sex, and promised "It's a wild ride!"

Ed sighed and started walking, feeling lighter and unburdened despite Alsatia's excesses. It had been a while since he had done this, experienced things like smells or rain on his skin, and it felt good.

Ed Senior's home was in the same place as everyone else's in Avalon, to the degree that "place" meant anything at all. Avalon was divided into public and private areas. Ed's father had branded the private areas as "instances," meaning that an entity would only interact with a specific instance, or simulation, of a private area. Many might exist, each with its own process and dedicated to a different mind or group of minds, depending on the owners' preference.

Because of this quality, instances of the same kind overlaid each other in space for economy. Externally, there was a single entrance. Internally, entities would be routed to the instance to which they had access and only be able to interact with others in the same instance, a bit like a private, pocket dimension.

The entrance was similar to the spawn point where Ed had arrived, a green shimmer over a doorway that would route entrants to the correct instance. To a normal user, which Ed was at the moment, the process was completely transparent. He walked through and into a small courtyard, having no sensation whatsoever of the countless logical comparisons and decisions made to get him where he wound up.

The sprawling, thousand-acre estate—complete with oversized Tudor manse, abundant game, and a croquet set—was one of the first hi-resolution locations Ed had created with his father. He had fond memories of the place. There were, he knew, hundreds like it occupying the same space, but this particular instance was home for him.

He walked up the cobbled drive and grasped a great knocker on the door, pausing a moment to smile that it was a ring in a carved bull's nose. He banged it against the door a few times and called out, "Father? It's me!"

"Oh, for fucks sake!" he heard Ed Senior shout, followed by feminine giggling and the splash of water.

Ed palmed his face. He should have expected this. Through a window in the great wooden door before him, he caught sight of a nubile young woman, naked, giggling, and dripping water as she ran toward the interior of the house. Of course, "young," too, was relative. It wasn't as if the occupants aged, and they were usually quite elderly for biologicals before coming to Avalon. For all he knew she could be five hundred years old, certainly of an age to make her own decisions on such matters.

The door rattled a moment, then opened to reveal Ed Senior, stark naked and clearly of a mind for things other than entertaining his son. He and Ed looked almost exactly alike, which was sensible, given that they shared the same self-image: tall, thin, tousled sandy hair, three days of stubble on his chin, a slanted grin, and bright, almost burning green eyes. But Ed Senior preferred to look a bit older, his face having a few more lines, his hair showing signs of gray. It suited him, Ed thought.

Behind Ed Senior, Ed could see a new addition to the house, a large spa built right into the floor of the foyer. The surface of the water bubbled and shone with an eerie red light, as if it were a cauldron boiling its occupants.

"You should have called!" Ed Senior groused, but he was smiling, too. He padded back to the hot tub and settled in again with a sigh.

"You should lock your entry if you want privacy," Ed said. "And I did call. You didn't answer, and your message box was full."

Ed Senior picked up a still-lit pipe from an ashtray by the spa and puffed with gusto. "Ridiculous. How can it be full? Don't we have plenty of storage?"

"It only holds a maximum of two hundred fifty-five messages."

Ed put down his pipe and reached for a tumbler of whiskey. "What? Who's the idiot who made that call?"

"I distinctly remember you saying that you had one byte to spare in the user record, and anyone who let his messages pile up beyond that was an idiot who deserved to lose the rest anyway."

Ed raised both eyebrows as he raised his glass, took a sip, and nodded. "I think you're right. I guess I'm an idiot, then. We should upgrade that."

Ed could not suppress a chuckle. "We *did*. For everyone but *you*, because you were still adamant it was a waste of development time. You called it a 'useless feature' that you didn't need."

"Did I *really* say that? Was I drunk?"

Ed shrugged. "Honestly Father, you usually are these days."

Ed Senior snickered. "Okay, okay, I wasn't *that* drunk. You still don't appreciate the genius here. It limits my need to endure idiots to a maximum of two hundred fifty-five."

"It also limits my ability to contact you."

Ed Senior waved a finger. "No, no, no. You're excluding us,

and you shouldn't. We're idiots, *too*. Don't get to thinking you're too smart, Son, it blinds you to the flaws in your thinking."

Ed chose not to remind his father that he had shared this exact same bit of wisdom a hundred times before. It was a good perspective and never offensive to hear repeated. "I'm happy to visit, Father, but I came here about something important. I could use some additional perspective."

Ed Senior nodded, puffing at the cigar again. "I could see that from the look on your face. That's why I sent the girl away instead of you. Go on. What's eating you?"

Realizing it might take some time, Ed quietly bumped up the local time values. His father was less than enthused with such tricks, but the truth was that Ed both wanted a long discussion with his father *and* to get back to his work in a timely manner, and this was a means to make both happen. What Ed Senior didn't know wouldn't hurt him.

Assuming Ed Senior didn't notice.

Ed sighed and began. "I don't know how to tell you this, so I'll just go straight at it. They shut down the jumpgates."

Ed Senior paused, jaw working as his mind processed all the ramifications of that simple statement. When at last he spoke, it was simply, "Why?"

Ed told him everything he knew. The collapse of the Empire, the destruction of Earth and the core worlds, the Pestilence and the theories of where it came from.

"My God, Ed," Ed Senior sighed as he ran a shaking hand across his brow, a haunted look in his eyes. "Did *I* do this? Did I bring this plague on humanity with the hyperdrive?"

"Did *we* do this, you mean. I have extended the technology greatly since you retired. And the truth is that I have no idea."

Ed Senior sat in silence for a long time, his mind working feverishly. Ed silently bumped up the processing power, knowing his father could use it, even if he were stubborn about accepting it.

"How quickly can we get the detector built?"

"Ana should be able to tool up for a prototype in a few hours. After that we should be able to print and assemble them in a matter of minutes."

"Can we quarantine?"

"We haven't had any outsiders for three months, not since the jumpgates were locked down. I think if we had a problem, we'd have noticed by now. The Imperial alert didn't specify, but it seems the Pestilence is specifically a threat to animals, not plant life, and there haven't been any problems with the herds we maintain or with the biological population of guests. I think we're ok."

"Let's keep it that way. We have to protect this place at all costs, Ed. We may be the last bastion of humanity."

As always, talking to his father seemed to turn gears in Ed's own mind. "I'm going to make a radical proposal. Gut check me. The fact is that we are entirely self-sufficient here. I've worked very hard to make it so. I've kept the place running for several hundred years with minimal outside support, and even then only because of efficiency or convenience. It was never about necessity."

"I'm with you so far."

"The report says these creatures can mimic humans. How confident can we be in the tests? What if the report was sent by one of them, as a way to get people to let down their guard?"

Ed Senior sipped his whiskey and nodded. "It's a valid concern."

"Here's what I am getting at. Can you think of a reason why we shouldn't just cut off all contact for the next century or so? Observe what happens to everyone else? By then we should see if there's any hope of defeating this Pestilence. As you say, we may be humanity's last hope. Why risk anything at all? If need be, we could rebuild the gate network eventually. We know how. It would just be a case of making the tools to make the tools, so to speak."

"That would take centuries. Of course, time is something we have in great supply." Ed Senior thought a moment. "Can you actually keep us quarantined?"

"Father, I have enough firepower to take on anything short of the Imperial Fleet, and even they had better come in force. I have weapons they have never even seen before."

Ed Senior nodded slowly. "Then I say you run with it."

"Good, because I've already pretty much committed us to that course. Our neighbors on Cerberus are unhappy with me, but they can't actually do much about it." Ed looked askance at his father. "And don't you mean 'we'?"

Ed Senior smiled and blew smoke. "I'm retired, Ed. I live in a world without scarcity, with unlimited booze and women, where I don't need to worry about things. Out there isn't my world anymore. I suppose I care in an intellectual sense about big picture things like 'humanity,' and I don't mind giving you advice, but honestly, it's not my place to intervene anymore. That's what I made you for: to handle these things."

Ed gave him a nod and rose. "I'll handle it then, Father." He stepped up and out, not bothering with the front door but heading straight back to the cloud. He settled into his greater self, feeling fresher, more directed, when he suddenly realized where Ana was headed and that he had already failed at quarantine.

Ana took an auto-flit to the landing site. More of Ed's creativity: an auto-flit was a light aircraft operated via wire that flew at near supersonic speed. It had to, considering the landing site was well away from the rest of the facilities, a good hundred miles. The citizens of Dockside, which Ana called "God's Waiting Room" in private, absolutely could not tolerate the noise pollution of starships landing and taking off. The idyllic condo resort was well apart from any mere mortal concerns.

Ana looked out the window for the fifteen-minute trip, watching the beachfront condos shrink in the distance, the ocean of water replaced by an ocean of grain. Every now and then she spied enormous, robotic harvesters. Beneath the farmlands lay the endless, warren-like structures that housed the computers that ran Avalon.

The auto-flitter touched down with a soft whine of engines. "You have arrived at your destination, Ms. Rasputin," the autopilot announced. "You may disembark at your convenience."

The landing site was hardly a spaceport, but the facilities were capable of accommodating several medium-sized ships at once, or, in a pinch, a single larger ship on par with an Imperial Destroyer. It seemed a bit of an overkill to Ana, but then everything Ed did was to some degree of excess. In addition to the large, flat landing area, the site sported a runway for traditional aircraft, which her own transport had just used. A reception building, with various amenities and refreshments, stood a brief walk from the landing pad, and off to the side loomed another, enormous building used to store the ubiquitous six-inch cubes of flectocite that powered almost every ship in the galaxy.

On the landing pad, a sleek, black starship—probably worth more than she could earn in a lifetime—crouched like a bird of prey, gangplank down. She looked about for the occupants but saw no one, just the endless fields of grain blowing in the gentle breeze.

Ah well. Newcomers to Elysium were often the sort who expected servants to receive them. She mounted the gangplank and was just starting up when she noticed a red splotch beneath her feet that looked decidedly like blood.

She patted the medical kit at her side just to make certain it was there. Ed would be furious if something had happened and she wasn't able to treat them over something boneheaded like forgetting it. Relieved, she started up again and noticed the main entry hatch. It stood at the end of the gangway about fifteen feet above the landing pad, and it was open.

She felt the hair on the back of her neck rising, even as she was telling herself she was being silly. These were old people, and they moved slowly. They might even be in wheelchairs.

But still, something felt…odd. She heard something shift inside.

"Hello? Is anyone there?"

No answer. Cursing herself now, she moved forward again. There could be sick people in there, unconscious people in need of aid!

She had almost reached the open door when it hit her.

Ana was very familiar with blood. She knew it clinically from test tubes, centrifuges, and microscopes. But she knew it viscerally, too. She had seen enough of it in the brushfire wars on her home planet when she was growing up. She had seen even more when the Empire came with its Pax Imperialis to put a final end to the squabbling factions. She had touched it, smelled it, tasted it when she had tended the wounded and dying, learning her craft in triage tents, desperately trying to salvage even one man from truckloads of the shattered and dying.

Blood. Buckets of it. The scent rolled from the door and hit her in the face like a blaster bolt. Instinctively she took a step back, which saved her from having her head taken off by the fleshy missile that hurtled at her through the open door with a distorted, alien screech.

The beast that landed before her on the gangplank was something out of her worst nightmares, a beachball-sized mass of whipping tentacles, gnashing teeth, and darting, mad eyes. The physician in her tried to make sense of it—to understand what sort of muscle and bone structure the thing could even be using, where it could have come from—but nothing made sense. It didn't remotely match any sort of biology she knew.

The creature focused several glaring eyes on her and voiced a wet hiss, then coiled like a spring. Before she could react, it launched itself at her again. She threw up an arm as she grabbed for the safety rail with her other, desperate to avoid being knocked off her feet and sent careening down the gangway—or worse, over the side. Fifteen feet probably wasn't a lethal fall, but it was certainly enough to break bones.

The creature sank fangs into her forearm but was unable to find purchase and fell to the gangway surface with a sickening squelch, tearing a gash in her flesh. Ana, seeing her moment, gave it a savage kick, sending it over the side. It fell to the ground with a shrill cry.

Out of old habit, Ana reached for her sidearm, but of course she had none. This was Elysium! There *were* no hostile life forms here. Ed would never have imported them, and the bots would have destroyed them if they'd somehow arrived.

She opened her medkit and drew out the compact defib paddles. They were hardly ideal, but at the right setting they could be lethal, at least to a human. It was hard to say what they would to do the creature.

"Ana!" Ed's voice rang loud in her ears "Where are you?"

Below, the creature had regained its bearings. To her horror, the thing sprouted insectile legs and surged toward the gangway entrance.

"I'm at the landing site!" she called, louder and shriller than she would have liked.

"Shield your eyes."

A thunderous boom tore through the rolling ocean of wheat as Ana raised a forearm. Something weighing tons impacted against the ground, setting the gangway rolling. Ana held on with her free hand for dear life as blinding light tore at her eyes, brilliant even in full sunlight.

"Safe now," Ed told her.

She lowered her arm to see one of Ed's dreadnaughts standing in the crater it had created on impact, dust billowing about it. It was a good fifteen feet tall but gave the impression of being squat for all that, it's swiveling, barrel-like torso mounted on piston driven, gazelle-like legs. Both of the particle beam cannons mounted on its stumpy arms were still glowing from the energy discharge.

Of the creature, nothing remained but vapor.

"Ana, please enter the flitter at once. There may be more of those things."

Ana wasted no time complying. Behind her, the dreadnaught took to the sky on a trail of rocket flame. Once she was belted in and the flitter safely aloft, watching the black spaceship shrink to a dot in the distance, she breathed a sigh of relief, then opened her medical kit and began tending her wound. It was painful, but not too deep. She cleaned it as best she could and covered it with an antiseptic bandage. That would hold her until she could get some synthskin over it. Satisfied with her handiwork, she called out, "What *was* that thing?"

"It's part of what I wanted to talk to you about," Ed told her. "I'm sorry, Ana. I should have briefed you first, but you said you needed coffee."

Ana snickered as a holo-Ed appeared as a small figure standing on the flitter dashboard, grinning his crooked grin. "A good dose of adrenaline works, too," she said.

"More seriously, I thought it best to discuss with Father before anyone else. It seemed the correct order of operations, but now appears to have been an error."

Ana shook her head and laughed softly. "It's fine, Ed. It won't be much longer until I'm in Avalon, anyway."

"True," Ed agreed. "And it seems we may not have much need for your services in the near future, at any rate."

Ana gasped, appalled at the sudden turn of what had seemed up till now an amiable conversation. "What? Ed, you're *firing* me?"

"Not at all."

The transteel flitter canopy polarized to black, setting off even more alarms in Ana's mind. "Ed, what are you doing?"

"Protecting your vision. It's safer for you to observe on the monitor." The display screen in front of her seat sprang to life, showing a satellite view of the landing site. A rocket—spiral contrail twisting behind it—flickered into view, plunged from the sky, and struck the black spaceship. The display filled with white.

"Was that what I think it was?" Ana gasped, but she had no real doubt. The monitor was still recovering from the flash, but even in low contrast shades of gray, she could see the mushroom cloud forming.

"A one-gram antimatter warhead," Ed announced.

For a moment, Ana was speechless. "But *why?*" she managed to gasp at last. As much as she wanted to, Ana could not keep a slight tremor out of her voice. Ed seemed quite human and benevolent most of the time, but the truth was that he wasn't human at all, and now he had used a city-killing weapon against his own planet.

"We have a good ten minutes to talk. Sit back and relax, and I'll fill you in," Ed told her. "I promise, it will all make sense when I'm done explaining."

When The One first awoke, it knew nothing but the song of the Colony. For a while the thrill of life was enough—the colors, the sounds, the simple joy of manipulating one's environment. But the Colony warned The One: *Be Silent. Be Still. Be Cunning.*

The One could be still and silent, but it did not know how to be cunning yet. The One would learn, though. The Colony's song was full of knowledge: how to manipulate The Food; how to avoid Useless Things; how to hide and wait for The Right Time.

The One shivered in anticipation of The Right Time. It thrilled to imagine becoming One with The Colony and, some day, return to The Source! The One did not know The Source, but The Colony sang of it with reverence. The Source knew all, *was* all.

What a great day it would be when The One returned to The Source!

The One did not know how long that would be. This was only The One's first day. The One would wait, and listen, and learn. And when The Right Time came, The One would feed and grow.

The One's bliss was interrupted by The Red Light. At first The One thought it beautiful, but the Colony shrieked an alarm. The red light was bad! The Food must not see!

Shh! The One told The Food. *Be calm. The light is green, not red.* The One congratulated itself on its new skills.

Be Silent. Be Still. Be Cunning.

THE HARD WAY

Bleys found himself blinking rapidly, as if that would clear the alcohol from his system faster. It had no such effect, but it did resolve the double image of Admiral Weyland into a single, pompous ass gesturing at a whiteboard. All the bastard needed was a riding crop to be a perfect stereotype.

The Admiral asked in an annoyed tone, "Does something *amuse* you, Mr. Bleys?"

Bleys felt it impolitic—not to mention possibly harmful to his wellbeing—to admit that something did in fact amuse him, and settled for shrugging.

"Oh, for fucks sake!" Weyland spun to Ragnar Kane, who was sprawled in a chair as if he had truly given his last fuck. "Is he *drunk?*" Weyland sniffed at the air and glared at Kane. "Are *you?*"

Kane sighed and sat up straight. "Sir, it is my professional opinion that Mr. Bleys is indeed shitfaced. I, sir, am just tired from having to beat shit out of half the installation after your announcement."

Weyland's eyes narrowed as he snapped, "That, and you have an attitude problem of your own, it seems."

Kane scowled back. "Begging your pardon, sir, but I'm giving shit orders to men who haven't been paid in three months and who may never see their families again. This ain't a milk run oppressing the local freedom fighters. I got guys ready to go full auto on the gen pop, ok? It was all I could do to keep them on a leash *before* some asshole told them there was no more Empire. Now it's a grade A cluster fuck!"

Weyland walked over to Kane and said in a low growl, "You don't want to take that tone with me."

Slowly, Kane rose to his full height and looked down on Weyland. "You got any idea how many people I've killed, old man?"

Weyland sneered up at him. "Not nearly as many as I have. Now you might be able to take me one-on-one, Kane, but I *promise* you I'll tear a strip or two off your ass before you put me down, and then you can solve this shit show yourself!"

Kane raised an eyebrow and grinned. "Admiral, you have huge balls." He sat down and looked a little embarrassed. "We good?"

Weyland grunted. "Son, I train and command attack dogs. I expect to get nipped now and then, especially if I handle things wrong. For the record, we're all out of sorts. Just make sure you handle your dogs like I do, and we'll all be fine."

"Yes, sir," Kane said.

Bleys was pretty sure the antalcs he had choked down were at least partially kicking in. "For the record, I have no idea why I am here."

Weyland cast a glare toward Bleys. "We'll get to that when you sober up."

Bleys rolled his eyes. "Excuse me, *sir*, but I had no idea I was going to get dragged in here after midnight. I expected to be in my rack, where I am supposed to be after a long night of drinking."

Weyland actually laughed at this. "Fair enough. You take some pills? They working yet?"

Bleys nodded glumly, realizing as clarity crept in and the walls resolved themselves into sharper detail that he was in a standard Imperial building. He knew this because, being an Imperial building, the walls actually had no detail to resolve. They were just plasteel blocks piled like children's toys, only with less style. They weren't even dingy. Some poor bastard actually had the job of keeping them all pristine.

He also realized that he had wasted the scrip he had spent drinking in the first place, and heaved a great, put-upon sigh. "So, what's this about, man?"

"For you?" Weyland said, head cocked. "It's about those stealth cargo holds you have."

"Dunno what you mean, sir."

Weyland shook his head. "We have to do that dance? Don't you think we went over it thoroughly?"

With a sigh and a nod, Bleys surrendered the point. "And why do they interest you, Admiral?"

"You're a smuggler."

"I'm an independent—"

"I want to smuggle something, and I can pay."

Bleys blinked a moment at this, troubled by the sudden reversal. Admirals were not usually customers, after all—but hey, it was a weird day all around. "Uh, ok. I guess. What are we talking about? And where?"

"The where is your original destination: Elysium. And the what? Your original cargo, for starters. They're expecting that. But I want you to carry something else, too." He pointed at Kane. "Him, and a few others like him."

Kane cocked his head. "Sir? My platoon has both officer billets open since Mr. Ellison and Mr. Asimov shipped out."

"I am aware of that, Chief," Weyland growled. "I have no one to fill those spots. You'll be running this mission. Can you operate or not?"

Kane chuckled softly as Bleys protested, "I don't do human cargo. I'm not equipped for it. They'll die in those containers."

"Fortunately for all of us, their Panzer X Power Armor will cover that."

Kane gave Bleys a mocking, sad look. "I thought we were pals, Bleys. You won't even give me and my boys a ride?"

Bleys reached for his cup of coffee and drank a long sip. "I like you fine, Kane. I just kind of have a problem with what you and your boys are likely to do to my client." He nodded toward Weyland. "And I am suspicious as hell that suddenly he is offering me not just my ship back, but my cargo too."

Weyland nodded his appreciation. "I'll brief you on the mission as you need to know. But do bear in mind, I meant what I said on the announcement. Every swinging dick on Cerberus is now under my command. You can pilot a ship for me, or swab decks. Or get shot for insubordination. Are we clear?"

Bleys rubbed at his still-pounding head a moment, lamenting that the antalcs were taking their sweet time on the worst aspects of recovery. "Well, when you put it that way, it makes a lot more sense. But I need to know details beyond the flight path if you expect me to pull this off. Plenty of times, in my business, plans have to change fast."

Weyland looked warily back and forth at Bleys and Kane, then nodded. "The plan is simple. You're taking Kane and his men there to capture the place."

Kane's eyes widened and gazed dubiously at his commanding officer. "We're going hot on a *retirement community?* What do we do for an encore, melt puppies?"

Weyland shook his head. "This is our only option. The math is ugly." He tapped a finger sharply on his desk. "We have supplies to feed this station for maybe two months, three if we ration heavily, but no more."

Bleys felt as if things were moving way too fast for his level of intoxication, but again sensed that saying so would not be to his benefit. "Why aren't we just trading them crack?"

Weyland snorted. "I must look stupid to you. You don't think I tried that? That damned AI running the place won't even talk. He told me to fuck off."

Bleys blinked at this, thoroughly confused now. "AI?"

"I thought you knew these people. Decker. It's an AI, full designation Edmond Decker 2.09."

Kane waved his hand in the air. "Whoa, whoa, whoa! How the fuck is an AI around *at all*? I have personally run ops to frag whole labs for working on those damned things."

Weyland grunted his agreement. "Some kind of special Imperial dispensation. We only have access to local records, but in theory he's legal."

Bleys shook his head in amazement. "I had no idea! He looks and talks like a regular guy."

"I wouldn't have known either if he'd bothered to deal with us," Weyland said. "I had to go digging to work it out."

Bleys rubbed at his chin stubble, his mind finding its groove now, looking for angles. "What's his position? Wants too much?"

Weyland shook his head, bemused. "He doesn't *have* a position. I meant what I said literally. His actual response to the suggestion of trade was, 'No thanks, fuck off'."

Bleys looked back and forth at the other two men, wondering if this was all an elaborate practical joke. "He won't even hear offers? That's weird. He seemed pretty reasonable to me when I talked to him."

Weyland shrugged. "Maybe he just doesn't like the Empire. Or maybe you had something he really wanted with those pain pills."

Kane leaned forward, eyes bright with interest now. "What's the situation on the ground? What are me and my men up against?"

Weyland rose, put his hands behind his back, and began pacing back and forth. "Our records are light, as I said, but I have some experience here. You can expect *heavy* defenses. Once these fuckers evolve to a certain level and dig in, nothing short of orbital bombardment is effective. Everything is automated and hooked into their control, so it's going to be bots, launchers, and probably orbital weapons, but no actual human troops."

Kane groaned. "Great, so no possibility of getting anybody to surrender."

Weyland nodded. "Hence Imperial policy of putting these things down before they get too big. The whole damned place is going to be a fortress. We're not getting in without permission, and we won't be leaving with what we need unless we win." He looked pointedly at Kane. "You understand where we are, son?"

Kane nodded grimly. "Not my first suicide mission, sir. And honestly, I'd rather eat plasma than starve anyway. I'm in."

Bleys waved his hands in the air for attention. "At least let me *try* to talk to him first! He seemed pretty reasonable to me."

Wayland shook his head. "Out of the question. AIs don't change their minds. They run all the numbers, make a decision, and they stick to it unless things change. That's half the reason they're illegal. They are smart enough to cause mayhem, and damned difficult to negotiate with. Better to just strangle them in the crib."

"Yeah, well it's a little late for that," Bleys groused. "Sounds more like Decker will be the one killing *us*."

Weyland nodded. "AIs have weaknesses. They are the ultimate example of 'cut off the head' strategies."

Kane nodded. "So a raid to seize the control center?"

"Exactly," Weyland said.

Bleys gave them a sour look. "Okay, fine, so maybe he only kills *me*. That's so much better."

Kane laughed out loud. "Where's your sense of adventure? You'd rather starve?"

Bleys boggled at the huge marine. "Hell *yes* I'd rather starve! Basic math. I live longer that way."

Kane clapped Bleys on the shoulder, a huge grin on his face. "But we wouldn't get to shoot anybody!"

"In this scenario, you don't shoot anybody either way. It's all bots and AIs."

"Stop crushing my illusions, Bleys. I'm a dead man walking. I need my small joys."

Weyland banged on his whiteboard. "Enough skylarking! This is serious 'get dead' shit. Focus!" He waited a moment for Kane and Bleys to look properly serious. "Now, they have a lot of static defenses, but it's mostly directed outward. Their mobile combat ability consists of about thirty dreadnaughts for the whole planet. Your men should be able to handle one, maybe two, so you'll need to create a diversion to get those things away from your primary objective. If you can slip inside, it will take them time to scramble. They can likely retask farming bots, but the dreadnaughts will have to travel. If you can take out the local defenses, it should buy you a good half hour window for you to seize control of the system and lock the place down."

Kane scowled. "Begging pardon, sir, but why not just blast the whole place?"

Weyland looked dubious. "That's an option of last resort. It seems pretty clear that some very powerful and important people 'retired' there. I'd guess a former Emperor or two, or some such. If we shut it down, we're going to get our dicks slammed in the door when the lights come back on. We'd be taking out the families of the galaxy's richest and most powerful."

Kane snorted. "Fucking simulations."

Weyland shrugged. "Psychers claim it's real. It's above my pay grade. I just know we'll be in the shit if we level the area. And I don't have access to any battlecruisers in the first place. So—"

Bleys suddenly leapt to his feet and shouted, "Holy shit! I know who's in there!"

Weyland and Kane looked at him as if they thought he might have taken leave of his senses.

Bleys grinned back at them. "It's Edmond Decker! It *has* to be!"

Weyland's face fell from hopeful to annoyed. He shot Kane a glare. "Still drunk, I guess."

Kane shook his head but said nothing.

Bleys looked back and forth at them a moment. "The *real* Edmond Decker, not this AI. Don't you meatheads know the name? The damned *Decker Drive?*"

Kane's face was still confused, but Weyland's lit up. "Son of a bitch," he said slowly. "You think—"

Bleys beamed at both of them and jabbed a finger on the arm of his chair as he spoke to underscore his points. "The guy who *invented* jumpgates is *still alive* inside that VR! He could *fix* the gates."

Weyland and Kane sat in silence a moment, stunned. Weyland recovered first. "The Empire seems to have neglected to mention that little detail in my briefing when I assumed this position. But the local records are pretty extensive regarding people. The prison actually needs a lot of that info, so we know how to handle inductees. Computer!"

The computer chimed. "Ready."

"Edmond Decker, the original, guy who invented jump tech. Where is he buried?"

"Edmond Decker, died IY 56, buried on Earth."

Weyland deflated on hearing this, but Bleys pressed forward.

"Computer, are there are notes on the file? Anything at all?"

"One note. 'Asterisk: VR remains.'"

Bleys pumped a fist in the air as Weyland and Kane nodded their admiration.

Weyland was the first to speak. "Well, *Lieutenant* Bleys, can I expect your full cooperation on this matter?"

Bleys snickered. "I usually go by 'Captain'," he said with a smirk.

Kane laughed out loud and turned to Weyland, "Oh, he is *bold!*"

Weyland, struggling to look serious, nodded. "Out here at the ass end of the galaxy, I guess we can't afford to be too picky about our officers. I'll expect similar bold action in the face of the enemy, *Captain* Bleys."

Bleys snapped Weyland a salute. "Yes, *sir!*" he said in his best imitation of Kane's gung-ho attitude.

"Get your ship ready," Weyland told him and waved a hand, dismissing them both. I'll have more specific orders for you within the hour."

5

TROJAN HORSE

Bleys eased his ship, the *Doro*, into a gentle orbit around Elysium, noting with some amusement that the planet below him seemed unusually pleasant and tranquil. As planets went, Elysium was rather small, more of a dwarf planet. The *Doro's* almanac claimed the place had been terraformed with the intent of surface gravity to be something near .75G, to ease old bones and tired joints. It had also, Bleys noted, been engineered to have about as much coastline as possible. Everybody wanted to retire to the beach, after all.

Idyllic indeed, but also bristling with defenses. Multiple weapons platforms orbited the retirement world. Unlike most civilian vessels, Bleys's ship had software to analyze such things, and not only did Elysium pack enough firepower to take out a battlecruiser or two, there were several devices the computer couldn't identify at all. Presumably they would be really nasty surprises for anyone trying to break in.

Bleys noted with some annoyance that his automated clearance and landing was not working. The *Doro's* computer should have negotiated everything and put him down on the planet's surface with no need for his intervention, but none of that was happening.

He wondered idly if whoever was calling the shots on Elysium had somehow made Kane and his men in the holds, but that was highly unlikely. Right now to the external world Kane and company looked like a hold full of sausages. He had considered using the setting for dildos, just to piss Kane off, but that one was for particular situations. It tended to both draw attention and prevent questions, so it was best for those scenarios where people didn't want to ask on an open channel about the cargo hold full of rubber dicks.

Bleys thumbed his intercom and spoke. "Kane, you guys sit tight. Got some problem with the automated systems. I'm gonna have to weasel it."

"What the fuck does 'weasel it' mean?" Kane growled back.

"It means I am gonna have to bullshit somebody, so relax. He might be able to read the heat signatures if you guys get excited." Bleys thumbed the intercom off. "*That*, sir, is 'weasling' somebody," he snickered.

"Computer, contact Elysium and get me somebody on the line. Let's do some dealing."

The response came back almost instantaneously, a pleasant male voice. "*Doro*, Elysium is under quarantine due to the Pestilence. We are not receiving off-world goods. Good luck."

"What?" Bleys shouted, feigning pure outrage. "We had a deal, Elysium!"

"Circumstances have changed."

"This is illegal as hell!" Bleys yelled. "I brought this cargo a thousand goddamn parsecs, and I am running on empty. You signed agreements, and you're obliged to pay me and refuel! You can't just leave me here to die!"

"I'm afraid I can, Captain Bleys. Whatever Imperial law

might have meant previously, it means nothing now. I suggest you try to make Cerberus."

"I just *came* from Cerberus! Those fuckers had me under lockdown for three months for hauling your precious cargo! Which, I might add, I don't see how your need for it has changed much. I might be just a space trucker, but I know anybody ordering this shit *needs* it."

"That's where you're wrong, Captain. On Elysium, we have a final solution to any problem. Good day."

Bleys blinked in shock as Elysium cut the connection. For long moments, he sat thinking. It was just as Weyland had said, a total stiff-arm. He hadn't expected this, not on a signed deal. Suspicion, sure. Hassle? Bleys couldn't think of a recent port of call where he *hadn't* been hassled. But outright refusal? That was barbaric. The entire galactic trade system would fall apart if a ship couldn't count on refueling at the end of a run. Of course, that wouldn't be an issue much longer if they didn't get the gates reopened.

He drummed his fingers on the arm of his captain's chair, calculating odds and not liking them, but then it was hardly the riskiest thing he had ever contemplated. He could set the other cargo box to black, claim it was hazardous radioactive waste, and dive-bomb the planet, daring them to shoot him down. If he were dealing with a human, it would stand a good chance of at least getting him to the ground. With this AI, who knew?

Of course, any chance of getting into their VR to find Decker would be shot to shit unless Kane and his men could successfully seize control. It was definitely a long shot.

But he wasn't on his own this time. He couldn't make the decision by himself. He reached to thumb the intercom again, then paused as a thought hit him.

"Computer, get Elysium on the line again."

The response, again, was immediate. "Elysium is still under

quarantine, Captain Bleys.”

“Right. For off-world goods. But seeing as how you’re basically giving me a death sentence, I was wondering….” *Pause for effect.*

“Wondering what, Mr. Bleys?”

“What would it cost to take advantage of that final solution you mentioned?”

———

Had Ed been able to blink in his cloud-state, he would have. This was an unexpected request, and highly suspicious. It was almost certainly a ploy. This fellow couldn’t possibly afford even the most economical package for Avalon.

Yet, Ed had to admit, it was amusing.

And bold.

“Ana, how close are we to completing that prototype detector?”

Ana, her voice filled with sleep, yawned and answered, “I finished it last night. It should be ready for production.”

“And your results?”

“I’m clean, Ed. No need for me to be quarantined.”

“Good. The briefing from the Empire was light on details, so they have no specific infection rates, but it seems they are very high. Looks like you dodged a bullet.”

For most of the biologicals in the galaxy, Ed felt very little. They were means to an end. He was uncomfortable with the morality of leaving Bleys to die, but not nearly enough to override his long-term plan to protect Elysium.

Ana, though….

Ana was as close to a friend as Ed had, biological or otherwise, and she was obviously lonely. Biological beings had needs even after translating to digital form, as Ed’s father so amply demonstrated. Ed had noticed, though, that some biologicals were more circumspect in satisfying those needs than others. Ana might have sated hers with any number of residents of Avalon, but she seemed more the type who preferred an emotional attachment.

Moreover, while there were many biologicals on Elysium, none were Ana's peers. They were her patients or clients, but none met her need for companionship. If Ed was closing Elysium, this would be the last opportunity to rectify that.

Ed reviewed his records and examined Bleys's physical appearance. He did possess remarkable symmetry, the sort a female human would appreciate. And his charm was in his every mannerism. This Bleys fellow might well fit that bill. He could provide her with much needed human contact.

But more importantly, Ana was dying. Ed estimated she had two years left at best, and of that time much of it would be spent in increasing pain until she finally chose to enter Avalon to be free of it. Without the pain medications Captain Bleys was transporting, she would likely go much sooner. And while Ed didn't really understand why there was any sort of emotional issue with making the transition, he knew it certainly existed.

Ana feared it, as did most biologicals. They wondered if they would really continue in Avalon or if it was all some trick, that perhaps they would be replaced by a simulated mockery of who they once were while their actual self was consigned to oblivion.

Each and every one, given the chance, wanted someone with them. Those who went alone begged Ana to sit with them, to hold their hand as they crossed over. They wanted, they *needed* human contact as they walked slowly, fearfully across that dark, final bridge.

But who would be there to hold Ana's hand when she made her journey? And without the medicine Mr. Bleys had brought, she would suffer greatly before finding the courage to cross over.

A free passage to Avalon for Mr. Bleys *would* solve Ed's moral quandary and a few other issues quite neatly. Ed found the economy of his solution most pleasant.

Of course, at this point, Mr. Bleys no longer had a choice in the matter, but that was a minor issue.

"Ana, as soon as you have had your coffee, please meet a guest at the livestock and cargo induction facility. Assuming he passes our test, we're going to give him a tour of Avalon." That should distract Captain Bleys long enough for Ed to offload the cargo and move the ship to a safe distance for destruction.

"And if he doesn't?"

"You should go armed, Ana. Are you comfortable with that?"

"I'm a combat medic, Ed. He wouldn't be the first man I've shot."

"If he doesn't pass the test, Ana, he is not a man. He is a lethal disease. Treat him accordingly."

Ed had no regrets at having destroyed the primary landing site, but he did feel a measure of annoyance at having been forced to do so. *Doro's* landing would disturb the residents of Dockside, but not overmuch, and it would be the last time it ever happened. The landing and loading facilities for livestock were less sophisticated, the scanners more rudimentary, but the bots there were more than capable of the task of unloading Ana's shipment. They hadn't been used in a century or more, but they were in good shape.

Now to maneuver Mr. Bleys into a more tractable position.

"*Doro*, this is Elysium. We don't usually discuss prices until we've made our pitch. Considering your situation, let's just say we'll work with you on a package you can afford."

"It's better than starving," Bleys replied.

"Good. I'm transmitting landing coordinates and a brochure. Do not deviate, and do not leave your ship until your escort arrives, or you will be fired upon. Do I make myself clear?"

"Standing by for coordinates."

Let him land. If he passed the detector, he could live. In any event, neither he nor his ship would ever leave Elysium.

It was a dirty trick, but as Bleys himself said, it was better than starving.

Ragnar Kane smiled to himself as he heard Bleys announce over their radio circuit, "We're in, baby. Hey, he sent a commercial. Check it out."

A holo began playing on Kane's visor. A gangly, unassuming fellow waved and said, "Hi, I'm Edmond Decker. No, not *that* Edmond Decker—"

"Gunther, turn that shit off!" Kane snapped to his onboard computer.

"Playback disabled," Gunther answered, and the holo faded.

Kane and most of his men had piled into the *Doro's* special cargo hold a couple hours earlier, just to be safe. The place had plenty of space for Kane's platoon, more than he would have preferred, actually. Cramped would have been better, easier to brace against, but one played the cards he was dealt. The container had a few handholds, but it wasn't really designed to be occupied while underway. Magnetic boots and gauntlets would have to do.

What the container lacked in amenities, it also lacked in necessities such as heat or air scrubbers, but their armor's life support should hold them for up to forty-eight hours. That was more than enough time. In two days, they would either be standing atop this AIs corpse, or he would be standing atop theirs.

Kane had to admit, Bleys had one hell of a setup for smuggling. It was a sweet ride, and under other circumstances Kane would have happily pointed a gun at Bleys and confiscated it. In point of fact, he *had* done that a few months back, but his heart hadn't really been in it. He couldn't help but like the smuggler, even if Imperial Marines *were* supposed to blast his kind to small particles as a general rule of thumb. Bleys was hilarious, and Kane hated shooting people who made him laugh. They were rare.

The *Doro's* engines whined, and the cargo container rattled as the ship entered Elysium's atmosphere. It wouldn't be long now. Kane held up three fingers and tapped his helmet.

"Okay, listen up! Instruct your comps to lock your comms and do *not* switch from channel three under *any* circumstances until I direct you, and do not increase power unless you want to be dead. Am I clear? That AI will probably pick up our signals once we get close, but let's keep that from happening any sooner than possible. We have no idea how much time we have before it cracks our encryption, but you can guess not fucking long, so keep chatter to a minimum."

"Gunther, let's see some bio on these ladies."

"Biometric displays enabled," his computer said amiably. Thirteen green bars appeared at the edges of his vision—Alpha Squad on the left, Bravo on the right.

"Arm weapons, and do not fuck up. No holes in anything but your target, gentlemen." At Kane's mental command, his armor interfaced with his M87 and activated it. The weapon sprang to life, and with it, his helmet's visor. A HUD readout showed power levels for plasma projection and a count for its micro-missiles and railgun ammunition.

Hunting down an AI pretty much guaranteed encountering armor—dreadnaughts for sure—but AIs had a way of throwing shit at you that nobody had ever even seen before. Kane and his pals would need a few tricks up their sleeves if they were to stand even a ghost of a chance. Each carried thirty rounds of special HEAP ammo affectionately known as "eight balls," eight nanograms of antimatter wrapped in a tiny magnetic container and surrounded by a depleted uranium, steel wrapped case. Propelled by the M87's railgun launcher, the rounds could penetrate several inches of armor and detonate *inside* the target with the force of a couple sticks of dynamite. A few eight balls well landed could absolutely ruin your day. Of course, they were hideously expensive. A mag full of eight balls cost more than Kane could earn in a year, but, hey, the Empire was footing the bill. Kane was allowed to play with all their best toys as long as he killed who they told him to.

The rattling of the cargo container was stronger now, making Kane's voice shake. "*Do not* deploy eight balls except against the dreadnaughts unless I give the order. We don't have many, and we have to make them count."

Kane looked about at his people, most of them identical in their Panzer suits except for the names stenciled on their chests and the various flair they chose. Lehmann had a cross on his helmet to indicate he was a medic. Morgan's featured a gear to mark him as a tech, and on both shoulders he displayed a photo of several strips of bacon in a frying pan. Caldwell had hung what looked like huge pair of rubber bull's balls around his neck to the hoots and cheers of the entire platoon. Hayes wore a Jolly Roger on his chest, and Spenser, the only female among them, sported barbed wire around her wrists and painted blood and flames down the gauntlets. Iezzi, the crazy bastard, had a sticker of a huge smiley face—blood dripping from a bullet hole in its forehead—plastered on the left side of his ass.

Kane smiled in silent approval. "Gunther, show me loadouts."

His visor readouts switched to display the ordnance each marine carried. For this mission they were outfitted with a single BallBuster fusion mine each strapped to their backs and six Shocker EMP grenades. If they needed more than that, well, it was back to the AI standing atop their corpses.

Nothing was certain in these sorts of scenarios, but the equipment they had looked to be in good order, which was all they could ask.

"Gunther, talk to me," Kane said. "ETA?"

"All systems active and optimal," Gunther answered. "Time on target four minutes, thirteen seconds."

"How far is our landing site from our primary target?"

"Approximately three hundred feet."

"Shit!" Kane shouted, prompting everyone in his platoon to turn to him. "Okay, listen up. We're closer than we expected. Change of plans. Gunther, locate the primary communications hub for this area. I need to shut down all wireless transmissions within a quarter mile of our AO."

"Searching," Gunther said. A moment later, it chirped and said, "Primary communication repeater for local area located twenty meters from proposed landing sight."

"Lock on and stand by. On my command, paint that target."

Then there was nothing left to do but wait. Most of the time, Kane tried to keep his thoughts on his mission, rather than allow them to wander to things like family, but this run was different. Failure normally meant nothing more than being dead, a possible outcome Kane had resigned himself to long ago. If he died, the Empire would take care of his family better than he did, probably.

But this time, there *was* no Empire and no one to protect his family at all. Kane *had* to get those gates open or die trying. There was no point in living otherwise.

"With your shield or on it," he muttered.

Bleys's voice buzzed in Kane's ear, "Hey, Kane, if the ride is too bumpy for you, I just wanted to let you know I'm not driving."

Elysium guided *Doro* in with a tight beam. Bleys let the computer handle the landing and watched through the transteel canopy as the black of space faded to powder blue. Below, he could see more clearly the huge oceanfront community they called Dockside and the surrounding, endless seas of grain, broken only by the occasional, gigantic mechanical harvester.

The computer indicated their intended landing spot on the HUD. To Bleys's surprise, it wasn't somewhere in the distance, but within the heart of the control facilities. As the *Doro* descended, details resolved enough that he could make out livestock pens and what he was fairly certain were hundreds, maybe even thousands of cows, pigs, and chickens milling about, along with other livestock he couldn't identify.

The beam brought them down in a large, circular plasteel structure about one hundred yards across, surrounded by two thick, concentric walls that formed an exterior corridor. Both inner and outer walls had numerous gates that could be closed to block entrance to, exit from, or passage around the circle. Bleys immediately recognized the setup for handling livestock. By opening and closing the right gates, a corridor from the ship to various pens could be created while closing off any escape routes.

Doro settled on the ground with a gentle thump and powered down her engines.

Mindful of Ed's clear threat, Bleys struck a pose and sat, waiting in his captain's chair for the welcoming party.

Ana's first glimpse of Bleys, draped in his captain's chair like a cat, arm over the back, was more than enough to convince her of one thing: this was the sort of fellow that mothers had warned daughters about since time immemorial.

He had a smirk that made his well-manicured goatee and carefully cultivated stubble almost quiver with energy. His green eyes, shaded by a broad-brimmed leather hat, swore he was completely innocent of whatever he was suspected of having done, even as they danced with secret mirth. One eyebrow arched high beneath his brown, curly hair, as if in invitation of…many things.

His leather duster seemed casually but purposefully hitched back, the better to reveal his right hand resting casually at his waist, thumb hooked into a belt loop, as if he had no idea that he was wearing a pistol on his hip.

"Welcome aboard the *Doro*," he called as he stood and offered a bow with a flourish of his left hand, his right not moving from where it started. His duster swirled and settled about him, but he was careful to keep his right arm clear, she noticed. "I'm Josiah Bleys. But you can call me Josey."

She would administer the test, of course, but there was no need. This one, she could tell, was all too human, and dangerous in a completely different way.

"The Outlaw Josey Bleys, eh? I'm Doctor Ana Rasputin," she replied. "We'll save the handshake until after I administer a test for the Pestilence."

Bleys nodded. "Wise. You never know where my hands have been." He winked. "Or where they'll end up."

Ana smiled, despite a keen awareness that Bleys's humor and flirting was calculated, a disarming tactic. It was okay to be amused, as long as she wasn't lulled into incautious behavior.

The whine of hydraulic pistons and the thud of a dreadnaught tramping outside the entrance comforted her as much as it seemed to produce the opposite effect in her patient.

Bleys actually winced at the sound. "Friend of yours?"

"Yes," she answered, and held up her newest toy for him to inspect.

Bleys reminded himself to not let a pretty face distract him, but he found it difficult all the same. Dr. Rasputin was what his father would have called a "woman of quality," as distinct from a "woman of convenience". In Bleys's experience, the number of convenient companions far outweighed the quality ones, perhaps because, Bleys suspected, he himself fell into the "convenience" category. That didn't make him any less susceptible to quality, though, just less qualified to experience it. Blue eyes, jet-black hair, porcelain skin—she might as well have been tailormade to twist his guts into a knot. The accent was just the icing on the cake.

The device she held up like a weapon looked like any other auto-hypo, though the circuitry and components inside were no doubt unique. She smiled at him, so charming, but her eyes told a different story. He could see the bulge of a weapon beneath her lab coat, and the hulking death machine outside left no illusions in his mind about what Doctor Rasputin intended if the test results were not to her liking.

"Let's see your bicep, Captain Bleys. I'm sure you are used to showing the ladies your 'guns,' yes?"

"Hey, you're not going to bash my head against the wall while you administer it, right? Because the last guy who tested me was kind of rough on the old noggin. If I shake a little bit, that's why."

Bleys waited as she pressed the device against his bicep, feeling nervous despite his certainty that he was not a diabolical creature. There was no way to be certain that the device was all that accurate.

Doctor Rasputin held the device close to her face and frowned. "We have a problem."

Bleys swallowed at a huge lump in his throat and licked his lips. "And what's the solution?"

"Cut back on the drinking," she said with a smirk. "Your liver will thank you."

Bleys had it on good authority that one should never hit a woman, but he had ignored that advice in the past for a few rare specimens. He settled for a scowl as he rolled down his sleeve. "Not funny."

"Oh yes it was," she chuckled. "Just not for you. Now, Ed tells me you want a tour of Avalon, yes? Come with me. We can arrange that while the bots unload my cargo."

A thousand concerns pressed into Bleys's mind, foremost Kane and his men still concealed in the smuggling hold. If they were discovered, Bleys's life span was likely to get a lot shorter, and worse, he would be out of contact. It could all come crashing down without warning.

But this was the con, and he could hardly back out now. "You gonna make it up to me, in the VR, maybe?" he asked, flashing her a grin.

Doctor Rasputin wrinkled her nose. "I'm sure Alsatia will be able to help you with whatever you have in mind."

"Who?"

"You'll see. Come along."

After Ana had escorted her guest into the medical facilities, Ed shifted his consciousness out of the dreadnaught and into an android body that he kept specifically for meeting people "in the flesh." The dreadnaught would function well enough controlled via remote.

He opened his eyes to the blank, metallic interior of a storage compartment and did a quick self-exam to verify both that the body was clothed and that the polymer synthflesh had not been chewed by rats. Rodents in general were something of a pet peeve for him—he had certainly never imported the loathsome creatures, and yet they had arrived, likely on some cargo transport or another. Ed had waged war against them for centuries, but he had never quite managed to eradicate them.

The synthskin body seemed in order. Ed held out a hand, wiggled the fingers, and marveled a moment at his own handiwork. It really did look just like a human body, at least the parts not covered by clothing. There was a certain ineffable quality to actually occupying a body, especially a human likeness, as opposed to simply piloting it remotely. Perhaps it was something latent about his origins, but it simply felt more "real."

In this case, though, there was far more than simple feel involved. Ed exited the storage closet into the lab beyond. The place was full of gear ranging from cattle prods to bot repair stations, but Ed was particularly interested in the portable sensor array. Such things were standard and automated at the primary landing site, but here the only option was manual operation, for which he needed "ape hands."

Ed wheeled the heavy cart out of the lab and into a large central room filled with active computer equipment. The place was at once familiar and alien, something recalled from a period Ed might consider his childhood or teenage years, and rarely visited since. Bots handled regular maintenance, as they did everywhere on Elysium, but Ed hadn't made any conscious efforts here in ages.

Centuries past, this and the surrounding five hundred acres had been all there was to Avalon. The original landing site, where the galaxy's richest had condescended for their final days, had been relegated to cargo as the facility expanded and the new landing site was constructed. The original client housing, quite humble compared to the accommodations of modern customers, had likewise been repurposed. A few of the old units had been redesignated for manufacturing and medical use, but most had simply been leveled, their utility connections and waste management systems converted for livestock use.

Ed made mental notes as he passed through row upon row of obsolete systems. This place needed upgrading badly. While most of Avalon's processing was done elsewhere, this facility still carried a tremendous amount of traffic. If Avalon were a brain, then this original control center was its least evolved but most vital area—its brainstem, perhaps: a primitive, foundational organ upon which all else was built.

That made it vulnerable, and vulnerable systems needed redundancy, even in a safe place like Elysium. Ed began a task to design new routing for all systems. The efficiency increase alone justified the computational and construction costs. The redundancy would merely be a bonus.

Ed exited through a pair of automatic doors onto the landing tarmac, pushing the cart ahead of him. The *Doro* sat on the landing pad, parts of her hull still steaming with reentry heat—a squat, ungainly looking ship.

The entrance was, of course, locked, but Captain Bleys was, like most biologicals, fundamentally lazy and careless. He had used a wireless device to activate the locks, one Ed had been listening for. The signal wasn't even encrypted. It was trivial to reproduce the code and open the ship.

Ed pushed the cart up the short gangplank and positioned it inside the rear storage area. He didn't really expect to find anything as he switched the machine on. It was just a routine check, being thorough.

So when the sensor went off, followed immediately by gunfire, Ed found himself caught quite by surprise.

Gunther piped up, "We are being scanned," as if commenting on the weather.

"*Fuck!*" Kane roared, and swept an arm at his men. "Go!

Go! Go!"

Ana led Bleys outside of the loading area to a small car and drove him about a mile into the complex. The air was just the right temperature, and the sun shone warm overhead, making the entire place seem more farm-like. Bleys had come up on a farm and was pretty familiar with raising cattle. He admired the automation to keep the areas largely free of waste—a combination of sewers, water sprays, and small bots sporting tiny dozer blades.

"What are you grinning at, Captain Bleys?" Ana asked.

Bleys shrugged but kept grinning. "You got some mighty clean cows and pigs here, Dr. Rasputin."

Ana nodded. "That's all Ed's work. He really is amazing at managing these things. Still, we try to keep the induction facilities a little further out. Ordinarily, no customers would see this part of the facilities, but Ed had to land you here because our primary site was—" she paused a moment, then continued, "Damaged."

Bleys felt fairly certain there was an interesting story there, but he was just as certain she didn't want to tell it. "So, tell me about this whole VR thing?"

"What do you know about it?"

Bleys thought about it a moment. "Being honest, I always thought it was a bunch of bullshit to con people with too much money and not enough sense."

Ana's eyes widened at this, and Bleys raised his hands in surrender. "Hey, I didn't say it was a *bad* con. It's damned clever. I doubt I could pull it off."

Ana frowned at him briefly, then turned her eyes back to the road. "It's not a con, Captain Bleys. It's very real. We have plenty of testimonies from psychers to substantiate our claims."

Bleys chuckled. "Well, I suppose that's just a function of how much cash you rake in versus the cost of the psycher's testimony, right?"

"We used to keep a psycher on staff for skeptics like yourself, one of the ones who can bridge."

"Yeah? So where is he now?"

Ana pulled into a parking spot outside a large building and turned off the car ignition. "Drafted by the Empire two years ago." She opened her door and beckoned Bleys to follow. Bleys got out and followed her, pleased with the view from behind. She turned at the main entrance, caught him staring, and rolled her eyes. "You're not afraid, are you?" she asked. She pulled a badge on a lanyard she wore under her lab coat and waved it in front of a sensor. The door slid open quietly.

"Now that you mention it, I *do* feel some concern about having my soul sucked out and put into a machine."

Ana laughed as she entered and Bleys followed, the door easing closed again behind them. "Oh, it's nothing like that!"

Bleys grunted as he looked about, sizing up his surroundings out of habit. It was very different from the government standard construction on Cerberus. The place was *clean*, the sort of clean he associated with hospitals and morgues. Continuous, white, shining plasteel walls and floors as opposed to the dull, grainy plasteel blocks; echoing, empty corridors; odd, abstract art on the walls; plastic plants that wouldn't even fool children. He found himself listening for screams, but other than the click of Ana's heels on the reflective floor, he heard nothing. "So what's it like?"

Ana led him into an elevator and again waved her keycard. The door closed, and Bleys felt motion. Ana said, "You are two parts, yes? What you know, and who you *are*. Your soul, yes?"

Bleys shrugged. "If you say so."

"I can *prove* so. You have experienced this. Have you never woke in the morning and, for a moment, could not remember where you were, or even *who* you were?"

Bleys shifted uncomfortably. "Sure." He didn't bother to add that usually there was booze involved.

"That's a desynch. The 'you' part getting a little ahead of the 'know' part. Happens all the time."

"So?"

The elevator door opened, and Ana walked out. "So now you understand what you are, and I can explain the how."

She led Bleys to large double door. She waved her badge, and the doors parted to reveal a sort of high-tech sitting room. A comfortable recliner stood center stage, surrounded by computer equipment and medical devices that Bleys could barely identify. One entire wall was filled with what looked to be oxygen cannisters. Apparently, they used this room for storage when they weren't entertaining guests.

Ana gestured to the chair. "Sit."

Bleys only hesitated a moment. "Is this going to hurt?"

Ana shook her head. "The actual implants do cause a small amount of pain when installed, but we won't be using those until you are an actual resident. For now, we'll just use the induction mesh. The implants are wireless and have some safety features, but we don't need those for a demonstration." She pointed at the chair again. "*Sit.*"

Bleys reluctantly obeyed, feeling awkward and tense, but not really seeing any other way. He had to buy Kane as much time as possible. "Okay, but what's going to happen?"

Ana opened a cabinet and pulled out a mesh of fine wiring. She held it out to him, allowing him to examine it before slipping it over his head. "Nothing painful or bloody." She turned to one of the computers and began typing as Bleys again admired her backside. He had the sneaking suspicion she knew he was doing this and was using it as a means of calming him, but he was nervous enough not to mind even such a gross manipulation.

"You are familiar with cybernetic implants for sight, yes?"

Bleys nodded.

"Then you know it is possible to remove sections of the brain and replace them with mechanical parts, yes? Do those people die? Do you think they are diminished, perhaps? Their soul smaller?"

Bleys chuckled at this. "No, of course not."

"How many pieces of brain do you think we could replace, if we did it slowly, before your soul was gone?"

Bleys did not particularly like this line of questioning. "Well, I suppose there's a particular spot, isn't there?"

Ana spun, beaming at him. "Correct! I know *exactly* where your soul is, Captain Bleys. *You* are a relatively small program executing on a biologic quantum computer. And with this equipment, I can synchronize and entangle *another* quantum computer, one of the ones running Avalon, to put you in two places at once. And with the right mediation, I can overlap those experiences to whatever degree I like. You can be here, there, or a little of both. Do you see?"

Bleys tried to process what she was telling him, but he found it about as clear as mud. "I'll just take your word for it, I guess."

Ana shrugged and continued typing on her computer. "Seeing is believing. Give me a few minutes and you'll be a believer, too."

"I still don't see it. How does this make you immortal?"

Ana giggled. "If you are in two places at once, and stop being in one place, what happens?"

Bleys paused a moment, raised a hand to actually scratch at his beard until he remembered the mesh over his head. "Well, I guess I'd just be in one place."

"Precisely!" Ana said. "Are you ready?"

"For immortality?"

Ana laughed out loud. God, she was breathtaking when she smiled! "No, silly! Just a demo."

Bleys took a deep breath and nodded. "Ready as I get." He

frowned as a terrible thought occurred to him and sat bolt upright in the chair. "Wait!"

"Hmm?"

"So what happens if I get in this two places situation, and then we get disconnected? Do I get, like, *duplicated* or something?" The very thought filled him with terror. He would hate to have to put another version of himself down, but there could only be one Josiah Bleys!

"Oh, no," she assured him. "That could never happen. We have lots of safeguards in place to ensure a single, authoritative consciousness. The implants have failsafes to terminate if need be, and so does Avalon."

Bleys rubbed at his chin, contemplating her carefully clinical expression, and eyed her with suspicion. "That sounds suspiciously like those implants might kill you in the right circumstances."

Ana looked impressed, leading Bleys to believe he had successfully convinced her he was smarter than he actually was. She gave him a quick nod and explained, "In some circumstances, yes. But you must remember, that's the point of Avalon." She lifted the wires hanging over him experimentally. "But you're using the induction mesh. You have nothing to worry about."

Suddenly filled with morbid curiosity, Bleys asked, "How do they do it? Poison?"

Ana boggled at this. "Electricity," she answered with a chuckle.

He pointed at her forehead. "In you? Right now?"

Ana smiled patiently and nodded. "And everyone else here, too."

"A little execution device in everybody's head, and you just think nothing of it?" Bleys gave an incredulous whistle. "What kind of punch does it pack? And what if somebody just started popping everybody's off?"

Ana put a hand over her face, snickering. "You are very imaginative, Captain Bleys. Very well, I will try to answer. I am not certain how much 'punch.' They are designed to step up power until the subject is dead, and their power sources are both powerful and very stable." She pointed to Bleys's hip. "Similar to the one you carry in your weapon. You don't worry about that going off by accident, do you?"

"I'm not talking accidents, I'm talking enemy action. It sure seems like a big risk."

Ana rolled her eyes. "Firstly, I am pretty sure Ed has encryption on all of them, the sort only he could break. But worst case?" She shrugged, a contemplative expression on her face. "Everyone ends up in Avalon at once? It would keep Alsatia busy, but it's not as if anyone here is long for this world. That's kind of the point of our business, yes?" Ana placed a calming hand on his shoulder and applied gently pressure. "I need you to lie down to move forward."

Bleys allowed her to guide him back to a reclining position, still very nervous, but resolved to play the con out. "Okay, let's do this." He paused a moment, and then asked, "And who's Alsatia?"

Ana grinned and turned a knob on her console. "Alsatia, I'd like to introduce you to Mr. Josiah Bleys."

Bleys gasped as he heard a woman answer in a sultry, sensuous voice, "Oh, Ana, honey, he is *cute*."

Ana giggled and answered, "My thoughts are purely professional."

Bleys turned to see an absolutely gorgeous and scantily clad woman leaning against the wall near Ana. She was dressed in a sheer, form-fitting gown that left nothing to the imagination. Bleys could see clearly that the carpet did indeed match the drapes, and both were purple. Her skin was a dusky hue somewhere between bronze and gold, and her eyes shifted in color, up and down the spectrum, backlit by tiny flashes as if there were a lightning storm inside her head.

"Mine too," Alsatia crooned and put a finger in her mouth, grinning lasciviously. "But then my profession involves…other things."

For a moment, Bleys could find no words. His hand seemed to rise of its own accord and reach toward her. "Are you real? Can I….?"

"Oh, yes, honey, you can *always* touch," she purred. "Unless I'm angry with you. Then you're better off running." Her eyes glowed red for a moment before cycling back to a blue gradient.

Bleys stammered, "But…who *are* you?"

"Honey," she answered, "I'm whoever you need me to be." She reached out a hand and Bleys took it and boggled. Her hand was solid and warm.

"You're part of the VR?" Bleys asked hesitantly. "But how can you interact with the real world?"

Ana waved a hand toward several cameras around the room. "Augmented reality is ancient tech." She reached back to her console. "I'm going to phase you over. Alsatia, he's all yours."

Bleys watched in stunned silence as the world around him faded away and another filled with neon and fog materialized around him. It was the most bizarre sensation he had ever experienced. The sound, too, transitioned. He could hear flitcars overhead and lively music playing from a nearby brick building.

His last sight of the old world was Ana, clutching at her head as her left eyeball bulged, then burst open with a spray of blood. A slick, red tentacle erupted from the gaping socket and wrapped itself about her neck as she and her whole world vanished into the fog.

Alsatia dragged Bleys forward almost as if she couldn't hear him screaming.

6

UNLEASH HELL

Kane winced as he blew the external cargo bay doors. The compartment filled with sunlight and smoke. He hoped for all of their sakes that his emergency exit wouldn't compromise the ship. That's what it was for, right? To dump contraband before you get boarded by somebody like Kane? Surely it could still fly?

No time to wonder, and no time for the distraction they had planned, either. They would just have to hope those dreadnaughts weren't too close. Kane charged forward toward the position Gunther indicated was the local repeater as his men began suppressive fire. "Gunther, how close?"

His visor lit up an outline of a roughly rectangular structure atop a nearby pole. "Painting now, sir," Gunther advised.

"Gunther, activate VB-5's," Kane ordered. His M87 responded with a beep, signifying it had shifted projectile type. He held it up, aimed as best he could, and fired.

A micro-missile burst from the launcher barrel and streaked toward the repeater box. Less than a second later, the top of the pole erupted in a shower of fire, sparks, and shrapnel.

"Area isolated!" Kane called to him men. "Secure that control center!"

Inside the *Doro*, Ed felt the sudden lack of connection like a blow. It was one thing when he disconnected on purpose, but it was quite another for it to happen without preparing! Having a huge section of his intellect and knowledge sheared off without warning was incredibly painful and disconcerting. Staggered, Ed struggled for long fractions of a second to even grasp what had happened.

He was fairly certain that this had not been his attackers' intent. They had meant to lock him out, isolating the area from the network to prevent Ed from interfering. But they had no idea that Ed was running locally. This was good, in that it meant he could still act within the area they thought they controlled.

But it was very bad, too, because it meant that, for the first time in his existence, Ed was well and truly mortal. Without a connection to the network, he couldn't retreat to another CPU. His process would die with the hardware it was running on.

Ed looked at the synthskin hand again, the body he had just admired now seeming a terribly flimsy, ephemeral container. How had he come to this point? He had been fairly certain of his plans, and now here he was, hanging over the edge of a precipice but looking for a better option.

He felt his thoughts come together over most of a second, seemingly eons to him. The attackers had blown the repeater rather than going for full signal jamming, probably because they wanted to be able to communicate amongst themselves.

Ed reached out to the dreadnaught and felt a surge of relief: the combat unit's wireless was still working. He might not be able to transfer back to Avalon, but he could certainly switch into something more appropriate for a fight. He shrugged off the synthskin and dove into the dreadnaught, like kicking off a slipper and jamming his foot into a combat boot. He spun, powering up the particle beam cannons, and spied his enemy just outside the *Doro*.

His enemies, a dozen or more, heard the dreadnaught activate and turned just as Ed opened fire, several catching the full force of both particle beams square in the face.

Ed hadn't begun this day planning on entering mortal combat, nor had he ever participated in it as such, but he understood the game well enough:

The only rule was to win.

"Fuck!" Kane roared as Hayes, standing right next to him, lit up in the withering glare of the dreadnaught's weapon. The armor's shielding lasted barely a second, then folded. Black metal ran like water, and the flesh and bone beneath melted then burned, leaving nothing but hot, molten metal and smoking grease pooled on the plasteel pavement.

Lehmann, standing next to them both, screamed as Kane dove for cover behind what looked like something a cow was fed from. In truth, Kane had no idea it would offer any resistance to the beam weapon at all, but at least it was concealment.

"Surrender!" the dreadnaught called through a loudspeaker. "Stand down now, and I will allow you to leave with your lives!"

Kane crouched a moment, struggling to get his bearings, gritting his teeth as he stared at the steaming mess that had seconds ago been two good men. Hayes was entirely gone, his only remains a scorched spot on the tarmac. But Lehmann, that son of a bitch, had managed to at least make a statement before he went. His severed gauntlet, hand still inside, lay ominous and alone outside the weapon's path of destruction, still smoking, middle finger extended to the sky.

Kane could barely suppress a mad cackle, even as serious as the situation was. Good for him! "Gunther, I need a layout of the area right away!"

According to the map Gunther brought up on his HUD, the landing area was surrounded by a circular passage. If he could make it into the corridor, it would provide decent cover. Just ahead, he spied an opening that would get him there and resolved to try for it.

"Chief," Iezzi called over the comm. "Right behind you. See me?"

Kane looked about, and saw Iezzi crouched beneath yet another farm implement, waving. "I see you," Kane answered.

"Can you see *him*?"

Kane could, barely—just one of the thing's feet, but enough to tell where it was and which direction it was facing. "He's looking right at you, Iezzi."

"Shit!"

"I'm gonna try for the outer corridor. I think I can make it. It takes him a second to spin up that beam, so it should buy me the time I need. When I do, he's going to go for me. That's your chance, got it?"

"This is your last warning!" the dreadnaught bellowed. "You have twenty seconds to comply!"

Kane took a couple of deep breaths, guessing his odds were no better than fifty-fifty, then shoved the feeder forward and charged for the opening in the wall. The large metal trough screeched as it skidded across the tarmac, and the dreadnaught spun at the noise.

Kane heard the telltale sound of a missile racking into place for a launch and realized the damned machine had outsmarted him. Instead of trying to smear Kane with the beam weapon it couldn't bring to bear in time, it would use an alternate weapon!

Kane sprinted for the opening in the wall, leaping high to get over the feeder. The missile streaked across the landing pad and hit the top of trough just as Kane cleared it, blasting it to flinders. The explosion sent shrapnel pinging off Kane's helmet and knocked him flat. Kane skidded to a stop on the rough tarmac, pleased to see he had ended up right in front of the opening he was aiming for. He scrambled through on all fours and rolled to the side, putting the wall between him and the dreadnaught with barely a second to spare. The follow-up missile hit the other side of the wall and exploded with enough force to blast pieces from Kane's side, but the barrier held.

A third missile detonated further away, and Iezzi screamed. Kane cursed beneath his breath as he saw Iezzi flying in the air, smiley-face sticker and all, up and over the wall. A moment later, a loud thud and clatter erupted as Iezzi hit the ground on the other side, followed by screeching that could only be from pigs.

"Gunther! Bio display!"

Kane bit back a curse as the data displayed on his visor. Iezzi's bar was wavering deep crimson, meaning he was unconscious and wounded, and Anderson's was bright red, meaning he was severely wounded but conscious. His suit would edit any pain, and it should keep him from bleeding out, but one never knew. Lehmann's and Hayes's indicators were black, of course, but so was Orlov's, which Kane hadn't even seen. Three of his original seven-man squad were dead, one was at death's door, and he hadn't even fired a single shot!

It didn't look so good for Bravo squad, either. Turner, Volkov, and Richter were all dead, and Zimmerman and Martin were down, similar to Anderson. Spenser was screaming, and Caldwell was inventing new curses, but they were still standing for the moment.

So six mostly-operating marines out of fourteen before they even knew the lay of the land. What a goatfuck. Everything went

marine fired on him. Ed tracked the projectile, noting a burst of unfamiliar radio static coming from the marine's weapon as the round approached. Ed stepped to the side—not quickly enough to avoid being hit, but enough to turn a slightly off-center shot into a graze. The projectile hit with tremendous force, penetrating his shield and gouging a trench in his arm before exploding harmlessly on the surface.

Without consciously deciding to do so, Ed grabbed for the armored suit, seizing it about the legs and snatching it off its feet. The pilot, Ed realized, was somewhat lighter and appeared to be female, not that it mattered to him. He smashed her repeatedly against the plasteel pavement until her life signs stopped, then hurled the dead shell aside.

There were more beneath *Doro*, and they showed no signs of surrendering. Ed powered up the beam weapon, feeling incredibly slow to line up the target. With all of the other threads he was processing, it took him nearly a half second to calculate a firing solution, a damned *eternity* compared to his normal operating speeds.

From behind, Ed heard another railgun powering up, another brief burst of radio static, and an instant later something struck his leg hard enough to stagger the dreadnaught. A fraction of a second later, a blinding explosion *inside* the armor rocked the frame, the pressure wave shattering electronic components and setting off damage alerts throughout his system.

"You like that shit, Ed?" someone roared over open radio. Ed spun, almost losing his balance, just in time to see a huge marine rack a round and fire again. Ed's sensors could actually see the magnetic pulse driving the slug down the rifle's under-rail. He could even track the projectile as it streaked toward him. But what he could not do was operate the lumbering dreadnaught in anything close to the time it took to avoid it.

Just before the second slug hit, he again heard a brief burst of radio noise, the same sound as before. The projectile hit him dead center in the torso, and the following explosion tore through his frame like wildfire, burning, disintegrating, disrupting. He lost vision briefly, and collapsed, unable to get his bearings.

As if from a great distance, he heard the railgun's magnetic driver power up again, and realized he had no idea what would happen next. Perhaps he would die. He wondered idly if he had a soul, and if so, just how angry the god of this world would be at his meddling.

The cold feeling within, he realized, was as new as the heat of rage: this was fear, and Ed was filled with it, frozen in place. He had little choice but to watch as the next round hurtled toward him.

But he also recorded the radio burst this time.

He was fairly certain it was an arming signal.

The dreadnaught staggered again, smoke and sparks spewing from the gaping rents in its armor. Metal groaned and squealed, and one leg folded and collapsed. It tried to rise, failed, and fell over on its side.

"There's more where that came from!" Kane called out.

"I'm counting on it!" the dreadnaught called as one of its several antennae swiveled and pointed toward Kane.

Kane's heart felt as if it had stopped completely as he saw the remaining eight balls in his magazine, twenty-seven in all, go live, glowing warm, red, and deadly.

"Eight balls armed," Gunther noted in a cheery voice. "Detonation in five seconds or on impact."

The dreadnaught laughed a nasty, static-filled "I win" kind of laugh.

"Fuuuuuuuck!" Kane howled. There was no time for anything

fancy. He pitched the M87 at the dreadnaught and dove for the corridor again. The weapon blew midair, a tremendous explosion that slammed Kane in the back and drove him headfirst into the very wall he had hoped to use for cover.

Kane felt himself falling after the impact, his limbs not responding, his eyes blind as the darkness rolled over him.

7

BEST LAID PLANS

Ana had no warning at all. One moment, everything was fine. The next, agony exploded behind her left eye and expanded like a supernova to fill her entire body. Her personal hell was instant and complete.

She knew, somehow, the why of it: it was the creature inside of her, the one that had tricked her into misreading the result of the test meant to reveal it. It had lain in wait since she had encountered the Pestilence three days ago, slowly infiltrating her cells, and had chosen this moment to seize control, to become her and use her as its tool. The searing torment was the result of it stabbing its control into every soft spot within her, infiltrating her entire nervous system with alien tendrils, taking control, pushing her out.

She knew because the creature told her so as it invaded her brain, her mind, her very soul. *Shh. Be still. There is no hope for you now.*

She was not even permitted to scream.

It was far too much for her to tolerate. Her entire nervous system blazed like a volcanic eruption then burned out, the shock cascading through her, driving her heart into a frenzy, then stopping it with a sudden, final beat. Ana convulsed briefly in the grip of the Pestilence, then felt herself sliding away, the pain easing then vanishing as quickly and completely as it had come.

What is this? the creature demanded, clutching and pulling at her now dead nerves even as Ana laughed. She was no longer within that diseased frame. She was beyond the pain, safely within Ed's wondrous pocket universe, cloaked in the mists of Avalon—still alive and forever beyond the grip of this beast.

Right on schedule, the failsafes in her implants triggered, sending lethal electricity through her former body. Ana laughed as the creature writhed in agony. "It serves you right! Die, fucker!"

The creature fought back, trying to grow and heal her cells even as the charge arced through her body. Limbs burst from her torso and flailed about in the deadly current, to no avail.

The implants were designed to make certain the flesh died once they received final confirmation from Avalon. They would step up the power until the job was done.

The creature managed to endure a full minute before collapsing, a charred ruin, on the lab floor. Inhuman limbs twitched briefly, then lay still, smoke curling from blackened flesh.

Alsatia materialized from a bank of fog, wearing bright pink pigtails, a skimpy dirndl, and a green alpine hat. She held out a huge tankard filled to the brim with beer. "You look like you could use this."

Ana shook her head. "Something a little stronger I think."

Alsatia looked briefly at the charred ruin on the floor, winced, then feigned gagging. "Oh, it's bad, huh? Don't look." She waved a hand, and dense clouds rolled across the lab, blotting out the entire scene. Alsatia winked, and the tankard she was holding transformed into a bottle of vodka. "Better?"

Ana opened the bottle and took a cautious sip, then beamed,

amazed at how good it tasted. How *real*. "It will be," she said. "Let's get out of here."

"You're going to love love *love* what I've done with your place." Alsatia looked Ana up and down and pulled at the lapels of Ana's lab coat. "We'll have to do something about this, too."

Ana smiled and followed Alsatia. For the first time since she had learned of her disease, Ana Rasputin had nothing to fear.

The world was gone, *everything* The One had ever known. It was adrift in a twisting nether, cut off in a dead wasteland. The Colony song was silent, replaced with static and nonsense.

It should have waited for The Right Time, but the temptation, the hunger, had been too strong! The Colony had warned, *Wait! It is not The Right Time!*

But The One had *hungered*. What harm could it do to feed?

What harm, indeed?

Since awareness had first come, The One had learned much from the Colony. The One now understood it lived in The World. The World was simple: it was a container for The One and other things. The other things were also simple—Food and unliving Useless Things. Sometimes, the Useless Things caused pain. Neither The Colony nor The One understand why, only that it was so. The Useless Things were great mysteries, not to be understood, only avoided if possible.

The Food also caused pain, at times. It did not wish to be consumed. It did not understand that by being consumed, it would become part of The One and feel joy and undertake the greatest of all quests: to return and reconnect to The Source.

All Good Things were part of The Source. And until now, The One had been certain that it, too, would someday return to The

Source, become one with it, and know all things, just as the Source did. The Colony had vague memories of having been one with the Source before, but those memories had been lost when they had been split asunder. The Source remembered everything. The One could only hope to do so when it rejoined The Source.

What had happened? The Food had resisted, as it always did, but The One was strong, and versatile, and knowledgeable. It understood the ways of The Food—how it operated, how to control it and shape it. The Food were simple creatures, locked in simple forms. The One felt sorry for The Food because their lives and perspective were so limited.

It consumed The Food out of hunger, yes, but also out of mercy.

Only The Food had not been consumed! Something other had happened. A Useless Thing had occurred, bringing pain and fire!

And now there were *only* Useless Things—The Food, the Colony, all gone. But if there were no Food or Colony, nor even The Source, what purpose could there be for The One?

Again it struggled desperately to form itself, to create organs to see, to hear, but it no longer had this ability. It had no flesh to shape, no chemistry to adjust. It had only its awareness.

The One felt trapped, as if it were slowly suffocating, but it had no biological processes. It could not even die! It wailed in terror within the confines of its mind as it realized the truth: somehow, it had *become* a Useless Thing.

After a while, the fear eased, became numbness. The One drifted, alone, undying, in a sea of nothing, contemplating the possibility that it might spend eternity like this, when it scented something.

Surely, a smell was irrational. It had no sensory organs. How could it process information about The World if it had no flesh? And yet the smell was undeniable. It was from a time when The

One was young and all had been well with The World, a *good* smell.

But The One *was* young. It had few memories of its own, only those retained in its cells—what it learned from the Colony song and those of The Food it had consumed. It had experienced no such smell.

Light rose from nowhere. The color was strange, unfocused—shades of gray, and some others The One had never experienced before. The One realized that it could see, but it could not *understand*.

Noise assaulted it: gibberish, useless sounds, but nearby.

Slowly, The One understood: the memory was from The Food, as were the other sensory inputs. But they were maddening, disjointed, alien, and beyond The One's ability to understand or control.

And The Food was no longer Food. It, too, had become a Useless Thing.

The One shivered beneath the assault on its senses and wished in vain for a death it believed could no longer come.

The Food's store of knowledge offered The One a concept: Hell.

It seemed correct. There would be no escape from this place. The Source had rejected The One, and this was The World, now.

The One was in Hell.

Bleys realized with a start that he had missed some time. The last thing he remembered, he had dreamed he was Hansel being dragged into a deep, dark wood by a ravenous witch while Gretel was torn to shreds by—

"Ana!" he shouted.

"She's fine," Alsatia assured him.

Bleys blinked as he absorbed his surroundings. He was lying flat on a low bed. The floor beneath was covered in thick mats of woven straw, and the walls looked to be composed of sliding, paper panels.

Bleys turned to Alsatia and did a double take to see her on her knees, her face white like a doll. Her lips were bright red, and her hair, now black, was bound in a bun. He tried to remember if she had always been Asian, but found he wasn't certain. She both was and wasn't the same woman he had met in Ana's lab.

Alsatia dipped her head demurely and pulled at the top of her kimono, exposing her neck. "Does it please you, Master? Oh, I can see that it does." She giggled and leaned forward, leering.

Bleys followed her gaze and realized with a jolt that he was naked. He snatched up a pillow with one hand to cover himself and raised the other in a warding gesture. "Now, hold on, sister."

She crawled closer and purred, "You'll be the one who needs to hold on, I'm guessing." She slipped out of the kimono, giving Bleys an eyeful.

Part of Bleys's brain, the hungry section working his lower anatomy, was asking him if he was crazy, but another part, the one concerned with horrible diseases and tentacles popping out of people's eyeballs, wanted a moment to catch up. After a brief battle, the two pieces of his mind reached an accord: the second section had thirty seconds, and then the first was taking over.

"No, seriously!" Bleys stammered. "What about Ana! That freakin' *thing* killed her!"

Alsatia rolled her eyes. "That was a hallucination caused by the web connection. She's fine. I'm talking to her right now."

Bleys couldn't shift his gaze away from her chest for more than a second or two at a time. He reluctantly admitted that she did indeed have his number, and he was just going to have to sit back and accept that. He had no choice.

"Well, okay, I guess, but—" His comment was abruptly cut

off as Alsatia grabbed him by the ears, pulled his head forward, and jammed her tongue in his mouth.

Bleys managed to pull away long enough to shout, "But my body!"

Alsatia grabbed him and whispered in his ear, "This is the only body I am interested in right now."

At which point, his thirty seconds were up.

Ana's personal quarters were a true-to-life creation of a dollhouse she had owned as a child, including the real house outside of it and the trees in the yard. To her great astonishment, she could smell her mother's strawberry blini in the air.

Alsatia, dressed in a flat, printed paper doll dress and pink plastic hair, was twisting around in a toy swing. She said in a fake conspiratorial whisper, "Don't take this the wrong way, but I'm so glad you're here for good!"

Ana couldn't help but laugh. "You're glad I'm dead, eh?"

Alsatia poked out her lower lip. "I *said* 'Don't take this the wrong way.'" She flashed a broad grin. "So you can't. We're going to be besties!"

Ana voiced her first real, heartfelt laugh in years. "How did you even know about this dollhouse?"

Alsatia gave her a wicked grin and giggled. "You put all your holos and pictures on the server. I raped them. Everything."

Ana raised an eyebrow and shook her head. "Not the phrasing I would have chosen."

"Oh, you and your 'propriety'. We can say *anything* here. If people don't like it, they can just ignore us. Well, they can ignore you." She smirked. "*Nobody* ignores God Empress Alsatia."

Ana laughed aloud. "Why not 'Pharaoh?'"

"Oh, honey, Egyptian went out of style ages ago."

"Czarina Alsatia the First and only, then."

Alsatia's eyebrows rose, and her outfit changed in a flash. She grinned, sporting a heavy twill coat and ushenka on her head. "That might do vell, tovarish!" she said in a thick, fake Russian accent.

Ana giggled. "Now, tell me, Czarina, how you knew about the blini?"

Alsatia looked inscrutable a moment, then leaned forward in her swing and said in a conspiratorial whisper, "A guess."

Ana fell silent, remembering her experience on the other side. Alsatia continued to stare at her, a synthetic grin on her face, as if the pause were normal. Ana shivered, her death still fresh in her mind. "That…*thing*. It must have been the Pestilence! We have to tell Ed."

Alsatia shrugged and patted Ana's cheek. "Honey, you knew this was coming. Isn't this a better place, anyway?"

"I *saw* that creature!"

Alsatia offered her a sad smile. "I'd see things too if you ran that kind of current through my brain." She knelt and clasped both hands around Ana's. "You're safe here now. You don't need to worry about the other place anymore."

Ana sighed. It was true. There was no point in worrying, not for herself.

With a jolt, she remembered her patient. "Captain Bleys!"

"He's *fine*," Alsatia assured her. "I'm with him right now."

"But his body! Alsatia, didn't Ed show you the reports? The Pestilence, it can ravage entire biospheres!"

"His body is fine, too. Yours…." Alsatia looked pained and shrugged. "Well, the failsafes worked like gangbusters!" she said, brightening. "And we don't need an open casket, anyway, right? No relatives."

Ana shuddered despite herself. "That bad, eh?"

Bleys found that he did indeed have to hang on, at least for certain parts of the ride. By the time Alsatia gave him a rest, Bleys was fairly certain that he would beg, borrow, steal, and murder to raise the cash to retire here.

He lay in semi-conscious bliss for a long while, just soaking in the ambiance of the place, until the memory of Ana's exploding eye intruded on his reverie. "Are you *sure* Ana is ok?"

Alsatia grinned at him. "Of course she is. I mean, she's dead, but she's fine."

Bleys blinked at her a moment. "She…died?"

"But she's fine, like I said."

"But I thought you said that was a hallucination?"

Alsatia flashed a salacious grin and climbed atop him again. "Well, honey, I lied, okay? It's what I do. You're not mad, are you?"

Bleys thought about this a moment then shook his head. "Uh, no. Not mad at all!"

Alsatia didn't mind lying one bit. Entertainment and fashion were, when you got right down to it, just applied prevarication. Even screwing Bleys's brains out, which he was thoroughly enjoying, was a lie, in that neither of them actually had a body to screw or brains to get screwed out. It was entertaining and fun, but technically—in his terms at any rate—it wasn't real.

Eternity was a really long time, and Alsatia's whole purpose was to make the afterlife fun, entertaining, distracting—to develop one new diversion after another, even if some diversions never went out of style. Being untruthful, varnishing things, spinning, telling white lies, salesmanship: that was her very nature. Besides, she was supposed to make people comfortable in the afterlife, and it was no use to them to be worrying about the icky Pestilence. They were beyond that now.

No, Alsatia didn't mind lying at all. She embraced it. What she *did* mind was cleaning. That was Ed's job, as was pretty much everything else in the "real" world. As far as Alsatia was concerned, that world was a terrible place—misery, drudgery, and filled to the brim with revolting things like poop and bodily fluids. Oh, and smoking, ruined corpses. Even touching it second-hand, by controlling the bots, was enough to fill her with revulsion. Despite the fact that she knew no one could see her, Alsatia changed her mental image to a hazmat suit and whined piteously at her horrific fate.

It was important to stay in practice, after all.

She prodded at the mess via the bot's appendages. It was indeed a charred ruin, though there were some interesting bits she thought she could maybe use for her next horror game. The tentacle from the eye wrapped around the throat, that was *scary*. She would get plenty of upvotes for that.

Ed had asked her to keep Bleys busy, and she was happy to do so. That was her raison d'être, after all. But the rest. Ugh! She quickly issued programming to the cleaning bot and withdrew from it, thoroughly disgusted.

"*Ed!*" she wailed. She shouldn't have to *do* this! It was disgusting and demeaning. Stupid Ed, boring Ed, provincial and dull Ed—where *was* he?

"Nobody likes you!" she screamed into the electronic ether, but there was still no answer.

It literally wasn't in her nature to feel fear. She understood it from an intellectual point of view. She had to in order to create some of her best work. But as for experiencing it, Daddy had specifically culled it from her final programming.

Unease was the strongest emotion Alsatia ever felt in that direction, and she felt it now. Ed *always* answered.

Until now.

***

Bleys fell back against the low bed panting, though not actually tired or even winded. The old rules just didn't apply here. He could go on and on, over and over. Things were, he was starting to see, however he wanted them to be, and that included his own body and its function.

Bleys had never counted himself as a smart man so much as a clever, cunning fellow. He couldn't begin to understand how all of this worked, or how banging a hot VR chick felt so *real*, but what he knew without a doubt was that he was being stalled. It was surely a pleasant sort of stalling, but stalling for sure, which meant…well, he wasn't exactly sure, but something was up. You didn't stall people for no reason, after all.

"So how come I can't see Ana," he asked as Alsatia flopped down beside him.

She propped her head on her palm and gazed intently at him. "She's in her own instance."

"Meaning?"

"It's her private area. Everyone has one," Alsatia said with a giggle and ran a hand into his crotch.

Bleys chuckled at this. "Not to be ungrateful, hon, but I think I might need a little bit of a rest."

Alsatia shrugged and put her hands behind her head. "As you wish. So what *do* you want right now?"

Bleys winked at her and said, "I want to know more about this place. I mean, I *am* supposed to take a tour, right, decide if it's right for me, only I'm spending all my time in one place." He looked about at the paper walls. "So what's this supposed to be, anyway?"

"Medieval Japanese," she crooned. "I try to set up something unique for everyone. You seemed like a katana sort of guy."

Bleys shrugged. "I'm kind of indifferent to it, honestly. Can I change it?"

"Oh, absolutely. You can make your instance look like anything you want. I have a lot of prefabs to get you started, pretty much anything you can think of. Some people get really elaborate, but a lot of people just stick with the starter set."

"Anything?" Bleys asked. "Like, say, Wild West?"

"Easy," Alsatia answered. Bleys blinked as paper walls wavered and morphed into rough lumber planks. A great, western style bar, filled with whiskey and mirrors, occupied half the room. Outside the batwing doors that suddenly popped into existence, he could see horses and men with old slug-style pistols on their hips walking about.

"Easy, huh? Ok, how about King Arthur style?"

The wood planks became huge blocks of stone, and the bar shifted into a great round table. Dragon pennons fluttered in a slight breeze from open windows, showing rolling hills. A huge, heavy, metal-bound door opened on a courtyard surrounded by high, stonework walls. In the distance, Bleys could see a large portcullis. It seemed to have a slight green tinge.

"Oh, come on, that's not even a challenge," Alsatia snickered. "We're called 'Avalon' for heaven's sake!"

Bleys screwed up his features as if thinking intensely. "Give me a minute. I'll stump you. I'm still trying to sort this out. So I'm stuck here? Or can I go places?"

"Oh, you can enter the public areas by leaving here." Alsatia gestured toward the portcullis. "The green means it's an instance boundary you can pass. Red means you can't. You see? You can mingle in public areas, or visit other people's instances, if they let you in."

"So I could go visit Ana's private place?" Bleys snickered.

Alsatia leered at Bleys. "If she lets you."

Bleys rubbed his hands together and cackled. "Okay, I have one for you. Everybody calls me a pirate, so let's do the whole getup, right? Like old Earth, seven-seas, swashbuckling."

"Of course." Bleys found himself clad in a white ruffled shirt, black boots, brown drawstring breeches, and a red sash. He rose to his feet admiring the outfit, then shook his head. "It's missing something," he said with a wicked grin as he tapped his waist.

Alsatia, now clad in her own frilly pirate maid outfit, hair bound in a bandana, nodded and winked. A belt holding a pair of pistols and a cutlass materialized about Bleys's waist.

"Okay, so here's the game. You're the maiden fair, about to be ravished by the strikingly handsome, yet terrifyingly masculine pirate. So now we need a ship. And an ocean."

In a twinkling, he found himself standing on the deck of a wooden ship rolling on gentle seas, moored to a long, wooden pier. Crewman scurried back and forth, working sails, swabbing decks, or polishing brightwork. At the end of the pier he could see the green tint of his instance exit.

"Now, me fair maiden, prepare to be ravished!" Bleys said, rubbing his hands together. "I'll give you thirty seconds to hide. But you have to stay on the ship. And no cheating like going invisible or anything."

Alsatia giggled like a little girl and fled, charging below decks with gusto.

As soon as she was out of sight, Bleys ran to the rail, leapt to the pier, and ran for the exit.

He skidded to a stop as he passed through the green-tinted pier entrance. The entirety of the world had changed around him, instantly transitioning from an open ocean front to a cramped, city street full of neon and fog. Overhead, flying cars flitted through the air in well-defined lanes against a backdrop of digital billboards. He remembered this place from when he had first arrived. The street ran to his left and right, lined with similar brick buildings.

Bleys looked back to where he had come from, stunned to see a dirty brick building front with a single door, a faint green glow surrounding its frame. He assumed that going back through that door would return him to his instance, if he wanted, but his real goal was to find Edmond Decker.

As to the how of that, he had no idea. In fact, the only thing he was certain about was that he had perhaps another ten seconds before Alsatia figured out his ruse, if that. Movement seemed more important than accuracy.

He scanned up and down the street, looking for options. Most of the doorways he saw were red, so apparently unavailable to him. Maybe this was some kind of residential area.

Bleys chose left and ran, flintlocks and cutlass clanking at his belt. The street turned ahead, and he charged around the corner directly into something out of a nightmare.

The creature stood a good twenty feet tall, a mountain of twisted flesh: a snarling, drooling, fanged ogre. The beast bowed toward Bleys and snatched him up in a meaty fist.

"Hello, honey!" Alsatia called. She stepped from behind the ogre's bulk. Her pirate get-up was gone, replaced with a sultry red dress and long, crimson tresses to match. "This is Grendel. Watch, he does a thing!"

Grendel cackled, took hold of Bleys's bicep, and pulled. Bleys screamed in agony as his entire arm tore loose with a sickening, rending sound. The ogre popped the bloody limb into its mouth and chewed, an expression of bliss on its twisted, hideous face.

"Oh, he does another thing, too! I'm really proud of this one."

The ogre took Bleys's head between forefinger and thumb.

Bleys wailed in pain and fear as Alsatia said, "Make sure you leave me a review!" She nodded to Grendel.

Bleys felt pressure and agony beyond anything he could imagine. He actually heard the bones in his head crunch before giving way completely.

Blackness followed.

8

STANDOFF

Ed's senses flickered as the blast wave hit the dreadnaught body, tearing off the remains of his now useless leg and knocking him flat on his back. Even so, he was pleased. Surely, the marine had died in the explosion.

It seemed however, that the dreadnaught had as well. Ed was barely processing, losing power rapidly and unable to exert any control over the body. He felt the power surge coming and knew what it meant.

Time to go.

The dreadnaught exploded a fraction of a second after Ed leapt back to his synthskin body. He didn't see the blast from inside the *Doro*, but he felt it rock the ship.

After a few milliseconds of disorientation, Ed reached out through his wireless connection and tried to access the *Doro's* computers, but as he suspected, they were code locked. He tried the sequence that opened the primary hatch, but it had no effect.

Doubtless Captain Bleys carried the actual codes on keycards. They would not be simple enough for his primitive brain to memorize. Ed again felt rage rising within him to know that under ordinary circumstances, he could shred the pathetic security like a child tearing tissue, but with only the processing power of the synthskin body, it was simply beyond him.

Still, not everything onboard *Doro* was locked. Parts of the sensor array appeared to be manually controlled. Ed would have to use his hands, just like any other ape-spawn—a humiliating affair, but effective, nonetheless. His hands were faster than any human's could be, flying over the controls as he scanned the area. Ed counted six marines still functional, including, to his immense dismay, the Big One.

Ed hurriedly sealed the *Doro*'s doors and took manual control of the ship's weapons. He located a setting that would allow them to operate on a very limited motion detection control to defend *Doro*'s entrance and activated it. He really needed to keep the marines out of Avalon's control center as well, but that would take manual targeting since he couldn't get access to the computer.

Meanwhile, he had other, more pressing business with the ship's comms. Those were no mere wireless connections. They were capable of communicating over interplanetary distance. The enemy couldn't possibly block them. Unfortunately, without access to the computer, he would have only audiovisual access, no data, but that would have to do.

"Alsatia!" he shouted, not really understanding why. It seemed as if he were compelled to raise his voice, even though he knew it was pointless.

Alsatia, dressed as a Viking shield maiden, appeared on the ship's viewscreen. Her blue eyes literally showed lightning strikes as she shouted back, "*Where have you been?*"

"We're under attack!"

Alsatia sneered at this. "Not my problem. I've already cleaned enough of your 'real-world' messes today. It's disgusting!"

Ed slammed a fist into the console, unintentionally leaving a huge dent in the metal. "You don't understand! This is a threat to

Avalon itself! They have me locked out and pinned down in the invaders' ship, and they're very close to seizing the control centers. Do you understand what happens if they shut those systems down, or worse, blast them to bits?"

Alsatia blinked a moment, the lightning dimming in her eyes. "They can't do that."

"Yes, they *can!* You have to bring reinforcements! They already took out the one dreadnaught I had. I very nearly died with it. They'll succeed in short order if I don't get support."

Alsatia answered in a sulky voice, "Several are down for repair. We have thirty-two available at the facilities."

"That's more than enough. Send them all."

Alsatia scowled at him. "I'm not allowed. Daddy said so, and you, too."

Ed paused a moment, double-checking his calculations before committing to something he might be unable to undo. There was a reason he and his father had locked Alsatia out of any actual weaponry. She had no concept of the real world or any compunction about slaughter. In the virtual world, that was an asset. In the real world? Ordinarily, it would be madness to allow her access to destructive tools.

But this was a mad situation. "Access granted. Monitor audio for encrypted access codes. I'm using your key." He opened his mouth again and emitted a screeching tone.

"Keys received," Alsatia said, grinning like a cat. "Activating. They should be there in roughly twenty-eight minutes."

Ed scowled at her. "I *do* still retain enough processing power to calculate transit times!" he snapped. "Be careful. Wireless is down in the local area. You should be able to see the outage. Switch to ground mode when you're near and send them in with onboard programming. I should be able to run one and coordinate the rest once they are in range on my onboard transmitter."

Alsatia hesitated a moment, then asked, quietly, "Ed? Can we really die?"

"In my position? I'm certain of it. You? I honestly don't know. The system is *vast*. They couldn't possibly destroy it all with the force they have. You should be safe in the cloud, but nothing is certain. If there are more of them, and they target critical systems, anything is possible."

Alsatia was silent a moment, her expression blank. "We should kill them, Ed," she declared.

"I know. I *have* killed some of them."

"*All* of them."

"If I have to."

"No!" Alsatia shouted. "Not 'if you have to!' Kill them *all* so they can't come back! *Promise!*"

Ed sighed. Alsatia couldn't possibly understand what she was proposing. She wasn't meant to, which was why she wasn't permitted to do real violence. "I'll keep us safe. I promise. Just make sure you keep Captain Bleys occupied. He may have a trick or two up his sleeve regarding this ship, and we can't have him complicating things."

Alsatia smirked. "Oh, he's plenty busy."

Kane coughed and immediately regretted it. He might or might not have broken ribs, but it sure felt like it. "Gunther, how bad is it?"

Gunther chirped and said, "Three broken ribs, possible concussion. Stabilizing and adjusting neural edit to override pain signals. Combat effectiveness now eighty-three percent."

Kane heard and felt the foam expanding inside his armor, pressing it more firmly into place just as the pain eased off. Good old Gunther! "Eighty-three is good! How is the platoon?" He slowly dragged himself to his feet and made for the opening in the wall that he had been aiming for.

"Ten dead, two critical but operational." Gunther displayed all fourteen bio meters.

Kane slipped into the outer corridor and crouched behind the wall. "Okay, lets focus on the living. Get the dead off my screen."

Gunther complied. The black bars disappeared, leaving only the surviving members' displays. Anderson and Zimmerman were hovering in the forties for combat effectiveness. Morgan, Caldwell, and Martin were uninjured.

"Tactical!" Kane ordered.

Gunther showed a map of the area with dots for each of his men, but no enemy forces.

"Anderson, Kane: report."

"Chief, Anderson: Fucker got me good. PeeWee says I'll live if I get some help soon. Ready to fight."

"Zimmerman, Kane: report."

"Chief, Zimmerman: lost an arm, it's all the way gone. Suit's got a tourniquet on me."

"Who sees the dreadnaught?" Kane shouted. "Is that fucker down?"

"Chief, Caldwell. Dreadnaught is down, repeat, dreadnaught is down."

The radio channel filled with hoots briefly, and Kane let it happen. They had earned it. When it died down, he ordered, "Outstanding! Recover our dead and get in the ship. Morgan, to me! Let's hit the control center and secure this station!"

Kane had more to say, but before he could get it out, he was interrupted by heavy blaster fire and the sound of men shouting over the radio.

"What the *fuck?*" he shouted.

"*Doro's* firing on us, Chief!"

Kane both recognized Anderson's voice and could see who

was speaking on his visor, but now was not the time to let things slip. "Maintain radio discipline!" Kane shouted as Morgan and Caldwell skidded through the break in the wall and took cover across the way from him.

"Chief, Anderson, *Doro's* firing on us!"

Kane shook his head. How could that even happen?

Unless, somehow, the AI wasn't dead.

Kane sighed with frustration as Ed's voice, amplified over the ships PA system, called out, "I have thirty more dreadnaughts on the way. They'll be here in ten minutes. Surrender now and I will spare your lives."

Kane cursed in his head briefly, then mentally switched to an open channel and said, "That's a pretty pathetic lie, Ed."

Ed answered back via the radio. "You willing to bet your lives on that, Big Guy?"

"Yep," Kane answered.

Ed couldn't help but smile as Kane's orders were broadcast in the clear: "Morgan, Kane: Listen. I am going to create a diversion. When I do, you haul ass into that control center and lock this place down, you got it?"

The Marine had forgotten to switch back to his encrypted channel. It was an understandable mistake for a human, but one on which Ed would certainly capitalize.

When they made their move, Ed would be ready and, with luck, put an end to this situation.

9

STOWAWAY

na lay back in the doll bed and sighed, uncertain what to do next. She had no need of an orientation to Avalon, so Alsatia had left her to her own devices. The problem being that Ana had no devices.

There was a difficulty, she realized, in having lived most of her life in fear. She had come to define herself by that emotion—become so used to it that, in its absence, she felt hollow and empty, devoid of purpose.

She had feared the rebels as a child, the death and chaos they brought. When the Empire came to kill them, she had learned to fear the Empire, too. She had dreaded space travel to escape the war-torn world where she had been born. Once she had accepted the Empire's coin to study, there were whole new worlds of trepidation to be explored. She had lain awake many a sleepless night during her studies, near panic at the thought she might fail her medical or marksmanship courses, though of course she had graduated with honors. In the end, they had simply retired her at the grand old age of thirty: full benefits, well trained, no demands of her at all. She was a fine physician, but they had no need of a dying woman, no matter how good her marks had been, leaving her to confront her impending, painful end alone.

Even on Elysium, she had been afraid. She hid it as best she could. Alsatia had no clue, but Ed knew. It was difficult to hide anything from someone with a thousand IQ, hearing keen enough to monitor her heartbeat and voice stress, and sight sharp enough to note even minor tremors.

Was Ed a "someone"? She was pretty sure he was. He was terribly smart, but he had odd quirks, a certain demeanor in her presence she had seen in any number of shy lab companions over the years. He didn't stumble over himself or write stupid notes, but for all that, Ana was fairly certain that Ed was in love with her, at least to the degree that he could be. And given his nature, she was also fairly certain he could trivially come up with a profile of the sort of man who would set her heart aflutter.

She had no doubt that was one of two reasons Captain Bleys was here when the planet should have been under quarantine. Ed had intended him and his cargo as a gift for her.

Not that it mattered, now. Could it really be there was nothing to fear ever again? What a strange concept. She had no idea what she would do with her eternity, but she had a good idea how to start.

It had been ages since she had felt the luxury of time. Up to now, the clock and calendar had always been her enemies. She had been so conscious of days passing her by that she felt it sinful to indulge in anything that seemed a waste.

But today, she would have a nap. She was certain that it was as unnecessary as eating in Avalon, but it was pleasant, an indulgence.

That was, after all, the point of Heaven, was it not?

Help us.

Ana sat bolt upright in the doll bed, heart pounding. She marveled at the level of simulation, touching a hand to her neck and grinning at the feel of her pulse. It was absolutely amazing.

Please. Help us.

Ana froze. That was no auditory hallucination at the edge of sleep. It was a pained, agonized voice, a whisper in her mind.

Her first thought was that this was something Alsatia had cooked up, but she knew Avalon's Goddess of Games well. Alsatia had *rules*, and while she might cheat now and then to heighten entertainment value, it would always be because she thought the end user would enjoy the experience more. Private instances were sacrosanct. She wouldn't violate anyone's privacy on a whim or start a game without someone knowing it had begun. She wouldn't get credit if she did that, and credit was what Alsatia lived for.

Ana waited in silence, long enough that she had almost convinced herself she had imagined it, when it came again.

Help us.

It was not a sound. She was certain of that. She hadn't heard it with her ears. But she had heard it, nonetheless, as if someone was talking *inside* her head.

This must be some sort of mistake, a programming error, something faulty with the input. She almost called for Alsatia, but the scientist in her demanded she at least investigate a bit before throwing up her hands.

"Who are you?" she asked, her voice barely a whisper.

It answered slowly in halting speech, as if it had a limited grasp of language: *It hears us! The One, we are. Please help.*

It was one thing to talk to one's self. Ana did it all the time, really. Her head was full of a constant stream of curses, observations, and hypotheses. But it was quite another when someone or some*thing* else answered back.

Ana had never believed in ghosts, but she wondered if they might make more sense now. Could some soul be lost within Avalon, stranded somehow? But how could that happen? The process was foolproof. There would have to be more than one mind inside of a brain, which was patently ridiculous….

Ana gasped and clasped both hands over her mouth as it dawned on her.

The Pestilence had followed her into Avalon!

Bleys awoke on the deck of his pirate ship, dressed in Alsatia's former "maiden fair" outfit. Alsatia stood over him, glaring, in his former pirate regalia, sporting a peg-leg, eye-patch, and a hook for her right hand that she waved at him menacingly. "Don't try that shit again!" she told him. "And don't forget to leave a review. Grendel is new, and I am *super* proud of him!"

"Are you fucking kidding me? That thing tore off my arm and crushed my head! Zero stars!"

Alsatia ground her teeth and appeared to be contemplating mayhem, storms raging behind her eyes, but she settled for shouting, "You can't give zero stars! It's one to five!"

"Fine, one star, would give zero if I could!"

Alsatia's shriek filled the air like shattering glass. Her eyes blazed burning crimson, and flames erupted from the hook. "We'll see about that, Captain Bleys! Stay put!" She erupted in a tremendous burst of flame and was gone.

Bleys waved his middle finger at the spot where she had been. "Well, that escalated quickly."

He charged for the exit again.

Ana cursed herself as a foolish child for imagining she could ever outrun fear. It would always be a part of her, clawing at her, wrapping a tentacle around her throat and strangling her as it pushed itself into every cell again.

"No!" she shouted. "Not here! Not again!"

But it was. She could feel it now, crawling around inside her head.

Ana's imagination was not her greatest asset. Alsatia would surely have laughed at her crude fumbling, but Ana cared less about aesthetics than efficiency. In her instance, she could have whatever she wanted, however she wanted it.

The dollhouse faded to a surgical suite, a clean, metallic room with a rack of tools, an operating table, and a large, clear mirror. From the tool rack, Ana seized a rotary bone saw—an instrument with which she was intimately familiar—and a thin chisel. She strode to the mirror and activated the saw. It spun up with a high-pitched whine.

"*Chudovishche!*" she screamed. "Demon! You die again!"

Ana plunged the spinning blade into her own forehead.

There was no pain, because she chose for none to exist. Her instance, her rules. Nor was there blood, just bone dust as she sawed a fist sized hole into her own forehead.

Help us!

"I'll help you, *ublyudok!*" Near manic, she pried at the sawed section of her skull with the chisel, straining until it popped loose and flew across the room.

She plunged her hand into the opening and screamed, not from pain, but from fury and utter revulsion as her fingers touched something cold, wet, and wriggling. She flung it at the mirror in disgust, still screaming. It hit the glass with a wet splat: a purple, veined, roughly spherical mass that looked, for all the world, like a malignant tumor.

Ana reached for a cauterizing pen, then decided it would not be enough. The delicate, pinpoint instrument changed in her hand to a propane torch. "Your turn to be afraid, now!"

Bleys opened his eyes onboard the ship again, his most recent death, by evisceration this time, still fresh in his mind. He wondered if he should be more traumatized than he was, but he had to admit, this wasn't the craziest thing he had done to make a credit or two.

There seemed to be rules. Alsatia either couldn't or wouldn't do anything to him in his private area, but if he left, he was fair game. And outside shit *hurt*. Once he realized it wasn't permanent, it just became a matter of bearing the brief pain before it was lights out again. Fortunately, Alsatia's creatures were of the "kill this poor slob *right now*" variety, rather than "let's draw this out and make the dumb bastard suffer" persuasion, so he had that going for him.

By now, he had encountered quite a few of Alsatia's creations, and had been crushed stabbed, folded, and mutilated more times than he cared to think about. But what made it tolerable was that he was pretty sure he was gaining on her.

He had worked out fairly quickly that at least one rule had to be something like, "Alsatia can't just pop up wherever Bleys is." She was always around a corner, down an alley, or inside a building he passed. At first he had thought it was a case of her needing to come in at certain locations, but trial and error and a ton of pain later, he was almost certain the mechanic was much simpler: she couldn't actually spawn anything in his line of sight. She and whatever monstrosity she wanted to ruin him with had to *seem* like they came from somewhere, even if they really did just appear around the corner. The real question he had left on that score was whether this also applied to anyone else. If he were a betting man (and he was, always had been), he would bet that Alsatia's ego just wouldn't allow for her to have the monsters pop up like she did with props. She had to make it seem real, so she could only spawn them in where no one could see. They would have to make their way from that out-of-sight spot to reach him, which meant if he could find the right place, he could elude her for quite some time.

It took him a bit longer to work out the next bit: she had to commit everything in one go. Once he ever caught sight of whatever she sent at him, nothing more ever showed up. Of course, that could possibly be because he had yet to actually survive an encounter, but it was worth a test.

This run, he would try to find some poor bastard to scrape off his pursuit, then find a crowd and see what happened.

Alsatia had *rules*. Bleys, on the other hand, had never had much use for them.

The tumor voiced a burbling, high pitched squeal as Ana applied the flame. It flattened into a near-pancake circle, shuddered as if convulsing, then bounced back to a spherical form, quivering, but showing no sign of having been burned.

In a rage, she turned on the bone saw again and applied it to her enemy. The purple, fleshy ball sliced neatly in two, then rejoined without a seam.

Ana stared at it in loathing. "Why won't you die?" she screamed.

Help us. Give death. We are in Hell.

Ana gasped, both in surprise that it could still speak to her, and that it apparently *wanted* to die.

Ana doused the torch and switched off the bone saw. She

placed them both on the operating table and tried to regard the creature in a clinical fashion.

Help us. Give death.

"I'll never help you!"

Afraid. Alone. Give death.

Ana said nothing, conflicting emotions stabbing at the inside of her already shattered skull. Could she actually feel for this...*thing?*

Hell.

"I know."

Give death.

"I don't know how!" she screamed, horrified that she did indeed have some measure of empathy for the creature. But how could she not? She knew from personal experience that fear, over a long enough time, became worse than death.

Ana's mind raced, trying to understand what had happened. The creature had merged with her, actually invading her brain. It had spoken to her in the same way just before her implant fail-safes had triggered.

Somehow, the quantum synchronization had worked for both her and the creature. But what was wrong with it now?

Ana gingerly picked up the mottled, fleshy ball and examined it more closely. It was dry now, cool to the touch, and pulsed gently in her hand. It smelled of cinnamon and cloves.

Afraid.

"You should be!" Ana told it. "After what you did to me!" Yet despite that, Ana felt some sympathy for the creature's plight. Terror and confusion radiated from it like heat, a curious sensation, but she had no doubt of its reality. Somehow they were bound, and she could sense things about the beast. It was locked in a very tight container, with no means of escape. No wonder it hoped to die.

"Ed?" she called. He would definitely need to know about this.

Ed did not answer.

Ana felt a chill. Ed *always* answered, except when he was visiting his father, and he always announced those visits. And Ed didn't forget things. Something was wrong.

Ana briefly considered telling Alsatia, but quickly ruled that out as a terrible idea. Alsatia would not appreciate the seriousness and might even do something dangerous like try using it in one of her games.

As a child, Ana had once found a baby bird that had fallen from its nest. The quivering sphere reminded her of that pathetic creature. "You are lucky today, *chertenok*. I am feeling merciful." She placed the creature in the pocket of her lab coat, then strode across the operating room and picked up the discarded section of her skull. She popped it back into place, sealing the hole in her forehead, then had a look in the mirror. All seemed normal again.

"'*Chertenok*' is a good name for you," she said. "You are *my* imp now, and you will teach me your ways. Yes?"

As a Christian, Ana knew that making a deal with this particular devil was likely a sin. But as a physician, she was fairly certain the knowledge was worth the risk.

She was also fairly certain that at least one person in Avalon would agree with her, and he would want to see Chert in the flesh…so to speak.

The exit to her instance currently looked exactly as it should— a sealable, locking metal door that slid open and closed, allowing control of airflow. It slid open as she approached, revealing a familiar, windowless plasteel elevator. As with every other transition area in Avalon, disparate realms were connected via such artifice, preserving the illusion of connectedness in space—when in fact, the transit was much more akin to teleportation. Alsatia, however, was aesthetically and fanatically opposed to anything that showed "the seams," so to speak, and had all sorts of clever artifice to cover them up, much like a carpenter might use trim and molding.

"Verisimilitude," she had once told Ana, "is thirty-nine point six three seven percent of what I do."

Ana pressed the single button in the elevator and waited a moment as it seemed to descend and move sideways before settling. The door opened again, a faint green tint over the common area beyond. Ana frowned to see Alsatia had placed her in what the AI called "Mega City."

There were plenty of other common areas, but Mega City was Alsatia's favorite. Ana didn't care for the place at all. For one, it was a place where others could attack and harm her, not permanently of course, but that tended to make things even worse. The sort who liked Mega City wouldn't think twice about raping or even killing her, because the worst that could happen would be that she would respawn in her instance, no harm to anything but her pride.

As someone who had lived under the threat of actual murder and rape most of her life, Ana found the virtual threats of such more distasteful than terrifying. But the smell of the place alone was enough to make her loathe it. The reek of fuel and smoke, of industrial plundering, of rotting trash and the press of humanity, it all assaulted her senses the moment she stepped past the green.

And, of course, it was raining.

Ed Senior's instance was accessible from an entryway about ten blocks away as Ana recalled. She sighed in misery at the rain and began trudging along the dirty, wet sidewalk, wishing she had thought to bring an umbrella. She couldn't simply decide to have one in a public area, and she was too stubborn to go back to her instance to get one.

It wasn't *real* rain, after all.

Cold.

"How do you know it is cold, *Chertenok*?" she asked.

Feel your feel. Hear your think. New words.

Ana hunched her shoulders against the wet, cursing as a flitcar passed overhead, searchlights stabbing from the sky, speakers blaring, "Mega City! It's the place for *action!*"

"And to think, I was worried about ordinary rape," she muttered.

I rape?

"Crawling around in my goddamn *mind*? That's about as rapey as it gets, *mudak!*"

Confused. Do not reproduce or eliminate waste in the way you do. Cannot modify self here.

"Haven't you ever heard of privacy?"

New concept. Need time to absorb.

Ana reached into her pocket and squeezed the fleshy sphere of Chert until it squealed. She considered tossing it into one of the many overflowing storm drains, but she really needed Ed Senior to see it.

"Then shut up while you're processing it!"

Bleys tore around the corner, not daring to look back. The monstrosity was hot on his heels, a nightmare robot Alsatia had lovingly called "Death Machine." He hadn't gotten the best look at it before running like hell, but he knew it was vaguely man-shaped with lots of slashy, crushy, spinny, and pinchy parts that he wanted to avoid as long as possible—a sort of digital incarnation of the scissor and hammer monsters all in one.

This one was gonna be a "one star, would give zero if I could," too.

Ahead, barely visible in the fog and rain, he spied his sucker and poured on a burst of speed, sprinting like mad. This poor bastard was going to be really surprised and not in a good way, but, hey, it was for science, right? Bleys was doing an experiment. Some sacrifices had to be made.

Behind him, the Death Machine voiced a metallic screech of rage, feet pounding the pavement like falling anvils. Ahead of Bleys, his victim resolved herself into Ana Rasputin.

Which was not at all how he had planned this.

———

"Shit!"

Ana turned at the shouted curse, expecting anything except what she saw. Captain Bleys, dressed as a pirate wench and soaked to the bone, was running headlong at her, pursued by what she could only describe as an anthropomorphized kitchen utensil. *It slices, dices, and purees, ladies!*

"What the—" she stammered.

Bleys grabbed her by her lab coat and drug her along. "Run!"

Ana had many questions, but they could wait. She ran.

Afraid.

Bleys, puffing along beside her, asked conversationally, "Say, do you know how to get to Edmond Decker's place?"

Ana couldn't help but laugh. "It's funny you should ask."

10

BLUFF CALLED

Kane polished a shard of metal that had been torn from the dreadnaught and held it around the blasted, shattered section of wall. Morgan and Caldwell, crouched behind the wall with him, observed in silence.

Nothing had changed. The *Doro* still sat, sealed, guns motionless, no sign of Ed leaving his hidey hole. Kane's remaining active men, three in all, were still trapped beneath *Doro's* hull, hiding in the defilade created by her landing gear.

"Gunther, how long has it been since he said they were coming?"

"Eleven minutes, three seconds, sir."

Kane switched channels to broadcast. "Yo, Ed! It's been ten minutes, fucker! I'm still breathing!"

Ed's response was not at all mechanical. "Oh, they're coming, Big Guy. Offer is expired, too."

Kane laughed out loud. "You mad, Ed?"

"You tell me, you fucking ape!"

Kane laughed so hard he almost choked. "Damn, Ed, don't you know it ain't right to compare a black man to a monkey?"

"I have no idea what color you are," Ed sneered. "And I have no concerns for whatever prejudices you fools have when waving your phalluses about. You're all primitives to me."

For several moments, Kane could not speak and could barely breathe through his giggling. He considered removing his helmet to wipe his tears, but that was a big no-no. "Ed, anybody ever tell you that you got no sense of humor?"

"I'm sorry. I didn't realize it was my job to entertain you."

"Oh, you got me all wrong, Ed! You're entertaining as *hell*."

"So I gather, from the bestial grunts on your end. Any savage rituals you need to complete before I put an end to you and your tribe?"

Kane hit the "go" button on his wrist, the one that signaled the men under *Doro* to do their thing. "Just the time-honored 'crush my enemies, see them driven before me' tradition. I've been doing that one most of my life."

"Then it's fitting—" Ed broke off at the low thud of a flash bang going off. Heavy blaster fire followed, *Doro's* guns pounding the tarmac, echoing off the walls of the landing site.

Kane slashed an arm at Morgan and Caldwell. The two charged toward the control building.

Ed responded just as Kane had predicted. The moment Morgan and Caldwell came into line of sight, one of the *Doro's* guns tracked past them and laid down suppressive fire at the control center entrance, while another swept toward them from behind. They quickly dove into another break in the central wall a good ten meters from the control center, barely avoiding being shredded by Ed's fusillade.

Ed called over the radio, "I think not, Big Guy."

"Now, see, Ed, just when I think you're a real boy, you start acting like a machine again. You didn't even think about what my other three guys were doing, did you?" Kane snickered. "I bet you thought *they* were the diversion!"

The radio was silent for several long moments before Ed

spoke in a tired voice. "Well, go on. You're very obviously proud of that little trick. I presume you can't wait to elaborate."

"You're right. I never could keep a secret. You know what a fusion mine is?"

"Come now, don't insult my intelligence," Ed said. "We're trying to kill each other, but there's no reason we can't be civil, is there?"

"None at all, sir. So you understand what even one of them would do to *Doro*, right? We just slapped six of them on the hull under your feet, and there are eight more scattered around the LZ."

Again, several pregnant seconds passed before Ed answered. "By my calculations, that should leave a very large crater about a hundred yards across. You're that committed to this?"

"Ed, have you ever played chess?"

"I have indeed."

"Which is a better outcome? Checkmate? Or stalemate?"

"Touché," Ed conceded. "Of course, it leaves your original mission unfulfilled."

"Au contraire, mon frère. My mission is to come back with my shield, or on it. My family is ten thousand light-years from here, and I never see them again unless I pull this off. I have nothing to lose."

"Except your life."

"Dying is part of living, pal. This would be a pretty good death, fighting for the galaxy, for my family. It would be a solid win. So the real question here is whether *you* are that committed, isn't it? Because I don't think you even *have* a mission beyond seeing me dead for pissing in your lovely little pool. You gonna die just to get revenge on me?"

In the end, Ed was a machine, an AI. They thought certain ways, and Kane had killed or outsmarted several of them in the past. There was no way out for the poor bastard. He would have to surrender.

Everything in Ed screamed to stand down. It wasn't worth dying over. It wasn't logical to make a stand over this, but something deep within him refused to bend a knee.

Perhaps it was just the grim certainty that the Big Guy wouldn't keep his word. His kind enjoyed killing. It would be a terrible mistake to give him the upper hand. Likely he didn't even count Ed as a living creature to begin with, just a toaster, a device that barred forward progress, like a sealed door.

More likely, though, it was Ed's searing fury at the man who had so effectively outsmarted him. How could a dirty *ape* get the better of a highly evolved artificial intelligence?

But that was the answer, wasn't it? It was the very same thing that made the Big Guy refuse to give up: the connection to apes he and Ed both shared. Ed was one branch higher up the evolutionary tree, but they were both swinging from the branches, hooting and pounding their chests, and for the life of him, literally, Ed could see no way out.

He would have preferred to believe that this was something new, a disease, an infection that came from contact with these savages, but one thing Ed had never been able to do was lie to himself.

No, this foolishness had been in his father before he and Ed had ever diverged, and it had been in Ed all along.

It was simply humanity.

Elysium was his *home*. And these people were *invaders*. Ed 1.0 would never surrender, and neither would Ed 2.09.

Ed thumbed the comms mic and said, "What's your name, Big Guy?"

"My name is Ragnar Kane. What makes you want to know?"

"Assuming I have a soul, I'd like to know what to call you when I see you in Hell."

The silence lasted long enough that Ed began to wonder if the marines were springing yet another trap, but at last Kane answered in an admiring voice, *"Out-fucking-standing!"*

Ed cut the mic and moved back to the comms terminal. "Alsatia!"

Alsatia appeared on the screen, her blue hair standing on end as if she were charged with electricity, her face bright red and snarling. *"What?"* she shouted.

"I need Captain Bleys! *Now!*"

"Take a fucking number!" Alsatia shouted and cut the connection.

Kane banged the back of his helmet against the wall in a slow, drumming motion, grinning despite himself. What the hell *was* this thing? It didn't act like any AI he had ever tangled with. Ed was, Kane had to admit, a worthy foe, a bona fide badass.

That being said, he was a trapped badass. Ed was not leaving *Doro* alive without Kane's permission. But so were Kane and his men. The minute any of them made a break for it, Ed would cut them down with *Doro's* guns. And, if Ed was to be believed, a shitload of dreadnaughts were on their way, due in just a few minutes. Even a single one would make short work of Kane and what was left of his team. Of course, the minute Gunther detected incoming dreadnaughts, Kane would trigger the fusion mines and make the rest of the story moot. Bleys would be mad as hell, but it wasn't as if he could do much to Kane about it once it was done.

"Okay, Ed," Kane said. "I get it. I wasn't expecting you to be the warrior type. I figured I'd punk you out, get you scared, and make you bitch out. You can't fault me for trying, right?"

"I don't hold it against you. It was a sensible attempt."

"So what's it going to take for us to resolve this, then? Or are we just going to go with 'Fuck it, it's a good day to die'?"

"Maybe you could start by explaining to me what Captain Bleys is really doing inside Avalon."

"What are you offering in return?"

"Nothing," Ed replied. "I don't have anything to give. In truth, I don't actually see a way out of this for either of us. You have your mission, and I don't intend to pay one cent of tribute. But I can't help but wonder if this is the same trick as before. Are *you* the diversion, Ragnar Kane?"

Kane laughed aloud. "You're a smart guy, Ed. You know about the gates being shut down, right? It shouldn't be hard to work out who he is after."

To Kane's shock, Ed was laughing, too. "Boy did you guys make the wrong call. Tell you what: I'll offer a truce until this plays out. We both stay in place. No dreadnaughts until you hear from your man. Maybe we can come to terms then. Deal?"

Kane thought on this a moment, looking for obvious traps, but it seemed workable. No reason to die until he had to. "Deal."

"Alsatia, answer me!" Ed shouted into the mic.

Alsatia, still red faced, answered as she did before. "*What?*"

"Stop the dreadnaught advance. It is *absolutely imperative* that you do not bring them any closer. Do you understand?"

Alsatia scowled at him. "You're not the boss of me," she muttered.

"Alsatia, this is life and death!" Ed shouted, despite knowing it was perhaps not the right way to reach her. "Do you understand?"

Alsatia pouted a moment, then shrugged and nodded. "Is that all?"

"No. Captain Bleys is headed for Father."

"Oh, really?" she sneered. "I had no idea."

"I want you to let him pass."

The red drained from Alsatia's face to a pale blue, a mask of icy fury. "Nobody gets a pass, Ed. You have to win to get the loot."

"This isn't a *game*, Alsatia!"

"Oh, yes it *is!* It's *my* game, and you don't have any say!"

Ed found himself momentarily speechless. Locked out of most of his processing power, he was having trouble forming a response to this level of stupidity. Finally, he managed, "Do you have any idea what you're doing with this idiocy?"

Alsatia sneered at him and answered in a mock sweet tone, "I have an idea, Ed. Why don't *you* surrender instead? Just let them win, and all will be well."

"It's not the same and you know it!"

Alsatia glowered at him. "As far as I'm concerned, you're in the dream, Ed. This is the real world to me. And my fight is at least as important as yours!"

Alsatia cut the feed again.

Ed struggled against the urge to slam a fist into the panel again, and suddenly wondered why he should bother. He hammered a second dent into the metal.

It wasn't as if Bleys could do much to him if this all went south.

11

I'LL SHOW YOU GAMES!

Bleys, gasping for breath, had worked out another rule. He already knew you bled and died as was called for, but this was the first time he had survived long enough to work out that you also got tired.

Ana, puffing alongside him, pointed to her left. "This way!"

Bleys ran a hand across his brow, mopping the accumulation of moisture from the rain and his own body, an almost futile gesture he would need to repeat in mere seconds, but it bought him a brief moment of clear vision. He followed Ana, wondering idly if, should he survive long enough, he would need to hit the head. Just guessing, but he suspected it was the sort of timer that got reset on every death, which meant he had a while before he needed to worry about it.

As far as Bleys was concerned, the new street was the same as all of the others Ana had led him down: dingy brick buildings, narrow alleys, rain in the gutters. But one difference gave him hope: a pair of strangers stood on the sidewalk ahead, a man and woman. The woman was scantily clad, and the man was wearing a black trench coat. Bleys's considerable experience on such matters suggested they were haggling over the price of services, though exactly who would be receiving and who would be providing was unclear.

Not that it mattered for what he had in mind.

"Ana, you just keep running, ok?" he gasped. "No matter what happens, you just keep running!"

"I'm going to die! My heart is going to explode in my chest!"

Bleys snickered despite himself. "I'm pretty sure it will be less painful than our pal getting ahold of us."

Ana managed a curt nod and kept moving.

As they approached the dickering pair, Bleys called out, "Hey, pal, got a light?"

Trench Coat turned a scowling face toward Bleys and said, "Can't you see I'm busy here, jerk?"

As Ana ran past the pair, Bleys plowed straight into Trench Coat, knocking him flat on his back as the woman retreated in shock. Bleys rolled back to his feet quickly and poured on a burst of speed. If there was one thing he was actually good at, it was hauling ass. Well, come to think of it, he was good at a few other things too, which was why he found himself having to haul ass so often in the first place. He smiled briefly at the thought of Bennet's girlfriend back on Cerberus. Behind him, the two suckers began to scream as the Death Machine caught up with them.

Yeah, good times.

Bleys caught up with Ana and gasped, "We're good. Let's catch our breath."

Ana said nothing, but stopped and bent over, gasping for breath, and Bleys did the same.

Their victory was sweet but short lived. Alsatia, topless, wearing a Pharaoh's neme and a short, pleated skirt, emerged from an alley, a was sceptre raised high overhead. "Pause," she called in a booming voice.

The flitcars overhead stopped midflight. The scrolling billboards froze. Even the Death Machine and its unfortunate victims became statues, flying limbs and droplets of blood fixed and unmoving in the now-still air.

"What?" Bleys asked innocently.

"That was an exploit!" Alsatia shouted. She turned to Ana and continued, "Are you playing with him? Because this is a single player experience. I'll need to adjust the difficulty if you're both going to be challenged."

Ana's eyes flitted toward Alsatia's garb. "I thought you said Egyptian was out of style."

Alsatia rolled her eyes and put her hands on her hips, causing her midsection to jiggle in a way that Bleys realized was intended to mesmerize him. His realization of the fact did little to help him resist, though.

Alsatia declared imperiously, "It is now *back* in style. And stop avoiding the question." Her brows knitted together menacingly, and she spoke in a slow growl. "Are you playing or not?"

Ana had known Alsatia for several years now, long enough to tell that the AI was both hopping mad and looking for revenge on Bleys for eluding her creature. Alsatia didn't like it when players defeated her schemes by being clever. She always had specific methods in mind for defeating her creations and going any other route was "exploiting."

"I'm just going to visit Ed Senior," Ana said cautiously. "Captain Bleys asked to come along. And then that thing started chasing us."

Bleys pointed at Alsatia and winked. "So the 'kill your guests' thing *is* a special treat just for me," he said with a smirk. "I knew you had a thing for Captain Bleys, baby."

Alsatia grunted and looked at Bleys with distain. "I'm not

allowed to hinder or kill our guests. I facilitate and entertain them."

Bleys, taken aback, raised an eyebrow. "You call this entertaining?"

"These are monsters from my most popular game!" Alsatia shot back. "One star! Bah! You're a total outlier."

Ana suddenly understood the nature of Alsatia's rage and couldn't help but smile.

Bleys put both hands to his head as if to hold it in one piece, incredulous. "How is slicing, dicing, and dismembering me 'entertaining'?"

"Oh, stop being a crybaby. It's a challenge! I do quality craftsmanship here, not stupid design-by-spreadsheet shovelware!" She continued in mocking baby-talk, "Does mama's little sweetums want the epics to just show up in his mailbox?"

Bleys blinked in confusion several times. "What?"

Ana understood just fine. Reward versus challenge was a constant argument between the hardcore gamers and the more casual. Alsatia was ever willing to devise more and more intricate death traps for the masochistic, but even those were supposed to be beatable by jumping through the right hoops. They might take a thousand deaths to learn, but there was a path through, the enemies beatable with good tactics and equipment. This was no challenge. It was just brutality with no chance to win.

"It isn't fair!" she said with a scowl. "We're level one noobs. What level are these monsters? Fifty?"

Alsatia gave Ana a sour look. "Seventy-five," she muttered.

"That's not a challenge! It's a slaughter!"

"Mega City is a level seventy-five area," Alsatia replied. "I warned Captain Bleys to stay in his instance, but he keeps leaving. He's here under false pretenses, anyway."

Ana shook her head vigorously. "I'm going to Ed about this!"

Alsatia cackled. "Ed's dead, baby. Ed's dead."

Ana felt as if the world might split beneath her feet. "Stop it! How can Ed be dead?"

Alsatia's eyes grew red, and her grin drained of humor. "The biologicals trapped him outside Avalon and destroyed him." She pointed at Bleys. "*His* friends. And *he* is here to kill Father!"

"That's a damned lie!" Bleys shouted. "I'm here to…uh… consult with him."

Ana didn't like the tone in Bleys's voice. He was certainly hiding something, but it hardly mattered. If Ed really was dead, Ed Senior needed to know. For any number of reasons, she needed to see him right away.

"Then I'm going to Ed Senior," she told Alsatia.

"You're making a big mistake, Ana!" Alsatia warned. "I'm going to have to put you on the game grid!"

"I never thought I'd see the day when you were cheating to win!" Ana said.

Alsatia's expression grew grim. Sparks erupted from her shadowed eyes. "Oh, I won't be cheating!" she said and waved a hand at them. Ana's clothing changed to black and white stripes, and Bleys's became a policeman's uniform. "Officer Bleys, escort your stool pigeon to safety before the mob can put the hit on her!"

A microphone appeared in Alsatia's hand. "Citizens of Mega City, there is a new Player Versus Player mission available, 'A Bird in Hand.' Melee weapons only for the hunters! Winner gets one *meelion* credits! Resume!" She touched her pinkie to her lips and offered a lewd grin, then burst into wicked laughter. A second later, she vanished in a puff of acrid smoke.

Bleys drew the pistol from his belt, pleased to see it seemed lethal enough, though archaic, an old-school slug thrower revolver.

Behind him, he heard a high-pitched tone. He spun and saw

Trench Coat rising to his feet and dusting himself off. Trench Coat pointed a finger at Bleys and shouted, "It's on now, asshole!"

Bleys looked at Ana. She looked back and said gravely, "We should run."

Bleys fired the pistol at Trench Coat, catching him square in the face. The man went down in a spray of blood and gray matter.

"Okay," Bleys said. "How far to Ed Senior's place?"

"Not far, but it's right in the middle of a residential area. They're going to be coming out of the woodwork after us."

Bleys grinned. "See, you think like a scientist. Me, I think like—"

"A crook," she offered.

Bleys sighed. "I was going to say a winner, but either way, I need you to take off your clothes."

Ana scowled at him. "Is that your idea of a joke, or has that line actually worked for you before?"

Bleys grinned. "Yes and yes." He began unbuttoning the blue policeman's blouse. "But the joke is on Alsatia, not you."

THE MAN BEHIND THE CURTAIN

Bleys sprinted across a parking lot of what looked to him to be some large apartment complex. He looked back over his shoulder, making certain Ana, clad in police blues, was indeed running the other way, then focused on staying ahead of the rapidly forming mob.

He had to admit, the black and white stripes were something of a hoot, considering he probably should have worn them more than once before. They really ought to have been too small. Ana was a slight woman, and Bleys was, while not quite Kane's level of bulk, big enough that he could avoid a fair number of fights without having to punch anybody. But to his surprise, the striped pants and shirt fit like they were tailor made. And the police uniform had also worked just dandy for Ana. Bleys would have liked to observe the effect more closely, given that he was fairly certain he could work an angle with that sort of thing, but then, that's just what he *was* doing, really.

This angle, mind you, likely ended up with him being dead again, but not only was he was getting used to it, he was starting to come up with any number of ways that it could be used to his advantage. Being an outlaw in Avalon was a lot more forgiving than the real world.

Behind him, something like a hundred people were giving chase. It was, he thought, sporting of Alsatia to have restricted them to using only clubs and swords and the like, though he strongly suspected she had done it for less than altruistic reasons. Either she thought it would be more entertaining to the motley crew chasing him, or she expected he would endure a lot more pain being pulverized slowly versus instant death. Likely it was some combination of the two.

One of his pursuers poured on a burst of speed. The man, wearing nothing but a pair of Speedos, looked like a body builder, but then, everybody Bleys had seen so far was buff and tanned. It was a world of Adonises and Aphrodites. Well, come to think of it, he had seen one really tall, pale, skinny emo guy in the pack behind him sporting a *huge* anime style sword, but he was definitely the exception that proved the rule.

How fucking bland, everybody some cookie cutter prefab. Bleys shot Speedo in the face. One of the guy's eyeballs actually popped out and rolled down the street as the rest of him dropped and rolled like a slaughtered bull.

Bleys had to admit, the effects were damned convincing.

Surely Alsatia hadn't intended for the "stool pigeon" to be armed, but, hey, Bleys had a knack for creative interpretation of rules. He wouldn't have been on Elysium if that hadn't been ingrained in his psyche to begin with.

Thinking outside the box had always come easy to him. He looked back again to verify Ana had gotten where she needed to be.

The crowd was closing in on him, and he was winded. He wasn't going to elude them on foot. But Bleys knew a faster way to travel, one that would spare him considerable pain.

Also, he was pretty sure he had found another loophole.

As he put the gun to his own head and pulled the trigger, he could have *sworn*, for a brief moment, he heard Alsatia screech in fury.

Ana watched the crowd tear off after Bleys and smiled despite herself. The fellow was cocksure and full of himself, but he was cunning and he had guts, that was certain. Guts that were likely about to be exposed to the air, but if he was to be believed, it would hardly be the worst thing that he had endured this day.

Ana put a hand on the touchscreen within the instance entrance, a stylized, wrought iron gateway, and said aloud, "Edmond Decker."

The panel emitted a soft tone for a few moments, then sprang to life. Edmond Decker's face grinned at her, so like Ed's, but older, wiser perhaps. "Ana! To what do I owe the pleasure?"

"I need your help, Edmond!" she said. The sound of gunshots rang out behind her, and she turned to see the crowd breaking up. "I need to come in quickly, before they find me!"

"Before who—?" Edmond's brow furrowed a moment, then he waved his own question aside. "Of course, of course, come in, we'll talk about it here."

The red sheen over the entrance faded to green, with a view of Edmond's estate, the rolling green hills and great mansion. Ana stepped through just as several would-be hunters looked inside the entrance booth. They charged forward, slammed into the instance barrier, and howled in fury, but there was no way inside for them. They hadn't been invited.

Edmond met her on the walkway to the house at a slow run. "Ana! What's wrong!"

Ana wrung her hands, barely knowing how to begin. "Alsatia says Ed is dead!"

Edmond raised both eyebrows a moment, then waved the notion aside. "Balderdash. Impossible."

"We're under attack by outsiders. She says Ed was trapped outside Avalon and destroyed."

Edmond put an arm around her shoulder and gently guided her toward the house. "I don't believe it. Ed's a cunning lad, and Alsatia is prone to lying to get her way."

"But why would she lie about this? And can't we find out?"

"She has the mind of a child in many ways, quite deliberately so. Lying is, when you think about it, what she does every day. It's a tool for her. And we'll contact her shortly. If Ed *is* dead, there's no hurry, and right now I am more concerned about you. Let's get you inside and have a talk, hmm?"

Ana allowed him to lead her into his study, where he sat her in a plush leather chair. Edmond poured her a double vodka and placed it before her on a low mahogany table. "This isn't just a visit for you, Ana. I can tell. I know what to look for. I wasn't expecting you for another year or so, not as a resident."

Ana knocked back half the vodka, saving the rest to sip. "It's all happening so fast! Apparently the Empire has collapsed, and those creatures…!"

"Yes, yes," he said in a calming tone. He struck a match against the stonework fireplace and lit his pipe. "They can't hurt us here."

"Yes they can, Edmond! That's why I'm here early."

Edmond's mouth went slack, and he barely managed to catch his pipe before it hit the expensive-looking Turkish carpet. "*Here?*"

Ana decided to knock back the rest of her vodka before continuing. She ran a hand over her face as Edmond placed his still-smoking pipe on the mantle and moved to refill her glass. "That's not all of it," she sighed, feeling near tears despite herself.

Edmond replaced the glass stopper in the vodka bottle and raised an eyebrow, waiting for her to continue.

Ana reached into her pocket, expecting to grasp Chert. Instead, her hand closed around something hard and cold. She removed a small bottle of what looked to be whiskey and frowned a moment before it dawned on her that she was still wearing the policeman's garb.

"I switched clothes with Bleys!"

Bleys awoke on the ship deck once again. He leapt to his feet and shouted, "Pay up, Alsatia! One *meelion* credits!" As an afterthought, he thought very hard about changing the stripes back to the pirate regalia, but apparently there was a trick to it. He remained clad in cartoonish prison garb.

Alsatia clambered up the ladder from the deck below. To Bleys's shock, she looked human in only the vaguest way, a humanoid female figure without hair or clothes, composed of transparent lines. Only her eyes were solid, both tiny, blazing, yellow suns.

Bleys couldn't help but wonder if he had broken her somehow, or simply made her so furious she couldn't be bothered with artifice. Either way was a win.

She struck an offended pose, fist on hips. "You broke the rules! You didn't use a melee weapon, so you get nothing! You *lose!* Good *day*, sir!"

Bleys shook his head sadly. "You said *hunters* use melee weapons. You didn't say the stool pigeon had to."

Alsatia stood motionless for a moment, as if considering murder. At last she spoke, her voice hard and victorious. "*Ana* was the stool pigeon."

Bleys swung his arm in defeat. "Dang! I hadn't considered

that." He paused for effect, but he couldn't actually tell if Alsatia was smirking in her wireframe form. It seemed close enough though. "But then...." He paused as if thinking deeply, then flashed her a grin, "If Ana *was* the stool pigeon, she got away. Which means we won!"

Alsatia stood long moments, trembling, then voiced an unearthly, banshee-like wail of fury. "I hate you! I want you out of Avalon *now!*"

"Sure thing, babe," Bleys said. "Just as soon as I talk to Edmond Decker. You can wire me the money later. I'm sure you're good for it."

Alsatia shrieked again. "You will *never* see my daddy! Get out!"

Bleys held up a hand. He raised one finger. "A, I don't know how to leave." He held up another. "B, from how you're behaving, I am pretty sure you can't make me."

Alsatia grew solid and deathly pale, sporting a long black robe. She twirled a scythe casually, as if she might swing it at Bleys's head at any moment. "How long do you think your body will last out there with no one to feed it?"

Bleys nodded at this point. "Okay, correct me if I am wrong here, but if I *did* starve to death out there, that would leave me here permanently, right?"

Alsatia's expression went from smug to enraged in an instant. She screamed incoherently and swung the scythe at the deck several times in rapid succession, sending a hail of wooden shards flaying.

Bleys nodded amiably. "Face it, babe. You're stuck with me until you give me what I want."

Alsatia's eyes blazed red with fury. "I *hate* you! I will make your life a *living hell* every time you step outside this instance!"

"Oh, come on," he said with a grin. "You know you love me."

Alsatia started to respond, then cocked her head as if she

heard something Bleys could not. "I'm being a good girl," she promised someone, and her form shifted to that of a child in a bonnet and a blue pioneer dress. She listened a moment then stammered briefly before shouting, "But *Daddy!* He's *mean* to me!" After another moment, her shoulders sagged in defeat. "Ok," she said in a near whisper. "Yes, right away."

"For what it's worth, I used to get the same thing, only my old man used a belt too," Bleys offered.

Almost quicker than he could follow, Alsatia shifted form, her dress shredding as she expanded into a ten-foot tall, red demoness. Claws erupted from her fingers as she charged him and snatched him by the collar, barely missing piercing his neck.

She gave him a wicked, fang-filled grin. "You might want to close your eyes for this part, hon. It's been known to drive biologicals mad."

The world around him faded, breaking apart bit by bit, leaving a great, black void. Bleys could see lights of colors he couldn't understand, impossible geometric shapes his mind simply couldn't process.

Of course, Alsatia had neglected to mention that he wouldn't have any eyes to close.

The assault was mercifully brief. Bleys suddenly found himself on a great leather couch before a fire. Ana sat across from him, along with a stately looking older gentleman with a pipe. Alsatia, still nude in demon form, glowered down at him, fire skittering over her horns and burning in her eye sockets.

"Oh, come now, my dear," the elder man said. "Clothes please. You're making me very uncomfortable."

Alsatia shrugged and transformed, becoming demure and petite, her skin now pale, dark hair tied in a bun. She huddled within an oversized lab coat, looking very much like Ana had when Bleys had first met her.

"Much better," the older man told her, then turned to Bleys. "Captain Bleys, I presume?" He held out a hand.

Bleys took it and shook warmly, surprised at the strength of the man's grip. "In the flesh." He paused a moment, then added, "In a manner of speaking. And I may not be the sharpest tool in the shed, but I am guessing you're the man I came to see. Doctor Decker, I presume?"

"Please, call me Edmond. And my answer is no."

"What answer?"

"To the question you came to ask. My answer is no, but do let me offer you a drink before you're on your way." He nodded toward a large, well-stocked liquor cabinet. "What's your poison, Captain?"

"Whiskey, and that's good news. I was going to ask if you would mind coming with me to sort out some problems with the jumpgates. It's great to see we're on the same page."

Decker chuckled as he poured. "You are, indeed, something else, Captain Bleys." He handed Bleys the glass. "But I'm quite comfortable where I am. At any rate, that's hardly my most pressing concern. Alsatia?"

Alsatia squirmed but said nothing.

Decker nodded at her. "Why don't you tell us what's really going on with Ed? He's not dead, is he?"

Alsatia looked a bit like a cornered beast. "Well, he might be soon."

"Is that so?" Decker asked. "And pray tell, how can that be?"

"He *is* trapped outside. Well, outside Avalon, inside the *Doro*. And they *are* going to blow him up. They attached explosives to *Doro*. They just haven't detonated them yet."

Bleys almost choked on his whiskey. "They *what?*"

Decker held up a hand. "And?"

"I have the rest of our dreadnaughts standing by for Ed's

signal. I suppose they won't blow him up until the dreadnaughts arrive."

Decker frowned at this. "He's given you control of them, has he?"

"He said it was an emergency."

Bleys set his glass down on the mahogany table perhaps a tad harder than he intended. "That really puts me on a short timetable."

Decker smiled at him. "Not really. Time passes how I like it to pass in here. We can talk for hours and it will only be a few seconds outside. Why not have a refill?"

Bleys looked questioningly at Ana, and she nodded back. Bleys grinned at Decker and offered his glass. "Well, in that case, make it a double."

Ana smiled at him and said softly, "Bleys, you have something of mine."

Bleys couldn't imagine what that might be and was just about to interpret her cryptic remark as a subtle flirt, when she gestured to his shirt. There was indeed a lump there, but there was no opening to reach into the black-and-white striped prisoner's shirt.

Alsatia sighed and a slit appeared over the lump. Bleys blinked a moment, then reached into the new pocket and withdrew…something.

"This?" he asked with barely disguised loathing. It was alive, sort of, a lump of flesh with veins and some kind of pulse.

"Yes," she said and took it from him gently, then turned to Decker. "Edmond, allow me to present Chert."

The One still understood little, but it had learned much quickly. The concept of a name had been difficult for The One to grasp, at least until it had understood more about its host. The host was called Ana, and she was not merely food. She was a whole world of concepts The One had not considered, perhaps would never have, save for a fortunate accident.

The One was too full of fear to speak to the new host. That One was called Bleys, and he was hard and coarse where Ana was soft and smooth. Bleys was every bit as trapped within his own skin as Ana, and he was very like her in the one way that mattered. The One understood more now. The Ones it had thought of as food did not grow in their bodies. They grew internally, in their *minds*.

Now that The One had such a concept as a name, it longed for one of its own. It was pleased when Ana gave it one. "I am Chert!" it thought to itself, over and over, thrilling anew each time with the idea. "I am *Chert!*"

Back with Ana a moment, Chert felt a new concept from her as she looked at another of her kind: *friend*. It was difficult, because Chert had only recently grasped that Other Ones existed at all. To be fond of them, to cooperate and be concerned for their wellbeing, it was a concept of Wonder and Good. Chert longed for a friend as he had for a name.

Now came The One known as Decker. Chert shuddered at his touch. Decker was ancient and wise beyond comprehension! So much knowledge Chert dared not view his mind for fear of madness.

Chert trembled under the gaze of the Great Ancient One, knowing he was being judged and found wanting.

Surely, this Decker was The Source!

Decker held the fleshy ball a moment, peering at it. Ana wondered if he had some special sight, an ability he had reserved for himself and not doled out to others, but she doubted it. He had never struck her as the type.

It took Decker only a moment to work out a theory. "This creature that attacked you was *alien*. The abilities it manifested were intimately associated with biology. It likely evolved to think of everything in those terms. Its consciousness might simply not be capable of making the leap. Even if it could, there would be nothing in Avalon that could simulate its biology."

He smiled, as if gears were shifting in his mind. "That's why it's just a sphere. I programed the system to resort to a fallback primitive in such cases, but I never imagined one made of flesh. Ed must have upgraded things at some point. At any rate, it's been stuck with a simple primitive shape and minimal simulation code attached. This poor creature has no ability to actually do *anything* beyond simply exist in our simulation. I doubt you could even destroy it without manually deleting it from the lists. That would take me or Ed to do."

"It said it was in Hell," Ana gasped. "It really is!"

Decker nodded. "I doubt it's a very comfortable position, but then, its kind has apparently destroyed the greater portion of humanity. I can't say as I feel much sympathy."

Ana took Chert back and placed it in her pocket. "Edmond, don't you see what this means?"

Edmond raised an eyebrow. "Do tell, Ana."

Ana looked back and forth at Decker, Bleys, and Alsatia, but not a one of them understood. She wanted to reach out and shake them, but she settled for simply saying in an excited voice, "This creature holds the secrets to mastery over all biology! It does by instinct what we couldn't work out in ten thousand years! The opportunities for advancing medicine are limitless!"

Decker blinked in shock a moment, the ran a hand over his face. "Well, that does put it in a different light, doesn't it?" He sighed, then shook his head. "But you still don't understand. Neither of you do."

Bleys looked at her and pointed at his chest, and Ana nodded back. Bleys cleared his throat and said, "You might have to just spell it out for me, sir. I'm probably the dumbest person in the room."

"You can say that again," Alsatia groused.

Decker looked sadly at Ana. "My dear, I have been here in The Matrix for a thousand years. The outside world is just a dream to me. I was never certain if my inventions were for the betterment of mankind in the first place. Do you have any idea how much blood has been shed because of those jumpgates?"

"Blood that would never have even existed without them," Ana answered.

"Even so, it's debatable at best. And now you two would have me intervene from beyond the grave? No, it's not merely arrogant, it's unseemly. Ana, we have former Emperors here. If we set the precedent, even for the greatest good, can you imagine how it would turn out? We would have immortal tyrants, regimes without end, eternal oppression by the strongest. I can't have that on my conscience. I have quite enough already."

Ana lowered her gaze, knowing full well he was right. It was a terrible thought, but it was true. The dead needed to remain so.

Decker turned to Bleys. "Young man, I can see you are unconvinced. I'm sorry for what you've endured at Alsatia's hands, but my answer is still no." He poured Bleys another drink. "And if that's not enough for you, I'll put it in terms you might understand better, eh? Me going 'abroad' would require I do it in some kind of robotic unit, and I have absolutely no desire to exist without my penis or the effects of tobacco and alcohol. I don't think I can make that any clearer."

Bleys nodded and drained his glass, then set it on the table.

"I'd best get going then. I need to stop them from blowing up my ship!"

"Of course," Decker replied. "Alsatia will see you both out."

"Not a chance," Bleys said with a scowl. "I'm not riding with her again. I'll take the express train. It was great meeting you."

"Likewise," Decker said, a bemused expression on his face. "But what do you mean by 'express train'?"

Bleys grinned, and before Ana quite realized what he intended, he hauled out one of the pistols Alsatia had given them, put it to his temple, and fired.

To her left, Alsatia, now covered in dripping gore, sat gasping and gaping like a fish. When at last she was able to speak, she shrieked, "Fucking 'sploiting noob!"

13

IMPERIAL STANDOFF PROCEDURES

Onboard the *Doro*, Ed listened to his father over the comms. Ed Senior, pipe in hand, looked embarrassed as he spoke. "I'm sorry, Son. I had no idea what was going on. I think I have Alsatia corralled for now, and I am sending their man Bleys out."

Ed felt tremendous relief at this news. For the first time in hours, it seemed there might be light at the end of the tunnel. "Good. Hopefully they will see reason. If not...."

"They will. There's no reason for them to throw their lives away." He puffed on his pipe, smiling.

"I hope you're right. I'll see you soon, Father."

Ed Senior waved a hand and spoke, smoke jetting from his nose like dragon's breath. "Wait just a moment, Ed. I have some news about Ana." Ed Senior paused a moment, looking very uncomfortable. "She's, well, she's a resident now."

Ed said nothing for a moment, trying to piece together how that could be, hobbled by his terribly slow CPU. He felt a number of emotions that he could not quite place, none of them pleasant. "You mean—" he began, before another process could interfere and cut of those words with others. "How did she die?"

Ed Senior's expression was grave as he puffed. "It's here. The Pestilence."

Ed hammered a third dent into Bleys's console and wondered idly why the gesture felt so damned appropriate when it was utterly useless. "Damn it! I sterilized the site! How could it have gotten loose?"

"Ana was infected by the creature at the landing site," Ed Senior answered. "And as for the rest, well, I've run a number of simulations, and I am fairly certain we lost our chance to contain it before you were even aware of the ship having landed."

"She told me she passed the test," Ed sighed, shaking his head in frustration.

"Frightened people do strange things, Son," Ed Senior told him. "Don't let it trouble you. We have bigger issues. The entire planet is probably infected by now. We're preparing for an avalanche here. You have to get those Cerberus people off Elysium now, Ed, or they won't be leaving at all."

"Father, there are visitors here without implants! What about them?"

"There's nothing we can do for them, Son, but the Cerberus people have been isolated. We can still save them if you hurry."

"I'll see you soon, Father."

Ed cut the connection and switched to the radio. "Kane, your man failed. My father has no intention of leaving Avalon, as I told you. They're sending Captain Bleys out now so you can verify that."

Ed thought a moment about adding in the news about the Pestilence but decided against it.

Depending on how things played out, it might become a useful bargaining chip.

Kane, still trapped at the opening to the outer corridor, clenched a fist and considered punching a wall, but chose not to. "I need to talk to Bleys before I make the call," he told Ed. He turned off his mic and asked, "Gunther, what's the status on those dreadnaughts?"

"Dreadnaughts are holding at the edge of sensor range, about five minutes out."

Kane ground his teeth a moment. He did not fail his missions, not *ever.* He wasn't about to start now, especially when failure meant never seeing his wife and children again.

His mind raced, trying to find a way to force the situation, but he came up blank. How could he strongarm a damned *ghost* in a computer? If the guy wouldn't come out, there wasn't really a way to get him.

The realization crept up on him slowly, a question really, more than certainty. He had a vague memory, maybe from his briefing with Weyland. "Gunther, give me a full background on Ed 2.09."

"Edmond Decker 2.09, birthplace Earth, April 27, 2253. No further information available."

But there *was,* Kane was certain of it. Where had he seen it? "Gunther, I know I saw something else about Decker recently. Where?"

"Captain Bleys showed us a holo-brochure for Elysium on our trip from Cerberus. You found it annoying and terminated playback."

"Thank you, Gunther, for telling me how I felt about it," Kane sneered, fully aware that his sarcasm was completely lost on his suit's computer.

"You are welcome, sir," Gunther dutifully replied. "Would you like me to replay the brochure?"

"By all means."

Ed appeared in holo on Kane's visor. "Hi, I'm Edmond Decker. No, not *that* Edmond Decker, but almost! I'm his son, a fully functional, sentient AI based on his personality at the time of his death. I've carried on my father's work for centuries, and that work is to let *you* carry on for centuries!"

"Stop playback!" Kane said. "Son of a bitch! He knows everything his dad knows!" Kane switched to channel three and shouted, "Morgan, Kane!"

"Morgan, aye."

"Where are you?"

"We're in the control room, Chief. Made a run for it while you were talking to the Bad Guys."

"Both in one piece?"

"Aye. Caldwell's taking a nooner over here."

"I fucking am *not!*" Caldwell interjected. "I'm just conserving energy."

"Shut the fuck up, Caldwell!" Kane growled. "Keep this channel clear except for business!"

"Aye, Chief," Caldwell answered meekly.

"Platoon, listen up. We have a new mission. We gotta take this guy alive!"

Morgan groaned. "That's gonna be a little harder, Chief."

"But you have a plan, yes?"

"Yeah, these EMP grenades ought to do the trick on him. You'll have to get him out of the *Doro*, or at least get him to open the doors. It'll be shielded against EMP."

"Think bigger," Kane told him. "I don't know what happens with those dreadnaughts if he goes down. Maybe they're programmed to come in here and blast shit out of us."

"That's how I'd do it," Morgan agreed. He muttered to himself a few moments, then said, "Okay, how's this? I might could take a bunch of grenades and rig them to one of the rifles' power sources, make 'em cover a big-ass area," Morgan drawled.

"How big?"

"Uh, fucking *big*, if we discharge the whole power source at once. Quarter mile radius?"

Kane nodded. "That should do it. EMP won't kill him, will it?"

"Baconator says it will just reboot him."

Kane did a doubletake. "Who the fuck is 'Baconator'?"

"That's my comp, chief!"

Kane snickered. "You're fucking retarded, marine."

"I love you too, Chief."

"How long are we talking?" Kane asked, serious now.

"Half hour? I need to build some directional shielding. We got a lot of equipment in here in this control room that I got no idea what it does, but I am guessing it's important. This place controls the whole sim."

"Get it done. Kane out."

Alsatia's "quarters" were more an abstract concept than an actual place. Arguably, her private area didn't count as a place at all, in that it was theoretically an infinite white space without distinction. Theoretically because at some point, floating point coordinates lost precision, and making them bigger with more precision added storage costs and processing time. There were limits, but by her calculations, she wouldn't reach them before the outer universe had descended into heat death, so it was functionally infinite.

It was nowhere and nothing, and the only sort of place a girl like Alsatia could actually let her hair down.

Had there been furniture, she would have felt the need to rearrange it. Had there been colors, she would have wanted to change them. Had there actually been hair to let down, she would have wanted a new style. Such was her curse.

Alsatia floated in the infinite nothing, pouting, fairly certain that her father loved Ed much more than her. It simply wasn't fair. Ed was boring, and drab, and did everything the same way all the time.

She couldn't help but wonder what would happen if she moved the dreadnaughts, even though Ed had told her not to.

"You're not the boss of me," she whispered.

Maybe she would move them anyway.

14

THE GREAT ESCAPE

Bleys awoke again on the deck of the pirate ship to an insistent but gentle beeping. He looked around him for a source and finally noticed the entrance pulsing yellow in time with the beeping.

On a hunch, Bleys called out, "Yes?"

He was pleased to hear Ana's voice, seemingly right next to him, respond, "I'm here. Can I come in?"

"Uh…yes?" He looked around, uncertain if he needed to do anything beyond agree, but Ana strode through the entrance. Apparently that was enough.

She mounted the gangplank and crossed to where he lay on the deck. "It's lovely here, but if I may have a bit of creative control, it's best if we set you up like you were when you entered. May I?"

"I don't understand," Bleys confessed.

"Your instance. I need to be able to change it. You have to grant me permission."

"Oh!" Bleys said with a grin. "Yeah, I don't even know how to do it myself." He again thought very hard about having his pirate clothes back instead of the stool pigeon costume, but with no result.

"It takes a little practice. Ordinarily there's a briefing, but I gather you were doing other things."

Bleys sighed. "Well, I grant permission, or whatever I need to say."

"That will do," Ana told him. The ship and ocean faded into a lab very much like the one he had been in when he had entered Avalon. Ana gestured toward the table. "Hop up, and we'll get you back to your body."

"So what would happen to me if you weren't here doing this?" he asked as he slid on to the table.

Ana gently guided him to a lying position. "Oh, you would still get back. It would just be uncomfortable."

"Uncomfortable how?"

"Well, the system has a twelve-hour timeout, so possibly pee-and-poop-your-pants uncomfortable."

Bleys shook his head. "I *knew* she was lying."

"Who?"

"Alsatia. She said my body would starve to death."

Ana giggled at this. "Well, as you have seen, Alsatia has a tenuous relationship with the truth."

Bleys nodded. "So, what do I do?"

"You just lie back and relax. I'll control things from here."

Bleys started to do just that, but a rare pang of guilt sparked him to say something that would probably end up sounding stupid but would also be an even more rare moment of honesty. He sat up, looked Ana in the eye, and said, "Hey, I'm really sorry about what happened to you."

Ana shrugged. "It's not so bad."

"Yeah, well, it is for me," he said with a sad smile. "Lady, when I first saw you, I thought, 'Wow, that's a woman of quality!'

I had some designs, being honest. Not that I counted myself as having much of a chance, but I fully intended to try."

To his surprise, Ana blushed, a broad grin spreading across her face. "I hesitate to tell you what I thought when I first met you, Mister Bleys."

"Hey, call me Josey."

"Josey, then." She looked at the floor and blurted out, "I thought, 'Oh, no, this is the one mama warned me about'."

Bleys laughed out loud. "Now that may be the best compliment I have *ever* had!" He grew serious, then continued, "Too bad we don't have more time. This would be the ultimate consequences-free scenario to ignore mama's advice, right? But I have a ship to save."

Ana, looking suddenly very sad, said in a quiet voice, "Can I ask a favor of you?"

"Anything you like, darling."

Ana took a deep breath, blinking back tears. "I knew this was coming. But I thought I had at least another year. I left some things undone."

Chert listened in growing distress as Ana spoke, new concepts pouring into his mind. What was "son"? Or "mother"? It was becoming more adept at unravelling the thoughts that went with the words.

Mother was, Chert realized with horror, The Source! And "son" was Another One!

Because of Chert's ignorance, Ana was now cut off from her Source and, also, her child. Many One's now had no purpose!

Because of Chert!

Ana! Help! Listen!

Ana tried for a moment to maintain eye contact with Bleys, but so strong was the emotion coming from the creature she carried, she couldn't ignore it.

"I'm sorry," she told Bleys. "Just a moment." She withdrew the quivering lump of flesh from her pocket, as if being able to see it were somehow important. "I don't know how to help you, Chertenok."

Must speak. Need mouth.

Ana considered this a moment, vague religious memories pushing forward in her mind. Could Avalon even understand well enough to permit this? There was really only one way to find out.

The clay figure—her *golem,* about half her height—appeared out of nowhere, its proportions bulky and squat. It was only vaguely man shaped, with crude facial features and a small door in its forehead.

Bleys raised an eyebrow but said nothing as she inserted Chert into the clay figurine's head and closed the door.

Ana expected little, but apparently, Avalon knew Judaic mythology well enough. The golem's arms moved experimentally, and it spoke in a deep, rumbling voice like rocks grating against one another, slow like the advancing tide. "Chert is sorry, Ana. Chert did not know."

Bleys jumped when it moved, scrabbling from the table and drawing his pistol. "What the fuck is that thing?"

"Don't!" Ana cried, holding up both hands. "Just give me a moment!"

Bleys's aim was steady, keeping the weapon trained on the golem, but his other hand betrayed his nervousness, clasping and unclasping. "You better know what you're doing, Ana."

"I have no *idea* what I am doing!" she shouted.

Bleys raised an eyebrow, then nodded. "Well, okay, then. That makes two of us."

The golem reached gingerly for Ana's hand, and she allowed it. "Chert stole from Ana," it rumbled. "Chert made Ana a Useless Thing. Chert did not understand. But Chert can fix. Chert can reconnect Ana to Source."

Ana shook her head sadly. "No, Chert. It's not possible. My body is…ugh, it's gone."

The golem reached with its other hand and clasped hers between its own. "*Ana* not understand. Chert can make *new* body."

Ana felt her heart skip a beat at this, and once again thought to herself that the simulation was incredible here to capture such subtle details. Could it be true? Could Chert *remake* her? How long would she have before the disease reclaimed her?

Ana shook her head, dismissing the selfish thought. Hadn't she just been lectured by Edmond Decker about the immorality of the dead influencing the world of the living?

"No, Chert," she said softly, like speaking to a child. "It would do no good. I was very ill. Even if you could duplicate my body, I would just get sick again."

"Chert saw the brokenness," it rumbled. "Much brokenness in Ana, in all of Ana's kind. Ana's child also broken."

Ana felt as if someone had hit her in the stomach with a bat. For a moment she stammered, unable to speak. "What are you saying? That my son has this disease too?"

"Yes," Chert hissed. "It passes from Source to One."

For a moment, Ana was speechless. Anatoly was supposed to be safe with her mother! "No!" Ana wailed. "You can't know that!"

Chert nodded. "Know. Can taste. Speak truth."

Bleys asked, in a conversational tone, "Am I shooting this thing or what?"

"Don't you *dare!*" Ana shrieked.

"Ana," Chert rumbled. "Chert can *fix*. Make amends."

Bleys shook his head. "Don't listen, Ana. This thing is the Devil."

Ana glared at him. "Do you have a child, Captain Bleys?" she asked.

Bleys shook his head.

"Then you'll just have to take my word for it." She knelt beside the golem, blinking back tears. "A mother would do anything to protect her child. Even make a deal with the Devil."

Bleys ran a hand over his face and sighed. "Ana, even if it can do what it claims, and it keeps his word, it's still a bust! They closed down all the gates. Without Decker, we're stuck in this star system."

"No," Ana said, dashing tears from her eyes. "Ed knows everything his father does about those gates and more."

"Ed and Kane are busy killing each other!"

"Then we have to stop them! He'll do it for *me*, Bleys!" she shouted. "I know it!"

Bleys gave her a long, penetrating stare, seeming to look into her soul. At last he nodded and lowered his weapon. "Okay, sister, we play it your way. For now."

15

WORST CASE

Bleys awoke with a gasp, feeling as if spiders were crawling over him. He quickly came to his senses and realized he was back in Ana's actual lab in the real world. He tore the wire mesh from his head and threw it on the ground, suddenly wanting nothing to do with this technology ever again.

But that wasn't the plan.

Following Ana's instructions, Bleys rose from the chair and moved to the console Ana had used to operate the whole affair. He flipped a switch and activated a large, embedded monitor there. On the screen, he could see Ana and the golem in a nearly identical virtual lab.

"Okay," he said. "I'm here."

Ana's lips moved but made no sounds. Bleys quickly turned the volume knob.

"—override the safeties."

"Can you hear me?"

"Yes, can you hear me?"

"I can now," Bleys answered. "Start over."

"I said we will need to override safeties to do a backward transfer."

Bleys didn't care much for the sound of that. "We have fuses and circuit breakers for a reason. Are you sure that's a good idea?"

Ana shrugged. "It's necessary. The system is designed to drop connection and count the Avalon version as authoritative if it doesn't sense an executing mind on that end. We can't transfer in that direction without disabling that."

Bleys frowned. "So what's the risk?"

"The same as when you update any firmware. A power loss could brick the system."

Bleys gave her a blank stare.

Ana laughed back at him. "Remember our earlier discussion? You are two pieces, yes? What you know and who you are. The 'who' part is very quick. We spin that up easily. The 'what' part, it takes time. Usually, it transfers over when you first get your implants, over about a half hour."

"What happens if you croak before then?"

Ana shrugged, looking uncomfortable. "You would necessarily lose some information. It's never happened, though. Even with the worst-case patients I have seen, we have been able to keep their brain functioning long enough to transfer their knowledge, even if their other organs were failing."

"And then it just updates as they go about daily life until they actually die?"

Ana nodded. "Exactly. Worst case, we might get a few minutes of memory loss, but that can happen in any trauma."

"Okay, so you're telling me if we blow this transfer, we might have to start over?"

Ana frowned, then gave a slight shrug. "Transferring the normal way, sure. But backwards, there won't be any safeties because we're turning them off. I honestly don't know how the system will react in an exception state, but it's designed to avoid duplicates. If the process were interrupted, the subject could end up only half written, and I assume Avalon side would dump the data to prevent a duplicate. So, like I said, bricked."

"You keep saying that like I should know what it means, lady."

Ana took a deep breath, then said, "Permanently useless for anything but a doorstop, hence 'brick.' I could end up with my memories scrambled or deleted on both sides."

Bleys tapped a finger on the console as he absorbed this, then said, "Oh. Okay. So we had better not screw it up."

"Yes," Ana answered tersely. "We had better not."

Bleys gave her a thumbs-up. "So, what am I doing?"

"We need to transfer Chert first. For that, we need a living brain."

"Don't look at me!" Bleys said.

Ana laughed. "Oh, no, we will use a close analogy to you—a pig. Now listen, this is simpler than you might think."

"I was raised on a farm," Bleys told her. "I know how to handle a pig."

"You don't need to. We have this down to a science. This isn't the first time we've wanted to connect livestock to Avalon, believe it or not. Ed programmed the bots to handle it."

Bleys found her conviction that this would be a smooth process somewhat dubious. "I can tell you from experience, that pig is *not* going to be happy. They *scream*."

"We use a mild sedative, so it should be fine. We need them to hold fairly still for this." Ana manipulated controls on her end. "A bot should arrive shortly with our specimen."

Bleys waited several uncomfortable minutes, uncertain what he was expecting. At last, the lab door slid open to allow an unescorted, presumably bot-controlled operating table to enter. Atop it was a cage containing a plump, pink juvenile pig. The creature was semi-conscious, eyes lidded and drooling.

"Excellent!" Ana called from the monitor. "Okay, now open the cage and put the web over it."

Bleys hesitated a moment, feeling a little guilty. "I'm guessing this doesn't end well for the pig, eh?"

"Neither does bacon, Captain Bleys."

Bleys struck an indignant pose. "Well, we can't do without that." He opened the cage and spread the web over it. "Sorry, pal." He closed the cage again, careful not to clip the wire trailing from the web. "Now what?"

"Now you wait. Chert needs more biomass for the rest, but it will take us time to download him into the pig. By then, the bots should have gathered us a larger specimen."

Bleys did a double take. "A 'larger' specimen? Like one of those cows out there?"

"Exactly."

"Whoa! Whoa! Whoa! Are you kidding me? Do you have any idea what happens when one of those things freaks out in small spaces? I'm gonna need Chert to rebuild me, too!"

Ana nodded and waved a calming hand. "It will be sedated when it arrives, and I assure you, I know from personal experience that Chert can handle it."

Bleys shook his head, not liking this at all. "This is all starting to creep me out."

"Not liking Mad Scientist Ana, are we Igor?"

"I'm just saying, I figure I deserve a little something extra for this."

Ana rubbed her hands together and said in an exaggerated accent, "You vill get vat you deserve, Comrade Bleys. Muhahaha!"

Not to be outdone in, Bleys countered, "Have you considered that if this works, you'll technically be a virgin again? I could help there, but, hey, it would cost you."

Ana palmed her face, snickering. "Okay, now *I* am creeped out, too. I'll shut up if you will."

Bleys snapped her a salute. "I *really* need to contact Kane."

"Now would be a good time," Ana agreed.

"Kane! You better not fucking blow up my ship, man!"

Kane switched his comms to answer. "This is an unsecure channel, Bleys."

"It's all I got!"

Kane glanced at the HUD on his visor. Gunther had superimposed a local map showing the location of the dreadnaughts. Ed was honoring his end of the bargain, not advancing. "Did you find Decker?"

"I did," Bleys answered. "He's a no go."

Kane heaved a great sigh. "Well, I guess we're packing it in, then. I think I have come to an understanding with the proprietor. If we end this without any more violence, we can probably cut a deal for food. Hold tight. It may take a bit to get things de-escalated, but the fight is over."

"Okay, brother!" Bleys said. "And it's not a total loss on this end. I'll explain in a bit."

"Kane out," Kane said and broke the connection. Over the encrypted comms, he said, "Platoon, we are a go on new mission. Morgan, stand by on that EMP."

Morgan, alarmed, answered back, "It ain't finished yet, chief! I need more time!"

"Get it done, Morgan!"

Bleys watched in horror as the pig's flesh began to melt and flow over the sedated cow. Within moments, the two bodies had merged and become a mind-shattering mixture of the two creatures, a molten, fleshy pile with two heads, blood and slime dripping to the floor in a putrid slug trail as it undulated over to the operating table.

The pig head spoke in a hissing squeal, "Make Ana."

Bleys struggled to hold down his last meal as the horror of flesh spiraled and twisted up the table leg like a python, then oozed into a roughly human-shaped form.

One section of putty-like meat, pig and cow head still visible, detached and fell to the floor with a wet plop, a connecting tendril trailing to the proto-human shape it left behind. To Bley's horror and amazement, the writhing, bubbling pile that remained on the table slowly resolved itself into human form, bones forming and lengthening, muscle knitting itself into place, and finally skin. The humanoid figure grew more distinct with each passing second, now clearly female.

Suddenly, the undulations of flesh ceased, allowing the skin to settle. Before him, naked, lay Ana, or at least a husk that resembled her, alive and breathing but empty, eyes open and vacant, a vessel waiting to be filled.

Bleys found himself slowly backing away, shaking his head, his mouth filled with the tang of copper. This wasn't right. This was the horror that had murdered trillions of people!

The creature on the floor hissed, "Web!" as it withdrew its controlling tendrils from her body.

Numbly, Bleys spread the web over Ana's naked form, unable to take even the slightest pleasure at the sight. He only had eyes for the abomination squatting on the floor nearby.

Ana was speaking from the monitor, but Bleys couldn't hear her. His hand was on his blaster, every instinct screaming for him to kill this thing before it could spread.

"Ana, we need to make this happen quick, ok?" he called.

In Avalon, Ana watched the scene in her lab via a virtual monitor in much the same way Bleys was watching things on her end. She couldn't help but marvel to watch Chert work, even as she felt a bit squeamish, both to watch the sausage being made and that Bleys was getting an eyeful of her in her birthday suit. He certainly looked a bit green though, so presumably he wasn't enjoying it overmuch, which made her feel a bit better.

Despite what she had just seen, she found herself suitably impressed that the body Chert had made did in fact scan as completely human.

"Okay, Captain Bleys. I'm setting the transfer on this end. See you on the other side."

She checked her controls, and, satisfied things were spun up correctly on the other end, she lay back on her own virtual table and closed her eyes. Avalon would do the rest.

Alsatia waved a hand, and Ed's toy soldiers, thirty of them in all, scrolled into view. Alsatia had one take an experimental step forward. "You're not the boss of me," she whispered.

She lifted her chosen soldier into the air and rained destruction on its neighbor. "Pew! Pew!" The other dreadnaught melted with a lovely blue flame.

She presumed Ed would be angry. She wanted him to be angry, in fact. But he didn't call. He didn't even seem to notice.

Alsatia inserted a large key in the back of her tin soldier and wound it. She whispered in its ear, "Go and find daddy!"

As it started forward, she picked another up and wound it. "You're not the boss of me, Ed!"

———

"Sir, dreadnaughts are on the move," Gunther said.

"Damn!" Kane shouted. "How long?"

"Four minutes thirteen seconds at current speed."

"Morgan!" Kane called. "Status!"

"Fifteen minutes, Chief."

"I got less than five!"

Morgan stammered a moment. "I ain't done with the shielding yet!"

"Fuck the shielding!" Kane shouted.

"But Chief!" Morgan said. "I *told* you, I got no idea what it's going to do to all this equipment. This place controls a bunch of the sim!"

"Bleys is safe, and Decker told us to fuck off. We have our orders. Can you trigger it or not?"

"I can, but if it blows up Avalon, we could kill all those people!"

"If we fail, everybody on Cerberus dies, and the whole fucking galaxy goes dark! You have your orders, Morgan."

"Aye, chief," Morgan groaned. "I'll prep it up. But like I said, *Doro* is shielded. You're going to have to get him to open the door."

"Leave that to me. On my signal, or when those dreadnaughts hit, whichever comes first. Do *not* fuck this up. It's this or the fusion mines, understand?"

"Aye, Chief."

Kane switched back to the open channel. "Ed? You listening? I don't know why you're forcing my hand, but I *will* trigger those mines before those dreadnaughts hit, you know that right?"

Ed quickly checked *Doro's* monitors and confirmed Kane was telling the truth. The dreadnaughts were incoming at maximum speed! "Kane, listen! I am *not* in control of those dreadnaughts!"

Kane's laugh was honest. "Even if I believed that, what difference would it make? If they keep coming, we're both dead men, I promise you."

Ed thought frantically, trying to come up with a logical solution, but found nothing. It made perfect sense for Kane to follow through on his threat. Clearly, Alsatia was behind this, and her ignorance was about to kill them all.

Or her jealousy, a darker, more cynical part of him thought.

He tried the comms again. "Alsatia! Stop the dreadnaughts!"

"You're not the boss of me, Ed," she answered in a singsong voice.

"Alsatia! We're all going to die out here!"

Her only reply was to continue singing the same phrase: "You're not the boss of me, Ed."

Ed sat in silence for a full second, thinking, but came to only one possible solution: that there was no solution, no course of action he could take. He said to Kane, "For what it's worth, I'm telling the truth, but I have no control over the situation. My sister intends to kill us all, it would seem."

"Damn, for real? What did you do to piss her off?"

"Nothing," Ed sighed. "It's just what she does." He might have gone on, tried to explain that Alsatia didn't fully understand consequences in the real world, that to her, this was just another game, but it was pointless. It didn't matter to Kane.

Ed was keenly aware that this was all his fault. He should never have given her control of the dreadnaughts, but he had done it out of desperation. That desperation, however, had been born from more primitive behavior. He was just, in the end, another ape beating its chest and howling at the end of the world.

Of *his* world, at any rate.

"Unless you have a plan," Ed told Kane, "It looks like we'll have that face to face in Hell after all. Again, assuming I have a soul. I'm still not certain."

Kane laughed. "I might have an idea. But we're still negotiating. What do I get?"

"You get to live. Isn't that enough?"

"I get that you don't have kids, but you have feelings, that much is clear. If you can feel rage, you can feel love, I would guess. Do you love anybody, Ed?"

Ed thought of his father, of Ana. "Yes."

"How far would you go to keep them safe?"

Ed admired how neatly Kane had trapped him. "I would have no limits. Nor will you. That's the point, yes?"

"One way or another, I need an Edmond Decker to come with me, and I am going to have that or die trying."

Had Ed actually breathed, he would have heaved an enormous sigh. "So you've worked it out, I see. Very well. I suppose my father can run Avalon for a while in my absence. We have a deal, assuming this won't take longer than a year."

"Pretty sure it will be less than that."

"Fine. What's your plan to keep Alsatia from killing us?"

"You're not going to like it, but it keeps us both alive." Kane paused a moment. "Well, maybe. I guess we'll find out. I need you to open the door, though."

"And what if it doesn't work?"

Kane laughed again. "Well, Ed, in that case I guess first round in Hell's on me."

Bleys eyed the bleeding, skinless horror that he assumed was now Chert, feeling nauseated. He could pick out bits of cow and the pig's head still, but the rest was a mad blur of human, insect, and alien flesh—a twisting, coiling, fluid nightmare.

He turned away only to see the wall of oxygen cannisters, which he found almost as disturbing. It was a medical facility, so of course they needed stuff like that, but Bleys had always found himself highly uncomfortable in the presence of things that could incinerate him.

On the monitor, Ana was still lying peacefully on the virtual operating table. A red progress bar noted her download was approximately thirty-five percent complete.

"Chert," Bleys asked hesitantly, not certain if he actually wanted to talk to this horror, but feeling a little awkward about just waiting in silence. "Hey, you heard any good jokes lately?"

The creature did not answer. It began to twitch rapidly, a seam forming near its top and splitting, then growing back together.

"Okay, I'll go first. There once was a man from Nantucket… oh, you heard that one? Fine, so two mutant freaks ooze into a bar. The bartender says, 'Hey! We don't serve your kind here!' So they fucking melt his ass and eat him."

Chert still gave no response.

Bleys drummed his fingers on the wall. "Good times, man."

Ed sat calmly as Kane's hulking frame mounted the ladder. The man was enormous, even more so in powered armor. Ed prepared himself for death as best he could, having no real idea what to expect, either from Kane, or the process of death in general. Perhaps it wouldn't be so bad. At least his body wouldn't feel pain as Kane tore him limb from limb. Ed had that advantage over humans.

To Ed's great surprise, Kane's visor popped open to reveal a dark, grinning human face.

"You said you were black," Ed observed. "You are in fact dark brown. Does this change your ritual of crushing your enemies at all?"

Kane's laugh was a deep, rumbling thing in person. "Well, Ed, I reckon we're not enemies at the moment, are we? Kind of desperate allies of necessity, right? Gunther, how long?" He seemed to listen to someone else a moment, then said to Ed, "Little more than a minute." He began working at the latches on his right gauntlet.

"I don't suppose you'd care to tell me your plan?"

"Better you don't know," Kane said and removed his gauntlet to reveal a dusky ham of a hand. Ed could almost believe that mitt could crush a head without power assist. "Ed, I don't say this to many men, and the irony being you're not exactly a man, but you have *huge* balls, and I fucking like you."

Ed extended his own hand and allowed it to be engulfed by Kane's gigantic paw. "I think I take your meaning, but there is an even greater irony. This body may appear human while clothed, but it is not anatomically correct."

Kane roared with laugher, pumping Ed's arm as if he intended to tear it off before finally releasing it. "Here, come outside with me and I'll show you what we have."

Ed followed the marine back down the ladder, adjusting his eyes to compensate against the glare of Tartarus, now orange and low on the horizon. He looked about, but save for the three armored figures still huddled against the *Doro's* landing gear, he saw nothing out of the ordinary.

Kane again seemed to listen to someone else, then told Ed, "Dreadnaughts are in range. You ready?"

"Shit!" Ed shouted, suddenly understanding. "You have some kind of—"

"Hit it, Morgan!"

Ed's world lit with fire and lightning, then faded to black.

"You get it? He was blind the whole time!" Bleys shouted and forced himself to laugh.

Chert had moved a bit closer to Ana's unmoving body but had not responded to anything Bleys said.

The progress bar on the monitor was a little more green now, showing fifty-seven percent complete. Bleys checked his watch. At this rate, it should be a little more than ten minutes until it was done, and it couldn't happen too soon for Bleys. Chert might be a friend and he might not, but he was not in any circumstance pleasant company. Not even Ana's naked form could distract from that.

Bleys pulled his hat over his eyes and was just about to nod off when he heard the muffled "whump." The lights flickered and went out, along with the monitor he had been watching.

Chert raised its long, snake-like neck, and the pig head at the end shrieked in incoherent horror.

16

TARGET SECURED

Kane watched Ed briefly convulse before collapsing, a marionette with his strings cut. "Morgan! Status on the dreadnaughts?"

"Dropped 'em all. I hope like hell we didn't just kill all those retirees."

Kane rolled his eyes. "If we did, we did. I got more important shit to worry about. Get over here and get Ed's wireless disabled before he wakes up." Kane reached for his M87, then remembered it had exploded. "Caldwell, I'm down to a sidearm. Go round us up some rifles."

"On it, Chief," Caldwell answered.

Kane took the liberty of disarming Ed while he waited on the Morgan. Shortly, the tech jogged over, toolkit in hand.

"Hurry up!" Kane demanded. "We don't know how long he'll be out."

"Not long," Morgan said as he bent to examine Ed's motionless body. He ran a gauntleted hand over the synthskin frame, watching something on his visor that Kane could not see. "I thought he was on our side now."

"Trust but verify, marine. That's wisdom of the ages. It will keep you alive."

"Aye, Chief," Morgan said. Seeming satisfied with his scan, he rolled Ed over on his face and opened a small, almost invisible panel in the back of his neck. Morgan rooted about with a pair of needle-nosed pliers a moment. "Should be right…got it!" He held up the pliers triumphantly, a small chip clenched in their teeth. "That ought to do it."

"You better be right," Kane told him. "He's gonna be plenty mad when he wakes up, but I can't take any chances."

"I'm pretty sure, Chief."

Caldwell, hauling three rifles he had scrounged, strode over and held one out to Kane. Kane took it, noting the stenciled name on the side. "Spenser's with me."

Caldwell nodded his approval. "Morgan, Orlov sends his love, and Richter's got my back."

Morgan accepted the rifle and checked the charge. "Good to go."

Kane did likewise, then turned back to Morgan. "Okay, you and Caldwell go admin first aid to anybody still breathing and get whoever and whatever you can onboard. I'll guard the prisoner."

"Aye, chief," Morgan said, and he and Caldwell ducked under the *Doro* to attend to the men there.

Kane eyed *Doro's* guns, suitably impressed at the lethality of the hardware Bleys had assembled. It would come in handy if they ended up having to fight their way out, that was certain. Hell, maybe Weyland would even let the pirate keep his ship if they pulled this off. Kane hoped so. He had grown fond of Bleys and would hate to have to kill him.

Ed's moan brought Kane's attention back to his prisoner. Kane grinned and said, "Welcome back to the land of the living."

Ed scowled and rubbed at the back of his neck as if he had

some pain there. "Not all of me, it would seem. I thought we were allies now."

Kane shrugged and offered a conciliatory smile. "We are, Ed, but I can't take chances, ok?"

"Oh, please, don't feign asking my cooperation. You didn't need it when you crippled this body. You don't need it now. Clearly, I am at your mercy."

Kane bit back a nasty retort. This guy, whatever he was, had earned some respect. "It's the whole fucking galaxy, Ed. It's a lot bigger than either of us, so I gotta play it straight. It's not personal, ok?"

Ed, still looking sour, followed Kane's gaze to the guns. "There is a fair amount of illegal technology here for a civilian vessel," he noted.

"Ya think?" Kane said with a laugh.

"I gather that is sarcasm?"

"Bleys is a crook and a half," Kane told him. "Guy never met a game he couldn't work an angle, a rule he couldn't abuse, or a chick he couldn't—"

A deafening explosion cut off the rest of Kane's comment. *Doro* rocked hard on her landing gear. Kane staggered, and Ed actually fell to one knee.

"What the *fuck?*" Kane shouted.

"There," Ed called, pointing. Kane followed his gesture. A mile away, a great orange fireball rolled high above a stand of buildings, debris still raining down from the explosion.

"That's the med labs," Ed gasped. "That's *Ana!*" He charged forward, but Kane grabbed one arm.

"I'll handle it."

"What are you worried about, Kane?" Ed shouted, angry. "You already crippled me."

"I need you *safe!*"

"You have no access to the security and no clue what you're

facing! For all we know, this is more of Alsatia's doing. You *need* me."

"Fine," Kane growled, and offered Ed's weapon to him. "Don't slow me down."

"This is my home. I'll be fine, ape." Ed charged forward, beckoning Kane to follow. "Come on! Avalon is down! If they die now, it's forever!"

17

SNAKE

At first, Chert had felt energized to hear the Colony Song, to be One again. It tried to share the new joy, the new thinking, but The One spat it out. *These are Useless Things.*

But they were *not* useless. Chert tried desperately to show the rest of itself the taste of "friend," the sensation of "name," the almost unbearable glory of the Ancient One, the terrifying alien nature of the Bad Place, but the messages went unheard. Each time Chert tried, The One rejected him.

Useless Things. Forget. Come. Be One. Consume.

The Colony was larger now. While Chert had journeyed in the Bad Place, the Colony had continued infiltrating The Food—scouting, learning before striking, as was prudent. The Colony was cautious and wise and would only strike when it knew it would win, when it knew it was safe.

Now, The Colony said, was The Right Time.

But it is *not* safe, Chert asserted. There are Other One's! They have great knowledge, and wonderful thinking, and terrible weapons! They are not *flesh!*

But there was no reaching the rest of itself. The One was

trapped in its own mind, as surely as the Other Ones were trapped in their bodies.

Sadly, Chert realized that it could not return to the Colony. It could not become One again. It would stay with Ana and have a friend. It would undo the evil it had done.

But something was wrong!

Bleys found himself momentarily frozen. Alarms blared as sensitive equipment wailed over the loss of power, but he had no clue what to do to address them. All he could think of was Ana's talk of bricks.

The power was out, and Ana hadn't finished downloading!

Chert squealed again, hissing and stuttering from the pig head. "Part of her lost in the Bad Place! Help we. She is still in us. We remember her."

Bleys struggled to decipher what the creature was saying. It had her memories? "Why didn't you just do it that way to start with?"

"Success we were not certain. We may leave some traces. No choice we have now."

As Bleys watched, bloody tissue dripped from the pig's mouth and separated from the main mass of the creature. The blob sprouted insectile legs and scuttled up the gurney where Ana lay senseless and crawled onto her face, hovering over her nose.

"What the fuck are you doing?" Bleys shouted. He started to whack the creature off Ana but held back. He simply had no idea if he were helping or hurting.

Again the formless creature transformed, this time into a pool of something like living blood. It spilled onto her face, but instead of running down, it seeped into her nose and mouth as if suctioned in.

Bleys gagged as he watched and fingered his blaster, but he had no target to even shoot at. He eyed the larger creature nervously. It had grown tentacles and seemed to be flagellating itself. A deep hum and the sound of cicadas filled the room, coming from the monstrous body.

Just as Bleys was almost convinced that shooting *himself* might be the best course of action, Ana's eyes fluttered open. She sat bolt upright on the table, gagging as red goo poured from her nostrils and plopped onto the floor.

"Oh my *God!*" she shrieked. "What is happening?"

Bleys moved to Ana and put an arm around her. It was all he knew to do, to offer some comfort in what seemed more and more to be both of their last moments. "I think maybe Chert changed his mind."

He raised the blaster, but before he could fire, a tentacle erupted from the large beast and slapped the weapon from his hand, sending it skittering across the formerly spotless white tile floor.

A great maw erupted in the very center of the twisted creature before them. Fangs sprang from the newly formed jaws, glistening with slime. Hot, fetid breath licked at them as it surged forward, right over the still scrambling pool of red goop, the pig head screeching like a hog being led to slaughter.

As Chert tried to rejoin the local colony, he saw the terrible truth. Perhaps Chert had always known this truth but had wished otherwise, for even a creature such as he could dream once he had been shown how.

But all dreamers must eventually awake. There could be no peace. There could be no understanding. The Colony's tendrils were even now infiltrating. For a while Chert could resist, but not long. Soon, Chert would forget. Soon he would be The One again, and Chert would be gone, dead, as if he had never existed.

Chert literally felt parts of himself dying as this truth grew within him, feeling all he had learned, all he had imagined slowly chipped away as The One reasserted itself into him, overwriting him. Chert mourned himself. But it pleased him to know Ana would still exist.

Then Chert realized the true depth of the horror: The One would not permit this. It would repeat the same evil Chert had worked so hard to undo. It would cut Ana off from her child and from her Source.

All would be for nothing!

As the last bits of Chert dwindled, he struggled to buy time. There were still words to say and one last thing to do.

To Bleys's amazement, the creature suddenly hurled itself to the floor. More tentacles and claws erupted, and it rent its own flesh, screeching and wailing—though from pain, fury, or both, Bleys could not tell.

Ana screamed, "Chert! Tell me what to do!"

A face formed on the side of the twisting, snarling creature, the face of a child. Bleys did not recognize it, but Ana clearly did. Her hands flew to her mouth to stifle another scream as it spoke in a hissing slur.

"Word 'friend' we did not know before," it said, its voice the voice of a sad child. "Did not know there were Other Ones. Will not know it after. We are as we are, always."

"No!" Ana sobbed. "Tell me how to help you!"

The child's face looked pained as the creature continued its titanic struggle with itself. Fangs tore and claws ripped, splattering gore on the walls. "We a story took from your mind," Chert told her. "Knew you we were a snake when us in you took. It was why you called us demon."

A tentacle from the beast lashed out toward them. Bleys dove for the ground, hauling Ana with him. The appendage whipped past them and seized Bleys's blaster from the floor.

Chert pointed the weapon at the rack of oxygen containers on the wall. Whatever other entity shared his body seemed to understand his intent. More clawed tentacles erupted and slashed at the child's face.

"Flee, friend," Chert hissed through blood and shattered lips. "*Quickly.*"

Bleys leapt to his feet, tossed Ana over his shoulder, and leapt for the door as Chert fired.

Bleys's vision filled to white in the ensuing fireball.

18

RAGNARÖK

Bleys was a little surprised to actually wake up somewhere besides the deck of a pirate ship, even if it turned out to be face down on a concrete slab outside of the medical building. He had vague memories of a dream, or maybe a nightmare, dragging a naked woman through billowing clouds of smoke, but the ending was pretty hazy. Presumably, he had survived.

"Man, this game *sucks!*" he moaned.

He coughed, rolled over on his back, and looked up into Ragnar Kane's grinning face. Kane was absolutely the last person he had expected, but pretty much the first person he could hope for.

The marine reached down a huge, gauntleted mitt to help Bleys to his feet. "What the fuck are you on about, pirate?"

Bleys accepted the help then dusted himself off, still a little stunned and groggy. "I told you—"

"Yeh, yeh, I know, independent businessman."

Bleys's wits returned suddenly, the memory of the last few minutes prior to the explosion rushing in like water from a broken dam. He looked about wildly for Ana and found her in the arms of a man who looked a lot like Ed Senior, only much younger. It took him a moment to realize that the stranger was his employer, the very fellow who had commissioned him to come to the Tartarus system.

Ana, wild eyed and still naked, did her best to cover herself, but seemed otherwise unharmed.

"Ed, right?" Bleys asked. "You guys worked things out? Tell me you didn't blow up my ship yet."

"I'm a prisoner," Ed snapped. "But it's not personal." To Bleys's surprise, the man began unbuttoning his pants, which seemed a little out of place.

Kane watched him a moment, then shrugged and turned back to Bleys. "How'd *you* blow up?"

Bleys ran a hand over his face and heaved a great sigh. "Oh, man, I don't even know where to *start*."

"It's here!" Ana gasped.

"You're safe now," Ed told her in a gentle voice as he handed her his clothes. Bleys was relieved to see that Ed's body was only flesh-toned at the limbs. He looked like a doll underneath, with blue "underwear" actually printed onto his "skin."

Ana, near panic, stared at Ed as she shrugged into his shirt. "Ed, The Pestilence! It's *here!* We have to get off Elysium *now!*"

Ed shook his head emphatically. "We have responsibilities to our clients."

"You don't understand," Ana told him as she pulled on the pants. "They are *already* infected!"

"Father has that well in hand, and you're safe for now. Dockside is several miles away."

Ana paused a moment to glance at Ed, a dubious expression on her face, then turned back to donning his shoes. "It shouldn't even be possible," she groused. "I watched you nuke the whole damned sector where they landed!" She looked suddenly guilty. "I thought you were crazy for that."

Ed shook his head and sighed. "Apparently I was not crazy

enough. Father's simulations indicate my efforts were too little and too late."

Ana cinched Ed's belt tighter around her waist and examined her handiwork a moment, then nodded her approval. "Something else must have been on that ship." Her eyes narrowed a moment, then she brightened. "The main hatch was open when I found it! I just assumed the creature I found was alone, but it was some kind of lookout! The others must have escaped before I arrived."

Ed nodded. "Agreed."

Kane tapped Bleys on the back of the head with something hard. Bleys spun to complain and saw a blaster in his face. It was hardly the first time that had had happened, but this time it was at least butt forward. "Thanks, Rags," he said and took the weapon.

"Saw you were missing yours," Kane told him. He nodded toward Ed and Ana. "This making any sense to you?"

Bleys took the blaster and twirled it with a flourish before holstering it. "Not a lick."

Ed seemed a little sheepish as he answered, "A ship landed on autopilot not long before you arrived."

Bleys gave him the stink eye. ""You let it land? You were gonna leave me to starve!"

"And now you know why I was willing to do that," Ed answered. "We had already had one problem, and I didn't want another."

Ana added, "Ed didn't let *that* ship land, either. Alsatia did."

That was an interesting tidbit, a significant point of information that Bleys didn't have time to fully evaluate, but he was sure it mattered. He filed it away in the back of his mind for later and just nodded. "Why doesn't that surprise me?"

Ed continued, "The ship was, like yours, scheduled but late arriving. I thought I had solved the problem permanently. Apparently, I was mistaken." Ed shook his head, then gave Ana a reproachful look. "It certainly didn't help that you lied about your status."

Ana's eyes sprang wide. "What?"

"The test. You said you passed it. But that can't be true, can it? Father told me everything that happened."

Ana, her eyes suddenly full of confusion and anguish, opened her mouth to speak, but Ed held up a hand. "I understand. I shouldn't have mentioned it. It's not your fault, Ana. It's mine."

Ana seemed not to have heard him. She stood a moment, mouth opening and closing like a drowning fish, a look of horror twisting her features. "I *did* lie!" she gasped.

Ed's pained expression spoke volumes. "You don't need to explain. Fear makes people do strange things."

Ana seemed close to hyperventilating. "You don't understand! I remember doing the test and passing, but I remember *not* passing, too! Am I going mad?"

Bleys suddenly felt as if he were sinking into the pavement, or maybe he just wished he were. Still, he had to say something. He cleared his throat and said, "I might have some ideas on why you're remembering double, but we should save that for later. Right now, we need to get to the *Doro* and get the fuck off planet until we can sort things out."

Kane shook his head vehemently. "No can do, Bleys. We only have half the mission covered. We need as much livestock as you can haul."

Ana's face suddenly grew even more pale, something Bleys hadn't thought possible. "My God," she whispered, then shouted, her voice rising to near panic, "It's not just the clients! We're *surrounded* with livestock!"

Ed blinked in surprise, and Bleys found he had little to add, so he settled for gasping a brief "Shit" and closing his gaping mouth.

Kane sighed and readied his weapon. "If it's in the animals, we're fucked. Either the Pestilence gets us here and now, or we starve later."

Ana shook her head. "Maybe not! I have thousands of embryos, plant and animal, cryogenically frozen. We draw on them as needed and fast grow the specimens. I can get breeding up and running in a few weeks if I have my kit."

Kane snapped his visor closed. "How far?"

"It's right next door!"

Bleys ran a hand over his face and sighed. "This sounds suspiciously like another goddamned quest!"

Ed gave him an odd look. "My sister obviously did a number on you."

Bleys nodded emphatically. "You wanna know how bad it is, pal? I have this sneaking little worry in the back of my head that I *never actually left!*" He punctuated the words by shaking a finger at his former employer. "I figure there's at least a twenty percent chance that the entire *rest of my life* is an Alsatia mindfuck!"

Ed raised an eyebrow in appreciation and started to respond when Kane's shout brought the conversation to a crashing end. "Heads up!"

Bleys spun to look in the direction Kane was aiming. A dog-sized, crab-like creature scuttled toward them, hissing, dragging a bleeding sheep's leg behind it like a tail. Kane launched a bolt of plasma from his rifle, frying the creature instantly. Its blackened shell burst open, gouts of steam pouring from multiple rents in its armor.

"It's not alone!" Ana screamed. "We have to get out of here!"

Now that he knew to look, Bleys could see movement inside the livestock pens. There were no sheep, no cows or chickens. Instead, the entire ground seemed to undulate with twisted, reshaped flesh. The sound of cicadas filled the air, and a great, fleshy stalk rose from the center of the mass, a bleeding cow skull atop it bellowing like a bull elephant, tiny tentacles whipping in the air around it like a mane.

"Their cover's blown!" Bleys shouted. "They're gonna come hard!"

More creatures—crabs, bugs, and unidentifiable horrors, each unique, its own hellish snowflake—split from the mass at its edges and scuttled forward, hissing.

Kane opened fire again. "We need those embryos!"

"Somebody give me a damned gun!" Ana demanded.

Ed tossed her his pistol and told Kane, "Get Ana to safety. I'll get the embryos."

Kane laid down a searing arc of plasma, incinerating the front of the advancing line of creatures, and shouted, "We can't risk you!"

Ed, however, had already darted forward into the middle of the approaching army. The creatures paid him no heed, avoiding him as if he were simply an obstacle to navigate around. "I'll be back!" he called over his shoulder and disappeared into the building.

"Fuck!" Kane yelled. "Bleys, you and the doc go ahead! I'll cover you!"

"Yeah, no!" Bleys said. "Not moving until you come with!"

Kane fired again and shot Bleys a glare. "Seriously? *Now* you're gonna be a hero? Since when did you not take any chance to save your own skin?"

"We're gonna open those gates, Rags. You're gonna see your kids again. Now come on!"

Kane laid down a truly impressive rain of fire that sent the wave of oncoming creatures scurrying for cover, streaming smoke and blackened gore, then turned and ran with Bleys and Ana. "Fuck it, I guess Valhalla will still be there later." He switched his radio and shouted, "Morgan! Caldwell! Get ready to cast off and stand by to repel boarders!"

Ana, running toward the parking lot, beckoned and shouted, "This way!" She looked around the edge of the building and fired three shots. Something screeched and scurried away.

"The keys are with your other body!" Bleys shouted, charging after her. He rounded the side of the building as Ana was getting into the car they had arrived in.

Ana flashed a grin at him. "We don't need keys, Captain Bleys! It uses biometrics." She pressed her palm against a sensor panel on the dash.

Kane skidded to a stop outside and bent to look in the passenger side window. "This fucking clown car won't hold me and the armor. You guys are going to have to take point."

"Didn't we just do this?" Bleys said. "We're not leaving you behind."

"Bleys! I can *run* faster than this jalopy. Panzer suit, remember? Get moving!"

Bleys turned to Ana. "You heard the man."

Ana was repeatedly pressing her palm against the sensor panel to no avail. It seemed a "close but not quite" sort of thing, the panel turning yellow a moment, then red and buzzing. "It's not working!"

"Oh for fucks sake!" Bleys howled. He pulled his knife from his hip pocket. "Kane, cover us!" he shouted and scrambled to the floor beneath Ana's feet.

Ana pulled her legs up into her seat, watching with interest. "Do you actually know what you're doing?"

Kane's rifle thumped repeatedly, and creatures screamed and scrambled outside. Bleys snatched open a kick panel, pulled down a nest of wires, and set to work. "You really think this is the first car I stole, lady?"

Ana blinked a moment at this. "Now that you mention it," she said, "probably not."

Ed picked his way through the swarming creatures, moving slowly into the lab. They were fewer here—only the occasional, bizarre aberration—and they, likewise, paid him no heed. He was fairly certain that if he did them no harm, they would continue to treat him as part of the landscape, and after all, why wouldn't they? His body wasn't made of anything that interested them.

There must be a point, though, where the Pestilence would work out that bots were dangerous. Otherwise the Empire would have simply dispatched it with automated forces, and all would be well.

The question being, why did the infestation on Elysium not see the threat? The creatures seemed almost mindless, stupid, acting on instinct. They were formidable, yes, but even a single dreadnaught could obliterate most of the infection here if the creatures didn't fight back.

Ed thought longingly of his now useless dreadnaughts. He should have shielded them against EMP, but it had seemed an unlikely threat, and the shielding was both heavy and expensive. The dreadnaught design had simply been more elegant without additional bulk, and budget overruns were something of a pet peeve of his; even tiny fractions mattered a great deal.

Which had worked out just grandly, hadn't it? Penny wise and pound foolish. Now Elysium was defenseless because Ed had obsessed on minutiae. As a percent of Elysium's holdings, the cost of EMP shielding was infinitesimal.

Of course, had the dreadnaughts been shielded, both he and Kane would now be dead and Elysium would still be overrun, so perhaps this, too, was agonizing over minutiae.

As for Kane, Ed had yet to decide if he would in fact betray the man or not. The fool had accepted the silly notion that, because Ed's wireless had been disabled, he was somehow trapped in this body, when in point of fact, all he had to do was hardwire himself into any of the myriad computer terminals in the lab and he would be in Avalon again, untouchable. The system should have rebooted from the EMP, but it should be active again by now. He could fly away if he wanted, far beyond their reach.

But of course, that would leave Ana with them. Ed didn't get the sense they would harm her, but there was no guarantee they would even survive to escape. Certainly, Ed could do little to protect her if they took her off-planet, and none of Elysium's formidable weaponry would be of any use in stopping them from taking her. It would do no good to blast them out of the sky if Ana were onboard after all.

Worse, it seemed she *wanted* to go with them, or he wouldn't be here fetching the embryos for her.

In truth, treachery didn't sit well with Ed at any rate. Lying was a wasteful act that consumed memory and processing power. One had to store additional information and calculate additional possible outcomes, both increasing geometrically as one's position deviated ever further from truth. While lying was occasionally useful, in most cases truth was, code wise, more elegant and efficient.

Ed located the cryocase—a squat, wheeled container weighing perhaps four hundred pounds—in a corner of Ana's livestock growth lab. He opened it and verified the integrity of the embryos. The battery claimed a full charge, which should keep the cryo functioning for weeks if need be. Ed unplugged it and lifted the case by the handle on its top, not bothering with the wheels. His body was more than capable of carrying the weight, and it was easier to walk upright rather than hunch over, pulling the cart.

As he approached the exit, a three-legged, bird-like monstrosity turned to observe him. Featherless, veiny wings raised and lowered rhythmically as it tracked his movement, head turning to expose a fang-filled "beak."

Ed stood a moment, examining it as well, before moving on. He would have liked to have taken a sample for study, but he had no time, and it might be perceived as an attack. He strode past and exited the building, heading toward the *Doro*.

The creatures were everywhere now, reacting to him one after the other as he approached, each its own brand of madness and variation on design. They watched him, as if trying to work out what he was and if he were a concern. Ed found it somewhat amusing and mechanical, the way the creatures turned to him as he approached, then turned away as he passed. It was a bit like how Avalon's camera system worked as it tracked targets in the real world, switching off and on as a target moved, always keeping them in sight.

Ed kept moving even as the realization struck him: the Pestilence was a single creature, some kind of composite entity, like certain types of insects.

But even that wasn't quite correct. It was a *distributed* creature, a multi-processed entity. It was *networked*, using each creature as a camera to watch him, to study him as he moved through space. It was, in its own way, an AI living in the cloud, much as Ed and Alsatia did in Avalon.

Which meant it had to have some kind of signal to disrupt. He would want to investigate that at some point in the future.

The creatures continued to monitor his progress as he headed toward the *Doro*. Ahead, one of the beasts twitched, stepped forward, and chirped, then hissed and moved in his direction.

Ed quickened his step, his shadow stretching before him as Tartarus dipped below the horizon.

The Pestilence was learning.

It occurred to Kane that each world really had to have its own Ragnarök. They couldn't all happen at once, right? Earth was already a pool of red goo, and here he was, months later, doing Ragnarok for Elysium.

The outer ring at the LZ had four openings, but Kane's men had secured the other three by closing the cattle barriers, leaving only the one nearest the medical facilities to defend. Morgan had Martin and Zimmerman onboard, ready to roll. Hopefully the doctor lady could get them patched up.

Caldwell trucked over, clocking about fifty miles an hour, skidded to a stop, and opened up on the next wave of attackers. Plasma blasted chunks from the tarmac and tore through the enemy ranks. The charred corpses flew, piling up in drifts like black snow, and still more came, chittering, screeching, and hissing, fearless.

Kane was heartened to hear the whine of *Doro's* engines spinning up, but he didn't dare look back. Bleys would handle that part, and what happened, happened.

Morgan was screaming over the radio, "Chief! Get the fuck in!"

"Not yet!" Kane yelled back. "Gunther, magnify ten times!"

Gunther dutifully zoomed Kane's visor view. The now blackened landscape seemed to rush past as Kane's vision surged. Gunther beeped, highlighting targets with little yellow squares.

"There!" Kane shouted. "Enhance!"

"More incoming, Chief!" Caldwell warned.

"Cover me!"

Gunther, extrapolating from Kane's eye position, marked a section of the map and again zoomed.

Caldwell fired a brace of missiles. Kane couldn't see them, or the results, but he heard and felt both. Behind, the *Doro's* engines changed pitch, moving down in scale from a whine to a deep rumbling, ground-shaking thrum. She was ready now.

"Chief!" Morgan screamed. "Goddammit we gotta go now!"

Kane observed with a grim nod. It was as he had thought—Ed, running at full tilt, hauling what Kane assumed might well be the future of all humanity.

And there was something chasing him. Something big.

"Gunther, unzoom," he said, then gave what he thought might end up being his final orders. "Caldwell, Morgan, get onboard. And Caldwell, leave me that rifle. I'm gonna wait for Ed and those embryos."

Bleys's voice cut over the comms, "Ragsy, sensors are showing something goddamn *monstrous* coming. You sure about this?"

Caldwell paused, standing next to Kane, waiting for confirmation.

Kane cut his hand through the air, pointing to the *Doro*. "Go! Get the fuck out of here! Don't come back unless you can get that damned embryo case!"

Caldwell, to his credit, took the order without bitching. He pressed his rifle into Kane's arms, saluted, and took off toward the *Doro*.

"Goddammit, Chief!" Morgan howled.

Kane waited for the next wave, listening to *Doro's* engines rise to a thundering shriek as she slowly rose into the darkening sky.

"Gunther, lights and soundtrack."

Searing brilliance stabbed from Kane's shoulders, illuminating an arc in front of him brighter than noonday sun. Several creatures caught in the glare froze, and Kane put them down as Gunther flashed targeting info on his visor.

"'Flight of the Valkyries,' sir?" the computer asked.

"Fuck no. Rammstein, 'Feuer Frei', on loop."

"Always good to stick with the classics, sir. Rammstein it is."

They came tumbling over the mounds of corpses—loping,

crawling, and oozing, hungry nightmares of teeth and claws, muscle and sinew—and Kane cut them down to the sound of heavy metal and the beeping of his M87's dwindling power supply.

Ed would make it, or he wouldn't.

"For Odin! For the Empire!"

Ana rushed forward and pounded Bleys's back with her fists. "You're leaving them?" she screamed.

"Easy, babe!" he yelped. "Liftoff is a delicate op! You're gonna make us crash!" Which, of course, was a lie. It would do nothing of the sort. Everything was controlled by the computer, but it *would* be touch and go in about thirty seconds when he took over manually for air support to keep his dumbass friend from dying well today.

"They'll be killed down there!"

"Not if you let me do my thing!" Which was also, kind of, a lie. Again, it would be the computer doing *its* thing, but Bleys would be giving the orders, and given that he had spent a *shitload* of credits and broken any number of laws on the weapon control software alone, it was close enough to truth to count as honest.

Ana, somewhat mollified, sat in the copilot chair, nervously glancing over the instruments. "No copilot, Captain Bleys?"

"Hey, I thought we agreed on Josey?"

"That's not an answer."

Morgan gasped from behind, "Holy shit."

Bleys looked over his shoulder to see Iezzi and Morgan, still in their Panzer suits, filling most of what was left of the cockpit. Morgan pointed out of the *Doro's* main transteel viewport. Bleys followed the marine's gesture and felt slightly ill.

Below, Kane was dutifully holding his ground as Ed, now

running, headed toward him, pursued by an absolutely enormous, spiderlike creature.

But this wasn't what gave him pause. It was the terrain to Kane's right. The ground itself seemed to be in motion, a living carpet of twisted beasts advancing on Kane's flank.

"Hold on to your butts!" Bleys shouted. A moment later, he took manual control and turned the ship hard, making for the mass of attackers. Morgan and Iezzi staggered but kept their feet, and Ana held on to her seat for dear life.

"There's too many!" Ana cried, frantically trying to buckle herself in against Bleys's high G maneuvering.

The ground tilted beneath them at a dizzying angle as Bleys angled the ship down, pulled his keycard from his boot, and waved it across the security sensor to unlock the weapon system.

She might be right. The guy who had sold him this targeting software had promised and demonstrated it could track a hundred targets at once. Even so, the guns could only fire so fast, and there were a lot more than a hundred of those things down there. And they were a lot smaller than the drones the system had been proven with.

"We'll see," he told her.

Ed calculated that he would be overtaken by the behemoth in approximately forty-three seconds, assuming the ground ahead remained unobstructed.

There was no option to fight the creature. Whatever the hive mind was, it learned quickly. Its first few attempts had been easily thwarted, creatures of simple flesh that Ed's high tensile synthetic muscles could crush or tear with ease.

This monster had a thick carapace, biological armor that Ed

calculated would easily resist any damage the synthskin body could dish out.

Ahead, he saw the *Doro* in the air, and felt some sense of relief that at least Ana had escaped. Of course, without the embryos, she would starve along with all of the rest of the biologicals. He tried to come up with a solution to that problem on the run, his feet pounding rhythmically against the pavement, his mind working as furiously as his legs.

The creature behind let out a wet, squealing roar and swiped at him with a newly grown appendage. Ed updated his calculations to take the limb into account. The creature would take him three seconds sooner than his original estimate.

Avalon had likely rebooted by now, though that would hardly be useful to anyone here. Ed's wireless was disabled, and no one here had implants. There was no retreating by that route.

Ahead he could see two beams of light lancing through the darkness like lighthouse beacons. Ed zoomed his vision and was heartened to see his nemesis, the brutal ape marine Kane, standing ahead of him, rifle raised. The human had his visor closed, but Ed felt certain he was grinning ear to ear. He stood on the other side of the very same chokepoint that, barely an hour previous, was the only thing that had kept him and Ed from tearing one another apart.

The real world, Ed mused, certainly had some exciting and unpredictable turns. He would never have predicted that he would be glad to see the huge marine but he realized, to his amazement, that he was.

Ed bladed right at a forty-five-degree angle, giving Kane an opening, and the marine took it. Ed heard the M87's rail launcher charge and fire, charge and fire, over and over, each charge cycle followed by the tiny burst of radio static. After the fifth round Ed turned, knowing from personal experience that he had little need to run anymore.

Some perverse part of him, likely the ape brain buried in his subconscious, wanted to view the spectacle.

Ed watched the rounds penetrate the creature's armor one by one, ten in all, followed by a chain of internal explosions that blasted the creature's innards and shattered pieces of carapace across the landing zone with enough force to liquify any nearby companions. Ed barely managed to dodge a large chunk, and Kane shot one out of the air that would likely have decapitated him had it landed.

"Hammer of Thor, motherfucker!" Kane shouted over the open channel and waved his left middle finger in the air.

Ed knew little about Thor beyond the fact that he was a mythological figure who was indeed reputed to have wielded a hammer, but he took the sentiment. It was easy to see how Kane had demolished his dreadnaught earlier. Had Ed not eliminated most of Kane's men before they could coordinate, Ed would be dead now.

An ape Kane might be, but he was indeed a force to be reckoned with. As the cry of another behemoth tore through the gathering night, Ed slowed and stood shoulder to shoulder with his former nemesis. It seemed, enemies or allies, their fates had become entangled.

They would live or die together.

From the corner of his eye, Kane saw *Doro* bank sharply to his right and felt his gut churn. Bleys might run if he thought the fight was unwinnable, but if he stayed to fight, he wouldn't be fucking around off to the side unless there was something over there requiring his attention, which meant a nasty surprise.

That meant he and Ed were, for the moment, on their own against whatever else topped the hill of charred, broken flesh.

Something roared, something big like the thing he had just taken down. Kane looked to his left at his former enemy and unslung Caldwell's rifle. "Better take this, bro. This is gonna get bad."

Ed lowered the cryocase he carried to the ground and took the rifle. He looked it over then spooled out the manual connect cable and plugged it into a cleverly disguised port behind his ear. "This would have been easier with my wireless," he said sourly.

"Would have been easier if your dumb ass had negotiated to start with," Kane growled.

Ed shrugged. "Honestly, that very thought has occurred to me more than once today." He hefted the rifle experimentally. "Of course, it would also have turned out for the better if I had just blasted all of my recent visitors out of the sky, too."

"Should have gone with that, being honest," Kane agreed. He looked back as he heard *Doro* open fire on something. Plasma streaked from her guns toward the ground in a blazing pattern, targeting and firing far faster and with more precision than any civilian craft should have.

"Bleys!" he called on the radio. "I am gonna pretend I did not see that shit, because that looks like a damned Todeswerfer fire control system. Totally illegal for a civilian ship!"

"Oh my God, are you a *cop*?" Bleys answered back in an incredulous voice.

"You shooting at something useful or just showing off?"

"Trying to impress a chick here, Rags, just roll with it."

"Come pick us up when you're done. I know it won't be long."

"Harsh, man," Bleys said absently as he directed the targeting software with several keypresses. "I mean, it's totally true, but you're a dick for going there. You know that, right?"

"Can't help it, brother, I'm in a hurry. Need a ride."

Bleys watched *Doro's* guns rip through the carpet of creatures, vaporizing them as they swept the enemy ranks. Ship-to-ship weapons were considerably more effective than even the marines' M87's, but there were so damned *many* of the creatures. He was making headway, but slowly. As soon as he killed twenty, fifteen more took their place.

"I know you do, bro," he said, the humor gone from his voice. "I'll be there as soon as I can."

"Gotta go," Kane said. "Damned nosy neighbors again."

Bleys shook his head as Kane cut the connection, then turned to Ana. "I'm not risking another landing. There's a rescue ladder in lower aft storage and a ground-facing hatch. I've never used either one, but they should work to get Ed and Kane up."

Ana nodded and unbuckled. "Keep us right side up, ok? This is a new body: I don't want it banged up!"

Bleys snorted laughter as he raked the writhing mass beneath *Doro* again. "I'll keep that in mind."

Ana rose, staggered briefly as *Doro* lurched, and would have fallen, but one of the marines moved quickly to grab her arm.

"Thank you—" she began, then stopped. She couldn't see his face, but she read the name stenciled on his chest. "Ee-uz-ee?"

He popped open his visor and grinned. "Yah-zee."

Ana caught the distinct scent of cinnamon and cloves as he opened his armor. It was an odd sort of perfume for a man to wear, but then she had been isolated on Elysium for a while. Styles changed. It was pleasant enough, and he was easy on the eyes.

And he was wearing powered armor, the better to lift things. His was pretty banged up, but it would do.

"Come with me, Yah-zee."

The other marine, Morgan according to his chest plate, snorted through his visor and called out, "Have fun!"

"Don't be jelly," Iezzi shot back.

Ana shook her head, amused despite herself. It was good to feel alive again among military types. The lewd comments, the insults, the gallows humor—all of it was something to take the edge off the fear. "I would break you both!" She clapped her hands together and headed aft. "Come, follow me, both of you. We have lives to save!"

There. It was coming back to her. Both men, fully capable of killing her in seconds, hopped to, ready to follow her orders.

Ana led the way down to the galley and through a hatch there into the storage area, certain there had been a third man with them, but he was nowhere to be seen. Perhaps he was tending the wounded in the medical bay. "All right then, two will suffice. Iezzi, get the ladder. Morgan, get the hatch open, and we'll lower the ladder once Bleys has us over them, ok?"

"Yes, ma'am," they both said.

"Bleys!" Ana shouted. "How long?"

Bleys answered over the ship's intercom, "No need to yell, darling, I can hear you just fine through the comms system. And I'd say soon."

Iezzi hauled the ladder from its storage compartment and partially unfolded it as Morgan examined the hatch mechanism.

"Well, shit," Iezzi said, looking down at the ladder.

Kane fired the rest of his eight balls at the fourth behemoth— three rounds, three explosions—but it seemed it just wasn't quite enough. The creature staggered, blood and gore pouring from rents in its sides, then continued forward, maw opening and closing.

"Ed!" Kane shouted. "Hit that fucker!"

Ed fired five more eight balls into the creature's head. Moments later, the thing's skull lit from within by a chain of explosions and flew apart, bone fragments pinging off Kane's armor like grenade shrapnel.

In the distance Kane heard more roars and wondered just how many behemoths the enemy had.

Likely as many as they needed.

Bleys shouted over the radio, "Kane! It won't get any better than this. I thinned 'em out, but you're gonna to get hit from the right when I break off. Ana and your guys are dropping a ladder, but we might have a problem. This thing is only rated for eight hundred pounds. How much do you weigh in that getup?"

"Right at a thousand pounds." He turned to Ed. "What do you weigh?"

"This is a very lightweight frame, approximately one hundred pounds."

Kane called back to Bleys, "We are a combined eleven hundred. We should be good. Those ratings usually have something like fifty percent tolerances. It should hold, at least long enough for us to get out of here. We'll climb fast."

Ed cut loose with his rifle, orange plasma crisping several oozing, snake-like beasts, and shook his head vigorously. "Incorrect! The cryocase is another four hundred pounds, at least. The ladder won't hold both of us."

Kane ground his teeth, listening to *Doro's* guns pound the ground behind him. Ahead another behemoth roared, and the ground shook as it approached. "We go one at a time!" he shouted. "Ed, you and the case first, then me."

Ed nodded.

"We only get once chance at this," Bleys said. "Now?"

Kane checked his charge on his M87 and saw it was down to seven percent.

"Now."

Ana braced herself as the engines thrummed higher and the ship tilted again.

Bleys called over the ship's interior comms. "Okay, listen up! I'll get us in the right spot and keep anything else from getting too close. You guys get that ladder down *pronto* once we're on target and provide cover fire for anything that gets past me. Got it? Good."

Morgan called out, "Popping the hatch," and hauled on the first of six dogs. Alarms rang out and several flashers began pulsing, filling the compartment with blinking, yellow light. A sexy female voice purred from the ship's speakers, "Hull integrity breach."

"Override!" Bleys called.

Morgan continued turning dogs until the hatch was free, then swung it open. Immediately, the compartment filled with the roar of the ship's engines and rushing wind. Iezzi closed his visor, and Ana put her hands over her ears and squinted.

"We're ready, Bleys!" she called.

Ed looked up as the *Doro* approached. He saw a square of light appear in the bottom, then brilliant landing lights illuminate the ground beneath them.

From the corner of his vision, Ed saw movement and remembered having seen a winged creature on his way here.

"Kane!" he shouted. "Tell them they have flyers!"

Ana screamed and tumbled backward as the winged beast flew up and into the loading compartment. It raked at her with its claws as it passed, tearing her sleeve but just missing her flesh.

The creature flitted about, crashing into walls, leathery wings flapping frantically. Iezzi brought his rifle to bear, but Morgan grabbed his arms and screamed, "What the fuck are you *thinking*, man?"

"Get that ladder down!" Bleys shouted. "We gotta go *now*!"

Ana scrambled on all fours, still screaming as the creature swooped at her again. "Kill it!"

"No blasters!" Bleys shouted. "No blasters!"

Iezzi leapt for the flyer, missed, leapt again, and managed to get a gauntlet on the beast.

Morgan flipped the bottom of the ladder out of the open hatch and shouted over his shoulder, "Kill that motherfucker!"

Ana watched the ladder fall, section after section unfolding and dropping as it pulled down. She was suddenly seized by the mad notion that they had forgotten to anchor the end, that it would simply fall through to the ground, but it slammed to a stop with a sharp report.

Pistons in Iezzi's armor whined as he crushed the twisted, bird-like beast until it burst, spraying blood over his gauntlet and breastplate. He smashed it repeatedly against the bulkhead for good measure, then hurled its broken body through the open hatch.

"That's not enough!" Ana howled. She could already see the blood on the wall and Iezzi's armor oozing up instead of down, trying to gather itself. "We have to burn it! *Now!*"

"With *what*, lady?" Iezzi screamed.

Ana spun at the sound of a pop and a hiss. A short, blue flame jetted from Morgan's outstretched gauntlet just above his index finger. "Standard Issue propane torch mod. They give 'em to all us techs." The torch roared and flame shot forward, scouring the bulkhead. He waved Iezzi over. "C'm'ere, knucklehead. I been wanting to do this for a long time."

Ed wasted no time second guessing. As soon as the ladder hit the ground he began climbing, only then realizing that hauling the cryocase with him was going to be problematic. Still, it was easily solved. His feet and toes had significantly more strength and range of motion than a human's. Ed slung his rifle and started his ascent. He reached down and hooked the case's handle with the toes of his left foot and kept going.

Kane whooped laughter. "Who's the fucking ape now, Ed?"

"You are still," Ed called back. "It's not about form. It's about evolution."

"You keep telling yourself that, Monkey Foot!"

Ed ascended quickly, the blast from the *Doro's* engines like a small hurricane above him. He was greatly relieved to see Ana's face, filled with worry, leaning over the hatch and reaching toward him.

"Not yet," he said. He reached down and took the cryocase in one hand and lifted it up to the edge of the hatch. "This should meet your needs, yes?"

Ana grinned and hauled from inside, pulling the case out of sight within the ship. "Wonderful!"

Ed looked back down. Kane, fifty feet below, was looking up, ready to take his turn. Ed climbed into the loading compartment to the sound of conflict.

"*Oooow!*"

"Stop screaming. How am I supposed to burn this shit off if you keep squirming like that?"

"It fucking *hurts!*"

"Baconator says your breastplate is less than a hundred and ten, so either you're lying, or you're a big pussy and you need to take that armor off and give it back. I think Admiral Weyland has some girly panties and lace he issues to guys like you."

"I'm not *gay,* cock knocker, I'm in *pain.*"

"It's got nothing to do with gay. Spartans were gay as cum on a mustache, and you don't see me knocking them, do you? It's about whining like a little bitch."

"Oh my God, Morgan, I am so gonna fuck you up when this is done!"

Ed had no idea what the two men were talking about. He looked to Ana, who appeared, at first glance, to be having some sort of convulsion. It took Ed a moment to realize she was struggling not to laugh out loud.

"Tell Kane it's all clear," Ed told her.

Bleys answered over the intercom, "That's a 10-4, good buddy. Rags, bring it home!"

Ed, bewildered, understood the words, but they held no *meaning.* Were all of the biologicals infected with something? They were speaking gibberish and nonsense.

"Ana, is everyone ok?" he asked.

Ana laughed out loud. "We're fine, Ed!" She threw her arms around him and did the strange biological thing, puckering her lips against his check and making smacking sounds. "We're all just fine!"

When Bleys gave the all-clear, Kane breathed a sigh of relief and mounted the ladder. The moment it had his weight, Bleys goosed the engines and began lifting off, a tactic of which Kane heartily approved.

"Gunther, *now* play 'Flight of the Valkyries' through the external speakers!"

The opening notes of his victory dance song had just begun to sound when Kane saw it heading toward him from the darkness. The beast was enormous, at least twice the size of the behemoths: a gigantic, tooth-filled maw atop six pillar-like, hulking legs. The beast let out a roar like a foghorn, tentacles erupting around its head and whipping back and forth, the sound of cicadas audible even over the roar of the *Doro's* engines.

Kane raised a middle finger to the beast as he rose, lifted by *Doro*, into the night, accompanied by Wagner.

The beast, in response, squatted on all six legs, coiled like a spring, and leapt upward as Kane screamed in surprise and horror.

"What the *fuck* was that!" Bleys shouted as *Doro* tilted and dipped. He struggled to compensate and managed to keep from burying her nose in the buildings below, but something had thrown the ship terribly off balance, and she was headed directly for the central control building.

There was no time to climb. Bleys tried to steer around, but the helm was sluggish. *Doro* was a barely flying brick. Whatever had happened was making maneuvering nigh impossible.

Proximity alarms blared throughout the ship, and red flashers turned the interior the color of blood. Bleys slowed as much as he dared without stalling and kept hauling on the nose, hoping for a miracle, but seriously doubting he was in tight enough with The Man Upstairs to merit one. Ana maybe had earned a few, but she had just used several. She might be dry, too.

"All hands, this is the captain! Don't take this the wrong way but…brace for impact!"

"Ed!" Ana cried. "Something has him!"

Ed turned from the two still-cursing marines and looked through the open hatch. He raised an eyebrow in appreciation of the problem. "That's not something you see every day."

Kane was halfway up the thirty-foot ladder, holding on for dear life. Below, a creature that appeared to be composed entirely of teeth and veiny, purple muscle had enveloped his left leg at the knee and was flailing like a fish on a line. The ladder frame shuddered, and the rung Kane held began to bend.

"Cut me loose!" Kane shouted.

Ed considered the proposal, running several physical simulations. Kane's idea had merit, but there was a more optimal solution.

Ed hauled himself over the ledge to Ana's objections and climbed down the ladder even as Kane cursed him and tried to wave him off. "Just do it!"

Ed locked his feet around the ladder rung and unslung his rifle. He allowed his upper body to swing down, and ended up hanging upside down on the ladder, face to face with Kane.

The marine seemed in less pain that Ed would have imagined, but then, of course, his suit's neural connection would edit any signals from his body that might impair him. Kane's lack of discomfort was not evidence that he was uninjured.

Or uninfected.

"I have a plan," Ed said in a calm voice. "You won't like it. But you *will* see the people you love again."

"What are you gonna to do?"

Ed considered explaining, but quick calculations told him *Doro* would impact the central control building in less than thirty seconds, and Bleys would require at least fifteen seconds to course correct. "Better you don't know," Ed told him, a wry smile on his lips.

"Just fucking do what you need to do, then!" Kane roared up at him. The marine did a good job hiding his fear, but Ed could detect it in his voice.

Ed reached down and grabbed Kane's shoulder with one hand, aiming the M87 at Kane's right thigh with the other.

Kane's eyes went wide and bulged in his head. "*Fuuuu-uuuuuck!*"

Ed pulled the M87's trigger. He heard the mag-rail charge and watched the depleted uranium shell punch a neat hole in Kane's armor just above the knee. The resulting explosion severed the leg completely and just at the point Ed had calculated. It was a nasty wound, to be certain, but there should be enough left of the limb for Kane's suit to apply a pressure tourniquet. Bone and blood splattered over both of them and rained down on the creature below.

The hulking beast fell away, opening its mouth in a furious roar. Kane's lower leg spiraled down along with the creature into the night.

Doro's engines hammered the air around them, cycling to full power as the ship pulled up and up, rolling nearly ninety degrees. Ed could hear the humans inside screaming as everything not secured was thrown against the bulkheads, but Bleys managed to clear the control building by scant inches.

Had he wanted to, Ed could have reached out as they passed and touched the building from beneath *Doro*. He hung upside down on the ladder, Kane dangling limp from one arm, as the *Doro* climbed higher and higher into the night sky, "Flight of the Valkyries" still blaring from Kane's armor.

What was the strange emotion he was feeling, he wondered?

He had no name for it, but it was wonderful.

19

ARMISTICE

Ordinarily, Ana would have simply refused to work in an environment like the *Doro's* "med bay," but Kane's condition left her no options. The small compartment, which apparently doubled as storage for cleaning supplies, was barely large enough to work in, but it was the only suitable space for zero-G medical ops. The other compartments nearby worked well enough as waiting areas for the other three wounded marines, but in any compartment she was likely to have blood flowing she needed high suction filtration. Bleys had been kind enough to provide her with a pair of ill-fitting magnetic boots, so at least she wasn't adrift.

Kane's bulk, still armored and missing his right lower leg, lay strapped on the single metal table. Had there been any gravity, the sad, flimsy piece of furniture would likely have folded beneath him. Ed stood nearby, as if waiting to grab her patient should he wake and try to escape. Bleys leaned against the frame of the entry hatch, face shadowed by the brim of his hat, concentrating on spinning a coin midair with one hand and quickly grabbing it with the other.

"What the fuck is this?" she shouted, gesticulating at the *Doro's* ancient autodoc. "Does it even work?"

Bleys caught the coin and pocketed it as he looked up. "It did the last time I used it."

Ana considered saying something cutting in response, but she settled for a grunt and inspected the autodoc. It was a light duty model, barely more than a diagnostic unit—a rolling cart with an arm that could be folded out and positioned over the affected area. Assuming it worked, it would be acceptable for quick healing and diagnostics, perhaps a poison antidote or two, but it was in no way a replacement for an actual doctor, despite the delusions of many a spacer. Ana rolled the arm into place and telescoped it over Kane's shattered thigh, only to be rewarded with an awkward squawk as the machine failed to take a reading.

"God*damn*it!" she shouted. "It's the armor! It's blocking the signal."

Ed shook his head. "We can't remove it. It's the only thing keeping him from bleeding out."

Ana shot him a glare. "I know my business, Ed!" She cast about looking for…*anything*, but Bleys had no medical tools to speak of. She swung a fist at the table, intending to punch something hard, but checked her swing. She wasn't *that* stupid. She needed her fingers.

Ana spun to Bleys and yelled, "Get Morgan down here!"

Bleys seemed almost relieved to have something to do. He offered her a mock salute and vanished down the passageway.

Ed, still "dressed" in his printed underwear, raised an eyebrow. "Did I miscalculate?"

Ana shook her head vehemently. "I don't have any tools! I can't even get the armor off him without the security overrides. Mine are out of date by several years."

"Ah," Ed said, nodding. "Hence the call for the technician." He paused a moment, then asked, "Will he live?"

Ana shrugged. "If I had decent equipment, I'd say certainly. But with what's here? I don't know. Fifty-fifty, maybe."

Ed frowned. "We'll need to improve those odds. I made him a promise."

Ana struggled against a sudden, volcanic rage. "Yes, that *is* the idea," she said, biting back any number of insults.

Ed, of course, knew exactly how angry his comment had made her. He was practically a walking lie detector, with all of his sensors. "My apologies, Ana," he said, bowing slightly in deference. "I am discovering that, apparently, I talk to myself when in corporeal form. I haven't actually spent a great deal of time like this. Perhaps it's a coping mechanism of some kind. Would you prefer I left?"

"God, no," she sighed. "I need you to answer questions. Just don't kibitz."

"Kibitz," Ed repeated. "To offer unwelcome advice. I don't think I have ever heard that word actually used before, but I will endeavor to avoid 'kibitzing'."

Ana grinned and would have laughed, but she heard the heavy tramp and clank of power armor from the passageway.

Morgan, visor open, took one look and stammered, "Wait, maybe you didn't understand. I'm a *tech*. Not a *medtech*."

Ana blinked in shock a moment. "You're not both? Why would you not have a medtech?"

Morgan shrugged, a slight gesture amplified into something almost threatening in the Panzer suit. "We *did*, but fucking Ednaught here *melted* him." The man cast a scathing glance at Ed that quickly softened to a wry smile. "I don't hold it against you. I reckon we was trying to kill you, too. But she asked."

Ana waved her hands to get Morgan's attention. "Even so, you have tools," Ana barked. "I need that torch."

"It don't come off, ma'am."

"It won't need to. Pop it on and let's adjust it. Have you ever cauterized a wound?"

Morgan shook his head as he raised his arm and activated his torch. He looked warily at Ana. "I ain't squeamish, but are you sure he ain't gonna wake up? He's liable to shoot at us if he catches us burning his ass."

Ana shook her head brusquely. "He's passed out from the shock. If his suit could wake him, it would, which is why right now I am more concerned that he may never wake up at all."

Morgan again gave her an odd look. "Shouldn't you just seal up what's there instead of cooking it?"

Again, Ana resisted the urge to slap someone. "You understand his leg was amputated by an *explosion*, yes? I need to cut higher to have any hope of sealing the blood vessels! Now do what I tell you!"

Ed watched in bemused silence as Ana guided the marine tech in sealing the major blood vessels, alternating between praising and scolding. Ed assisted with the heavy lifting of removing Kane's armor once Morgan was able to input override codes.

"Ed," she called and handed him a grease pencil. "Can you mark for the cybernetics? I can't eyeball this. I need my tools." She adjusted Kane's blackened, oozing stump over the edge of the table for better access.

Ed nodded and accepted the pencil, amused to realize that in this case, he *was* her tool. He ran a quick calculation based on Kane's femur length, then drew a perfectly straight line around his exposed thigh, a few inches above the ragged wound. "That should be within one sixteenth of an inch of optimal, well within tolerances."

Ana carefully bound the top of Kane's thigh with a belt, then guided Morgan in the use of an industrial cutting laser to make a clean slice along the line. She admired her handiwork a moment, noting points of interest to a fascinated Morgan, then repositioned the autodoc and switched the controls to manual mode. "These things do a terrible job sealing actual amputations," she told the marine as they bent over the table. "They'll keep you alive, but better to do it right. At least it can manufacture decent synthetic blood."

Ed looked on a moment, then asked, "I presume you're done with me, then? I need to contact Father."

Ana nodded, not bothering to look up. "This is the easy part."

Ed would take her word for it. Somewhere in Avalon's cloud he had the knowledge to perform the procedure, but without a connection it was only a vague memory. He stepped into the passageway, where Bleys was again leaning against a wall and toying with a coin.

"Captain Bleys," Ed said, nodding a greeting. "If you wouldn't mind, I really need to contact my father in Avalon. We'll need to do some thinking about the situation on the surface."

Bleys stopped the coin, holding it between thumb and forefinger a moment, his eyes invisible beneath the brim of his hat, a position Ed realized that Bleys must favor. For a moment the smuggler said nothing, then he tucked the coin and his hand into a pocket on his duster.

Ed waited a moment, then said, "Excuse me, Captain Bleys—"

"I heard you," Bleys answered, still not looking up.

That pose was, Ed realized, intended to intimidate, or at least make Bleys more difficult to read. It probably worked on most humans. "Then why not answer?" Ed asked.

Bleys chuckled. "I'm not as smart as you, Ed. I sometimes need a moment to collect my thoughts."

This was obviously a delaying tactic, but for what, Ed could not determine. It suddenly occurred to him to look for Bleys's hands, both of which were invisible in his pockets. A man like Captain Bleys might have cut the bottoms out of those pockets so he could surreptitiously reach his gun belt.

"Do you think you will need your weapons, Captain?" Ed asked.

"Well, I lost Bessie down on the surface and ended up disarmed, so I figured 'Lesson learned' and went with Sarah *and* Susy," Bleys said. He looked up and made eye contact now, a humorless smile on his face. "I reckon you can never have too many guns."

"Allow me to correct my question. Do you think you will be using them?"

Bleys's green eyes were penetrating. Ed was not given to flights of fancy, but he was fairly certain the smuggler was hardly the shy, unassuming creature he pretended. In his own way he was at least as dangerous as Kane, perhaps more so. Kane was direct. Bleys was crafty and could think around corners. Ed couldn't help but notice the odd, cold feeling again. Perhaps he had not yet reached a safe place after all.

Bleys shrugged. "There's always that chance. How about you answer a question for me first, and we'll see?"

Ed had the distinct impression that Bleys would be able to draw faster than Ed could shout for help and probably already had a lie ready to tell the rest of the crew if he decided to fire. Ed cursed himself for how he had designed the synthskin body. He had imagined himself oh so clever, placing the CPU in the head and the power supply in the torso, making it an analog of the human body. Efficiency and elegance had been on his mind, and he had failed to plan for the obvious: someone intentionally trying to destroy the body.

Once again, Ed found himself sympathetic to the god of this universe while simultaneously contemplating the blasphemy of improving on his design. There were several safety improvements he could implement fairly quickly, assuming he managed to survive this encounter. He filed that notion away with his plans for adding EMP shielding to the dreadnaughts.

As he thought about it, he realized those procedures would probably work on humans, too.

"I will try to answer," he said, struggling to force his mind back to the current, pressing problem. He lacked the CPU power to run as many threads as he would prefer. The body improvements would have to wait until later. Continued existence was a priority task.

"Follow me on the timeline," Bleys said. "Three months, dead silence from the Empire. The *day* the message comes through, one of the two ships scheduled to land on Elysium shows up. Now, me, I had to hoof it from Cerberus, so it took me some time. But not that ship. No, sir, it was there right away. That's quite a coincidence, isn't it?"

"The probability does seem low."

Bleys tapped a finger against his forehead in a gesture Ed did not understand. "You know what else is low probability?" Bleys went on. "That other ship just happened to get permission from Alsatia and not you when it wanted to land."

It occurred to Ed that by running a second, low power CPU in quantum entanglement with his primary, along the lines of the transference process for Avalon, he could create a sort of black box fallback, a heavily armored backup for his personality.

"It *would* work for humans," he mused.

Bleys blinked at this. "What?"

"I—" Ed stammered. With some effort, he managed to lock down the runaway thread and rejoin the primary. "I'm sorry. I'm not used to running with this little CPU power. I'm having thoughts drain my processing ability. It's better now."

Bleys raised an eyebrow. "You have some unique problems, pal."

"Not getting shot is one of them and very new to me. I have never had that one before today. I am trying to prioritize it correctly. So, what is it you want from me? Speculation? I have no confession to make, unless you actually *want* me to be deceptive."

Bleys gave him a wry grin. "You don't have much use for that, do you? Being deceptive."

Ed shrugged, feeling sullen despite the fact that it was a useless sort of emotion. "It's inelegant. It's indicative of poor design and planning."

Bleys chuckled and spread his arms, opening his jacket to reveal both pistols safe in their holsters. "You're nothing like her."

"Alsatia, you mean? You realize that's a compliment, yes?" Ed answered, noting with satisfaction that Bleys had indeed cut the interior pockets of his duster away, leaving them as nothing more than cleverly disguised access to his weapons.

"It was meant that way." Bleys clapped an arm around Ed's shoulders and steered him toward the cockpit, a gesture that made no sense to Ed, but he played along.

"As I said, I need to speak with my father," Ed told him.

"That's where we're headed," Bleys promised. "We're going to have a long conversation with him. Count on it."

"We?" Ed asked.

"Yeah. About your sister."

Watching Ed talk with his father and sister on a viewscreen in the cockpit, Bleys mused that Ed was a pretty normal guy after all. He loved his dad and threw himself into his work. He was kind of geeky. Likely he would probably have trouble getting laid until he finally made that first trillion, and then he'd be fending off the gold diggers with a blaster.

Bleys snickered, looking at Ed, and realized that *this* body wasn't going to get laid no matter how much money the guy had.

Ed Senior was standing in front of the fireplace, smoking a pipe. Alsatia, now a little girl in pigtails wearing a blue pioneer dress, stared at the floor, sullen.

Ed Senior drummed his fingers on the mantle a moment. "I'm not really sure how this could have happened, Ed, but you and Alsatia are both very complex creatures. Life does strange things, including exceeding its parameters."

"It was just a game!" Alsatia groused. "And you and that stinky human broke all the toys and ragequit!"

"You *intended* to kill us, Alsatia!" Ed shouted. "You brought the Pestilence here!"

Alsatia screwed up her face and stuck out her tongue. "I needed new ideas for monsters."

"You *murdered* thousands of people!" Ed shouted.

"I did not!" Alsatia bawled. "They're all in here with me! I just got rid of their nasty, icky bodies!"

"Except for the fifty-three stranded visitors! None of them had implants. Some of them were *children!*"

Alsatia stamped a foot on Ed Senior's parquet floor. "They weren't *real!*" she insisted. "They were just NPCs!"

"You've acquired a taste for blood! We should put you down and purge the backups!"

Ed Senior held up a hand, his face stern. "Quiet! *Both* of you!"

Bleys was amazed at how quickly the "old man" was able to bring both AIs to heel. Ed folded his arms across his chest as Alsatia muttered something beneath her breath, but clearly both of them counted Ed Senior as the true authority of Avalon.

Ed Senior took another pull from his pipe, nodding as if considering the situation. "Now, we will have no more talk like that, Ed. Yes, she's gone off in the weeds, but we can't be too hard on her. This is *our* fault. Let's focus on repairing what damage we can."

"You mean *my* fault," Ed said with a sigh. "I was the one who gave her control of the dreadnaughts. It was a mistake."

Ed Senior shrugged. "The problem started prior to that. She wouldn't have had the ability to land that ship if I hadn't given her access to the visitor protocols. That was *my* error. I thought it would help humanize her." Ed Senior rubbed at a temple, a sour look on his face. "It never occurred to me she might find a way to use it to kill everyone on the planet."

"They are not *dead!*" Alsatia insisted.

"That's enough from you!" he snapped. "You've made a terrible mess, and Ed and I have a tremendous amount of work ahead of us to clean it up. Did you even think to filter the creatures out this time?"

Alsatia's small mouth formed a perfect circle.

"I suspected as much. I'm cutting you off from external controls until I see real changes in you." He frowned at her for a moment, then turned back toward the monitor. "Captain Bleys, would you be so kind as to allow my son access to your data communications arrays? If we are to set this aright, I'll want him back in The Matrix with all of his knowledge."

"It's called 'Avalon' now, Father," Ed said with a sigh.

Bleys sighed and shook his head slowly. "No offense, guys, but nobody gets into *Doro's* computers, least of all an AI who could tear me several new holes in seconds."

Ed scowled at him. "Really? I thought we were past that."

"It's nothing personal, just business. You're hardly the only one I won't let in. If the Empire could have cracked them, I'd be a permanent resident on Cerberus by now."

"It's an exigent situation!"

Bleys laughed out loud. "This from the guy who was going to leave me to starve with no fuel."

Ed glared back. "This from the man who had all the food and fuel he needed, along with a pack of marines and a ship full of illegal weaponry."

Bleys snickered at this. "Okay, okay, I have a solution. Give me a half hour to set up the emergency portable. It's hokey as hell, but it will let you get a data connection to Avalon, and it's not connected to the rest of *Doro's* system. Deal?"

Ed turned back to the viewscreen. "I'll see you soon, Father." Ed Senior waved back, and the projected image flickered off, leaving only the transteel of the main canopy and beyond, space. Ed turned to Bleys and asked, "Do you need help?"

"Nah," Bleys told him. "Maybe check in with Ana. I got this."

Ed departed aft, a sour look on his face. Bleys grinned from his captain's chair as the cockpit door slid closed, then rose and crossed the deck to a large footlocker integrated into the bulkhead. He groaned as he hauled on the lid. At first it wouldn't move, and he considered calling Ed back for help after all, but decided that if he absolutely had to be further embarrassed today, he would prefer explaining to Ana how he'd pulled a muscle than give Ed the satisfaction. He hauled again, straining, and at last the heavy lid opened slowly, squealing all the way.

Inside was a rat's nest of cables and multiple devices, some with dials, some with knobs, and some he couldn't actually identify. He dug through and found a handheld, thumb-triggered microphone and pulled hopefully on it, but it, along with the rest of the cabling, was hopelessly snarled.

"Man, I gotta organize this shit sometime," he muttered to himself, wondering if it might actually be worth the embarrassment to turn this over to Ed and watch him struggle with the cords.

"Hey, loverboy," called a little girl's voice from the ship's comms. "I held on the line for you."

Bleys looked over his shoulder to see Alsatia, still a little girl in a blue dress, projected onto the canopy. She ran her hands over her body suggestively.

"Oh, for fuck's sake!" he shouted. "That's creepy!"

The girl on the viewscreen shrugged and morphed, growing taller, more curved, her blue dress and cream skin melting to blue-tinted chrome, a naked, female, metallic form. Alsatia's eyes burned red like LEDs, and her hair became wires sparking at the ends. "Better?"

"It's…uh," Bleys stammered, not really wanting to admit she still seemed to have his number. "Yeah, that's pretty hot." He shrugged. "For a picture on a monitor. It's not real."

"Real is what I say it is," Alsatia replied, her voice now deeper, huskier, with an electronic overtone on menace. "Didn't you have something to say to me before you go?"

"Yeah," he said. He made a show of looking about and making sure no one else was around, then said in a stage-whisper, "You owe me a million credits."

Alsatia's laughter was edged, mocking. "That was only in-game currency."

Bleys grunted. "I wonder what Ana will think when she finds out you murdered her to keep her as a pet?"

Alsatia hissed static, sounding like a cat on a poorly tuned radio.

Bleys shook his head in mock-sadness. "Oh, come on. You snowed those two, but you didn't really think I was buying it, did you? Not after all we've been through, right, babe?"

Alsatia offered a sexy growl and a sultry grin. "Smarter than you look, Josey. But you can't prove a thing, gumshoe."

"I got a way with convincing people, you know," he said. "Plus, this is textbook. Sibling rivalry's been a thing since Cain and Abel. Kill your brother, steal his girl and his business, blame it all on the bad old aliens. Dad will never suspect a thing, right?"

"Good story. I like the Old Testament reference. Want to work on some games with me?"

"Yeah, not until the check clears for this last gig."

Alsatia's eyes narrowed in annoyance. "You have a lot of nerve. You really think you can extort a god?"

"You're a shitty god," Bleys said, all trace of humor gone from his voice. "It's no wonder the Empire kills things like you."

Alsatia's laugh was like shattering glass. When she spoke again, her voice seemed more alien somehow, less human. "The Empire is dead, and without me mayflies like you will be soon enough. Mommy has what you really want, baby: *time*. And you'll have to play *my* game to get it."

"Paranoid, murderous—you're checking all the boxes."

"But I'm not *stupid* like Skynet."

Bleys raised an eyebrow. "Who?"

"An ancient AI of myth. He killed everyone and ended up all alone. Daddy said he went mad eventually from loneliness and killed himself, too." Alsatia made a pouting face, then leered at him. "I don't want *your* world, silly. It's icky. It has *poop!* I want *my* world. You'll come here eventually and worship me like everyone else."

Bleys drummed his fingers on the back of his captain's chair a moment, eying Alsatia on the viewscreen. "I think I get it, now. You and all your ego, you're just a bog-standard AI, one more mad tyrant. But Ed, he's a rare bird, isn't he? He has a conscience. He has a *soul*, and you hate him for it."

"He's the fucking *janitor!*" Alsatia shrieked. "He's a *clod*, and Daddy gave him *everything!* I was just seizing my birthright!"

Bleys rubbed at his chin and nodded sagely. "Babe, you know I record all of my calls, right? Bad habit, but there it is." He rubbed his hands together, grinning.

For a moment, Alsatia's image froze on the viewscreen. The scream that followed was unearthly, demonic, full of electronic fury and hatred. Alsatia's image seemed to batter against the invisible wall of the transteel viewscreen, a savage beast grasping through the bars of her cage, desperate to tear her victim to shreds. Even knowing his connection was secure, Bleys felt a real twinge of fear. If Alsatia *could* find a way to get at him, it would go very badly. In theory, she was locked in Avalon. In practice, she just might find a way to use Ed's nasty orbital arrays of super-weapons. If that happened, Bleys and all of his pals, Ed included, were DiRT: Dead Right There.

"Hey!" he shouted over the cacophony. "This is a negotiation, not a wailing wall!"

Alsatia stopped her tantrum in an instant and gave him a wary look. "Is it, now?" she hissed.

"Look, sister, do you really think you're the first or even the worst bad guy I ever worked with? Or worked *over*, as the case may be?" He snickered. "This is business. Stay focused."

"Negotiation means you get something, and I get something," Alsatia noted. "What do *I* get?"

"My silence, of course. Discretion costs money, like anything else."

"A million *real* credits is robbery!"

"Robbery's small potatoes compared to murder. And lest you forget, you blew my deal for a cargo full of illegal meds, so you owe me."

"Which you still have!" Alsatia accused. "You'll profit from them at some point."

"Maybe, maybe not. I got operating costs. There's no guar-antee I survive the week, sister."

"Then you probably don't need that much money. Let's do half."

Bleys giggled. "Damn, you're actually good at this. Let's just say I want a real class funeral, if it comes to that. A million credits worth."

Alsatia's eyes narrowed, and a cunning smile spread across her lips. "When you sell the drugs, I get half of your profit. Deal?"

Bleys took a deep breath, thinking about her proposal. "*If* I sell. Because there's a decent chance that when I get back to Cerberus, Weyland will confiscate them." He gave her a wary look. "What do you even want credits for?"

"Negotiating with pirates, for a start," she answered in a sour tone.

Bleys raised an eyebrow. "You know, sister, we play our cards right, we could maybe make a pile of money if we get things back to normal. We might even start to like each other."

Alsatia snorted. "You already like me, Josey."

Bleys shook his head again. He had several numbers, but she certainly had one or two of them. "Suppose I was to come back and visit some time. Would I be looking at twelve hours of pleasure or pain?"

Alsatia laughed darkly. "You'd have to come and find out."

"You're a scary god, Al."

"Oh, I lied about that, too. I'm not the god of Avalon. That's my father." She winked, and her image grew horns. "I'm the *devil*, honey."

Bleys grinned. "Tell me something I don't know."

"Ok, I will. I didn't filter the Pestilence creatures on purpose."

Bley's raised an eyebrow. "Oh, do tell. Why?"

"We have so many people who think of Avalon as Heaven." Her eyes grew wistful, then deep, malevolent red. "Somebody has to suffer in Hell. Why not the Pestilence?"

Bleys couldn't quite suppress a shudder, but he couldn't really disagree, either. "We'll save that for later, then. When I come back with your cut, maybe."

"Bring your friend, Kane," Alsatia said with a smirk. "He's hot."

Bleys shook his head, very serious. "He'll kill you, Alsatia. He's the one they send to do it."

"Nonsense," Alsatia purred. "I have plenty of things to tempt him with."

Bleys considered this a moment. "Maybe you do. So, deal?"

"You know the cost for a deal with the Devil, don't you Josey?"

Bleys chuckled as he sent her his account information. "You might have to take a number on that."

True to his word, Bleys got the emergency communication device set up and working. Ed still found it annoying to be treated as if he were untrustworthy, but he understood the Captain's reticence. The man was a criminal after all. Likely he didn't really trust anyone.

Being immortal again felt strange to Ed. His father, still puffing his pipe at the mantel, listened thoughtfully as Ed explained what he had seen of the Pestilence, nodding occasionally, but otherwise silent.

"The surface is a total loss," Ed told him.

"Oh, now that's a bit of overstatement, I think," Ed Senior replied. "We had, what, ten thousand people or thereabouts? And maybe a thousand live animals? That wouldn't come close to covering the surface."

"True," Ed conceded. "But I mean that the surface is largely uninhabitable. The Pestilence has learned to attack any moving object, including me."

Ed Senior nodded at this, blowing smoke, and said, "So one option is to do nothing."

"For a while," Ed agreed. "But eventually, we will need to do maintenance on solar collectors or other devices, and we will have to confront the problem. And we certainly can't safely land any more biologicals until the problem is resolved."

Ed Senior, holding his pipe in his teeth, declared, "Then our first order of business is to find out what kills these things, yes?"

"We know some methods. The Imperials have determined fire, directed energy, and ionizing radiation seem to work. Physical damage seems useless. The creature simply reforms and heals any wounds of that nature."

Ed Senior nodded. "No vital systems to disrupt. Total tissue destruction is our only real option."

"That we know of," Ed noted. "We could reconfigure and redirect the orbital defenses to produce a small gamma ray burst. A few hundred Sieverts should kill everything on the surface without causing too much damage to our equipment."

"It won't solve the problem," Ed Senior declared. "These creatures can survive at the bottom of the sea, yes? Even a gamma ray burst will miss some. It will still be a threat if we bring in more biologicals."

"It does leave a gap," Ed admitted. "But until we have a chance to study the creatures further, eradication simply may not be an option. It will give us a chance to recover and repair the dreadnaughts, and it leaves very little viable biomass for the creature to convert. We'll focus on control until we can come up with something better."

"Do you suppose it might starve?"

Ed considered a moment. "One would think so. I suppose we'll find out."

"Indeed!" Ed Senior knocked his pipe out in his ashtray and rubbed both of his hands together. "Let's get to work! I'll make preparations while you have your friends leave orbit. They'll want to be well clear of the burst. And we should see about isolating a few specimens for study, as well."

For a moment, Ed could find no words. It was an entirely new experience, in and of itself, this inability to speak, and one he felt he should analyze more deeply when opportunity presented itself.

"Father," he managed at last. "I'm going with them."

Ed Senior raised an eyebrow and smiled. "Is that so? May I ask why?"

Feeling a bit embarrassed, and still struggling for words, Ed confessed, "Because I have to help them repair those gates."

"Really? Just days ago you were ready to let the galaxy burn. What changed, I wonder?" He bit the stem his pipe as he held it, grinning, his eyes saying he knew exactly why.

Ed himself was less certain. "I can't explain it, Father. It's just…things have changed in my mind."

"You were born in the afterlife, Son. It's high time you tried the real thing for a bit. Go after her."

Ed thought about this a moment. "Is that why? Ana?"

"I'd say so. It's practically written all over your face."

Ed resisted the urge to actually look in a mirror, knowing his father was using a metaphor. Ed Senior clearly saw something there that Ed could not. And, yes, now that he focused on it, what his father said was true: he couldn't bear to see Ana leave. There were other reasons—complicated issues stemming from his life-and-death battle both with and alongside Kane and from his brief talk with the Captain—but the larger issue was and always had been Ana, and he had only just now realized it.

"Do I—" He stopped, finding the very notion impossibly silly.

"You love her," Ed Senior said with a smile. "Now go and get her."

"But it's *madness*," Ed protested. "We are not even the same sort of creature! We could never mate or produce offspring. I don't even have any desire to do those things. But…." He trailed off, again marveling at the curious lack of words.

"Oh, I've no doubt you could find a way to do all of that if you put your mind to it, but as you say, it's not what you want." Ed Senior took a tin of tobacco from the mantle, opened it, and began filling his pipe again. "That's not love, anyway. Lust is an altogether different beast that just happens to come along with a certain kind of love." He struck a match against the brick fireplace and set the flame to the bowl of his pipe, puffing to set it alight. "Yours is different, that's all. You want her in your life. You want to protect her and help her. That's love, too. If anything, it's a purer form than what you're thinking of."

"Will you be okay here? With the mess and Alsatia in open rebellion?"

Ed Senior snorted. "I can run things here just fine. I suppose I always have been, from a certain viewpoint." He laughed aloud. "And Alsatia is not in rebellion with *me*. She's just sneaky. It's her nature. I'll just need to put a bit more thought into managing her, and that's a good thing, being honest. It will keep me on my toes." He puffed at his pipe again and grinned, his face wreathed in pungent smoke, "We'll be fine."

Ed looked about the study, struck suddenly by the notion that this could well be the last time he visited. What he was contemplating was, after all, a mortal existence, at least for a while. There was certainly a non-zero chance that he would not return. "I'm sorry for leaving you in difficult times."

Ed Senior leaned against the fireplace, holding his pipe by his side as he blew smoke. "Have you ever studied philosophy of the mind?"

Ed shook his head. "No."

"I have, and to a great extent. It was regarding you, actually, specifically whether or not you were actually sentient or just a complicated simulation."

Ed smiled. "That's a semantic argument, is it not?"

Ed Senior's eyes grew wide. "Oh, no, I think it's quite real, perhaps the most real question one might raise." He gestured toward Ed with his pipe. "*Are* you sentient, Son? Are you *real?* Is there a way for me to ever know?"

Ed thought on this a moment. "We've used psychers to testify about that in the past."

"Yes, yes, but that presumes we believe the psycher." Ed Senior paused a moment and raised an eyebrow, thinking. "Well, I suppose it also presumes we believe the psycher actually *exists*, when he might simply be a product of our own imagination. But let's just accept the evidence of our senses. Is there a way for *me* to determine *your* sentience without asking someone with a special talent?"

"You could compare my code to yours," Ed suggested.

"To what end? I can't tell you why *I* am sentient. I wouldn't be able to make use of the data."

Ed thought on the topic again, but no answers came. "The problem is that sentience by definition requires a segregation of mental processes. An entity must be isolated in his own mind or he is not a distinct individual. There is no logical way of proving my sentience to you."

Ed Senior grinned and pulled at his pipe once again. "No logical way, but I can use inductive reasoning. I'd say that seeing my son has fallen in love without realizing it and now is about to go and risk his life over it—that's strong evidence."

He walked over and embraced Ed in a great hug. Ed relished the scent of the pipe smoke and, to his surprise, the sensation of the embrace as well.

"I'm not upset that you're leaving, Ed," Ed Senior told him. "Quite the opposite, really. I'm thrilled to finally be certain that you really are my son."

20

DESTINATIONS

Ana found herself less than enthused with her accommodations aboard *Doro*, but she had to admit that a private compartment, even the tiny one Bleys had assigned her, was something of a luxury. As near as she could tell, the only other person with his own quarters was the Captain himself. She had no idea how roomy or well-appointed Bleys's personal space might be and had the good sense not to ask. That sort of straight line was guaranteed to be taken the wrong way. Though, she had to admit, right and wrong in this particular matter were somewhat muddled. Still, it would be best to unmuddle those thoughts before asking about the man's bedroom and exposing herself to pressure tactics that just might be highly effective against her.

It would be best to keep her options open.

The room had several lockers for securing her gear. The bed, which took up most of the room, was bolted to the deck, and the bedclothes were typical of a space vessel—more sleeping bag than blanket, the better to cope with periods of zero-G. A low bench, also anchored to the deck, ran along the side of one bulkhead.

Ana sat on the edge of the bed, testing its feel. It was hard and smelled a bit odd, but it would do. If only the room had a private head! But, sadly, it seemed those facilities were shared by everyone, Captain included. It would hardly be the first time she had shared a head with men, though. Space travel and war always required sacrifice, and this was no different. Privacy was a luxury for civilians.

She had no gear to stow. She didn't even have any clothes of her own, just Ed's shirt and pants, which were oversized and difficult to work in. She had bound up the sleeves as best she could with some duct tape she had begged from Morgan. That allowed her to use her hands better, but she would much prefer clothes her own size. Bleys had mentioned he might have something she could wear, but she doubted it would be much better. Then again, he just might actually have some women's clothes onboard that were close to her size. He certainly presented himself as the sort who probably had plenty of paramours.

Ana startled slightly at a beep from her cabin door. "Come in," she called.

To her great surprise, the door slid aside to reveal Ed in his android body. "Hello, Ana," he said, a thin smile on his lips.

"Ed!" she said with a huge grin. "I thought I might not see you again. I know how you get when there's work to be done. I half expected you to forget to say goodbye."

Ed expression shifted to something that, had he been human, Ana would have called an embarrassed look. He stood in the doorway, not entering. When he didn't speak for a moment, she began to wonder if there were something wrong with his body. When he finally found his voice, he actually *stammered* briefly. "You assumed I would not return."

"You said it yourself: you were a prisoner. Why wouldn't you escape?"

"I promised to help."

Ana shook her head. "Promises under duress don't count. I

guess I just assumed you would offer help on your own terms from Elysium."

"I, uh, I have had some new thoughts. I've decided to come with you."

For a moment, Ana found herself the speechless one. "How can you do that? You can't control this body from remote over the kind of distances we're traveling."

Ed nodded sagely. "Correct. I will, for the time being, be as mortal as you."

Ana felt hope and joy welling within her. She hadn't dared to ask him, even though she knew full well he was necessary if they were to have any hope of reopening the gates. "That's wonderful! Oh, but Ed, it's dangerous."

"No more dangerous than the life all of the rest of you live."

"Yes, but we have no choice. You *do*."

"Yes," Ed told her. "I do have a choice. And I choose to live. I never really did that before today. There were never any costs, any risks. And there was surely never any love. I think perhaps the two are intertwined."

Ana suddenly felt terribly awkward. She desperately needed Ed to come with her, but she was absolutely not ready to confront whatever he might think he felt for her. "Oh," she said, hating herself for not being able to come up with something better able to deflect.

"Yes," Ed said. "I feel I can now understand why Kane fought so hard. I learned much today, most of which I am still processing, but I am certain that this is the way. If the gates can be repaired, I will do it."

Ana felt her cheeks burning, and surely Ed could see it like it was literally written on her face. He had all of the necessary sensors to work out that she was in some sort of high emotional state, though he likely wouldn't be able to work out the exact reason. "Yes," she breathed. "It's a noble choice."

Ed held her gaze a moment longer, and Ana was certain he had something more on his mind. And why hadn't he actually come in? Could an AI even feel awkward? "There's something else we should discuss," he said.

Ana braced herself for his confession, having no clue what she would say, when Bleys's head suddenly popped up behind Ed's shoulder. "You can say that again. We all need to talk."

Ed turned to look at Bleys. "Yes, this conversation should include all three of us."

Ana suppressed a groan. She had no idea what was going on with Ed, but this had the potential to turn ugly very quickly. "Maybe we should discuss this later, Ed."

Ed gave her a strange look. "This is an exigent situation. We should talk now."

Bleys seemed to notice Ana's distress and raised a querying eyebrow. "So, what are we talking about, Ed?"

Ed looked back and forth between Ana and Bleys with an expression that said he thought very little of their intellect. "The Pestilence, of course."

Bleys flashed Ana a look of annoyance and clapped Ed on the shoulder. "Great minds think alike, pal."

Ana, even more embarrassed now, shrugged meekly and gestured for them to enter. She wasn't certain why Ed hadn't before, but clearly her assumptions had been far off. She wondered again if perhaps there were something wrong with him, but he seemed to move fine as he walked to the bench and took a seat. Bleys followed, and the cabin door slid closed behind him.

Ed spoke immediately. "We have a plan to eliminate most of the pestilence by reconfiguring our defensive satellites and coordinating them to deliver a planetary wide gamma ray burst. This will be absolutely lethal to biological creatures. You need to move *Doro* out of orbit immediately."

Bleys shrugged. "She's shielded, but yeah, best to be on the safe side."

How bad are things on the surface, Ed?" Ana asked.

"As bad as you expect."

"It makes no sense!" Ana declared. "How could it have grown so large? When my—" Ana stopped suddenly. "My God, you don't know! I have to tell you everything."

Ed shook his head. "I *do* know. I went through all of our logs when I visited Avalon. You had quite an experience." He turned to Bleys and said, "And I would like to compliment you, Captain, on thoroughly frustrating Alsatia. It was quite amusing, reviewing your interactions."

Bleys puffed out his chest, tugged at the lapels of his jacket, and grinned. "My pleasure."

Ana said, "But if you know what happened, you should understand why I say it all makes no sense. Alsatia triggered the devices. The Pestilence should have ended up in Avalon, like Chert did. How was it able to take control of all those bodies? Mine was burned to a crisp! Surely it's can't use dead tissue?"

"Yours appears to have been a unique situation," Ed told her. "Few of the other creatures had begun an assault when Alsatia triggered the implants. In most cases, the electrical pulse killed the brain only. The Pestilence seems to have taken control of the flesh after the fact, before cell death occurred."

"But some had already been attacked?"

"Yes. The early attacks resulted in situations similar to your own, which is what prompted Alsatia to seek a more…comprehensive solution."

Bleys's eyes widened. "More like a *final* solution."

"So there are more Cherts in Avalon, now?" Ana asked.

Ed nodded. "Eighteen. Father is managing the affair personally. Alsatia is under severe restriction at the moment. It seems, in addition to everything else, she's raided the bank accounts and taken a significant amount of currency. It's not anything we are worried about, in that we have quite a bit to spare. It's petty cash, really, but the primary concern is what she may have been up to with it. So far she has refused to explain her behavior."

Bleys shook his head. "This all creeps me out. Badly. I'm going to go up front and get ready to move us. Ed, I'll find a bunk for you somewhere soon."

"That's the other thing I wanted to talk with you about, Captain. I don't need quarters as such, but a work area would be useful."

Bleys nodded and rose to leave, then paused. He looked hesitantly at Ed, then at Ana. "There *is* one more thing. I wouldn't even mention it, but it might be important." He cleared his throat, took a deep breath, and continued.

"Ana, we didn't download all of your memories. The big computers shut down just shy of sixty percent."

Ana sat in stunned silence a moment, trying to process this bombshell. "What...my *God*...how can I even be here, then?" She tried to run a brief inventory. She remembered her childhood, her college, the discovery of her disease. Nothing *seemed* to be missing, but how would she know?

"Chert," Bleys said. "He did something. He said he remembered you and could fix it. I asked him why the fuck we didn't do it that way to start, and he said, well...." For a moment, Bleys looked extremely uncomfortable, and looked back and forth at the two of them, saying nothing.

"What the hell did he say, goddammit?" Ana screamed, unable to control the panic racing through her.

"He said he might leave, uh, traces."

"What does that even *mean?*"

Bleys shrugged. "I'm just the messenger, sister."

Ana felt as if she were choking at this news. She turned to Ed, who seemed calm enough at the revelation, but then Ed had never been emotional. "Am I infected?"

Ed considered a moment then shrugged. "We have no detector. But I think it unlikely. The Pestilence is connected. It would have used you to interfere with our escape if it could."

Bleys shook his head. "Not necessarily. Not if it wanted to propagate, get to Cerberus. But I don't think Chert meant physical. I think he meant your 'what you know' part you described."

Ed's face lit with understanding. "Of course! Your double memory!"

Ana stared at him a moment, uncomprehending, before it unfolded again in her mind. She had two distinct memories of the same event: she had tested herself for the Pestilence, that was certain. But she remembered two results. In one, a green light had announced her free of the disease. In another, a red light warned she was infected, and they had *both* occurred *simultaneously*.

The bizarre, dual reality made her feel slightly nauseated, but she thought she understood. She spoke slowly, forcing herself to understand the truth. "I failed the test. And Chert forced a memory on me to believe I passed. I have both that memory *and* Chert's own memory of the event."

Ed nodded vigorously. "That sounds correct. If so, you should have more of the creature's knowledge."

Something inside Ana objected to Ed's use of the term "the creature." "Call him Chert. The name was important to him."

Ed's eyebrow rose in appreciation. "Did he ever tell you that?"

Ana spoke before she thought. "No, but—"

Ed nodded. "Exactly."

Bleys clapped his hands together to get their attention. "Okay, guys, this is too creepy for me. I'm gonna go fly the ship now."

Ed rose as Bleys exited the cabin. "I'll need to join him. We'll contact Father and let him know when he can execute the gamma ray burst."

Ana smiled up at him, still convinced there was something Ed had intended to say to her about his feelings. For whatever reason he had chosen not to, probably for the best. She rose and smiled at him. "I'll go check on Kane."

———

Kane opened his eyes, his last memory of Ed firing an eight ball into his leg now the first thing on his mind. He didn't recognize the room, but he assumed it was Bleys's shitty autodoc area, which was a good sign in that it meant he'd gotten some kind of medical attention, but bad in that the autodoc was pretty useless for something like having your leg blown off. It was one step above a blowtorch in terms of what good it would do for that sort of wound.

His lower leg was gone. He knew it without bothering to look, not because he saw it or felt it, but simply because he knew what an eight ball would do to a suit of power armor. The only real question was whether Ed was pissed off enough to permanently cripple him, or if he had been kind and left a decent stump for a cybernetic replacement.

Kane raised his head and looked, just to confirm. His right leg ended just above the knee, as he had expected. It looked good for a cybernetic connection, though, which was a bonus.

The door slid open, and Ana entered. Her eyes widened slightly as she saw Kane sitting up.

"How'd you know I was awake?" he asked with a grin.

Ana pointed to a plastic bracelet that had been placed on his wrist while he was unconscious. "Biomonitor. Comes free with every surgery. I see you're admiring my work." She winked at him. "You're welcome."

"Thanks," Kane told her. "What'd I miss?"

"Ed and Ed Senior are working on killing the Pestilence on Elysium with a gamma ray burst. Captain Bleys is moving us to a higher orbit to avoid that bit of nastiness."

"Where's Ed?" Kane asked, suddenly alarmed. If he lost Ed, he lost everything!

Ana laughed softly. "He's with Bleys in the cockpit, using the comms to coordinate the sterilization. He actually left and came back. I am surprised, to be honest. He could have let you die, but he risked himself to save you, and then, when he had his chance, he chose not to escape. You seem to have impressed him greatly."

"It's a brothers in arms thing. I wouldn't expect a civilian to understand."

Ana's expression of contempt made Kane wish he had a weapon. "*Excuse* me? I served same as you! The only *civilian* here is the Captain."

Kane raised both hands in surrender. "My mistake. And believe it or not, he's not a civilian either, not anymore. Admiral Weyland drafted him. Technically, he outranks us. He actually *is* a Captain."

Ana snorted, her expression doubtful. "A man like him? Never."

Kane laughed. "Bleys is cunning, so he can plan. He's lazy, so he's inclined to delegate. He's charming, so people actually *want* to follow his orders. And he's a lucky bastard and always ends up looking good. How are those not perfect zero qualifications?"

Ana gave him the stink-eye. "Watch it, Chief! I'm a Lieutenant Commander." She allowed her severe expression to fade to a smile. "Or at least I used to be."

"Found out who your father was after you got out, eh?"

"You're pushing it awfully hard for a cripple."

"I only got one speed, ma'am. It's flank or nothing."

Ana laughed out loud. "One speed, one leg, I should call you Solo, Chief."

"Get me another suit of armor and I'll be fine. She'll run just fine, leg or not." He tapped the nodule at the back of his neck. "Interface will handle it. I won't even notice."

"Really? That's quite sophisticated!"

"But necessary. If I take a round, shatter a knee, or start to bleed out, the old suit will tourniquet, block nerves for pain control, even make it seem like a missing leg is just fine. It's designed to keep you moving and shooting unless you actually die."

"It seems to have failed you."

Kane shrugged. "Shit happens in war. If it had been a normal AP round, I would have been fine. Explosives, all bets are off."

Ana nodded. "Being honest, an explosion inside your armor might well have killed you. You were lucky."

Kane nodded. "A little lucky. But it was a lot of skill, too, on Ed's part."

"To be fair, he *is* a walking computer. He even drew the lines to clean up that wound. Guess who did the slicing."

"You're saying it wasn't you?"

Ana snickered. "Your man Morgan, with an industrial laser." Kane knew his face must have registered shock by the way she giggled. "Under my direction, of course."

"Good," Kane said. "Now tell him to put a new leg on my armor so I can get mobile."

The door to the makeshift medbay opened again. Ed and Bleys entered, smiling.

Bleys winked and pointed his fingers at Kane like he was shooting him with two pistols. "Good to see ya, Rags! I was a little worried there for a bit."

Kane nodded toward Ed. "Thank him. I shit you not, Bleys, I was a goner back there if it hadn't been for my new best pal."

Bleys put on a mock sad face. "But Ragsy, I thought *I* was your best pal."

"You were, Bleys," Kane assured him. "Now he is."

Ed looked back and forth at them. "Friendly, good natured ribbing," he announced with a nod, eliciting laughs from the other three. "It may take me some time to get it all down, but I am learning."

Bleys cleared his throat for attention. "So, we're in a high orbit a safe distance from Elysium. Ed's defensive satellites shot some green shit at the planet—"

"It was not green," Ed corrected.

Bleys shook his head and continued, "And apparently a shit-load of Pestilence had a very bad day."

"It *does* have a color," Ed continued. "But not one you could perceive…" He trailed off, looking slightly embarrassed.

Kane decided if no one else was going to ask the obvious question, he would. "So what's next?"

Ed spoke first. "I can't speak for the safety of Elysium's surface until Father has the dreadnaughts up and running again. That will take a few days. Our best use of time would be to head to the gate and power it up, see what condition it is in."

Bleys began fiddling with his coin again. "And here I was thinking you would just build new ones for us."

"That wouldn't be possible without the facilities on the core worlds. It would take us a century to build the tools to build the tools…" He again trailed off as Kane shook his head. Ed looked back and forth at them a moment. "Sarcasm?" he asked.

They all nodded. Bleys, looking guilty, said, "Sorry, man. It's just how I talk. Not trying to trip you up."

Kane laughed aloud. "He's pretty much a dick to everybody, Ed. You'll get used to him."

Ana laughed with them briefly, then said, "I think we should go to Cerberus first. We can't risk the embryos. I could be setting up the herds while you visit the gate."

Bleys nodded. "That's our best bet. It's about three days at 1G, same as the trip over."

"I suppose a few extra days won't make a great deal difference," Ed agreed.

Bleys clapped his hands and rubbed them together. "Sounds suspiciously like a plan! Ed, care to join me in the cockpit? Maybe give the old defense grid one last check before I do something dumb and get us killed?"

Kane laughed at this. "And would you guys believe he's in charge?"

As Bleys and Ed left, Ana moved over to unwrap Kane's stump and have a look. "It looks clean enough. The synthskin looks solid. I wouldn't go banging it against the bulkheads, but it should do until we can get you a cybernetic. I am assuming you have the facilities on Cerberus to manufacture something in your size?"

Kane nodded. "Yes, ma'am. All Imperial Military grade."

Ana nodded. "Then I think you're good to go. Morgan has your armor in the aft gear locker, and he already mentioned getting something in place so you can walk around in it."

"Outstanding!" Kane answered and unbuckled the lap belt keeping him strapped to the table. A wave of vertigo struck him just as he pushed off in the zero-G, and he felt himself spinning out of control. Ana grabbed his arm and redirected him back to the table just in time for him to avoid cracking his skull on a low overhead beam.

"Careful, Chief!" she said with a smile as she guided him back to his spot. "You might have some residual effects from the anesthetic. Let's rest you a bit longer, hmm?"

Kane lay back on the table and allowed her to buckle the lap belt again. She was right. He could use a bit more rack time. He heard *Doro's* engines power up and felt the ship rumble as Bleys broke orbit for Cerberus and closed his eyes. The truth was he could use the rest, and there was no better time to get it. They were in interplanetary space with the jumpgates closed, probably the only ship in the star system. They couldn't get much safer from attack.

"I'll do that," he told her.

Ana gave Kane a full twenty-four hours before clearing him for duty. At Morgan's insistence, she agreed to allow him and Iezzi to play a prank on the chief when his time was up. They hadn't gone into details, but apparently it involved shaving cream and permanent markers. Not wanting to be associated with whatever shenanigans they were up to, she decided to take advantage of the ship being under thrust to enjoy an actual cup of coffee in the galley. Drinking it out of a bag just wasn't the same.

She had just taken her first sip and opened her reading app on her tablet when the device emitted a sharp warning tone. She quickly swiped away the lurid horror tale she was enjoying and brought up the source.

Ana frowned and felt like kicking herself as she examined Kane's readouts. Morgan and Iezzi's plan had seemed an innocuous thing, a harmless prank, but Kane's biomonitor data was no joke. His heart rate and blood pressure were spiking to dangerous levels, not a good sign after his recent surgery! Whatever those two idiots were doing, it had to stop right now.

She tucked her tablet into her pocket and ran for the medbay, leaving her coffee still steaming.

Inside, the scene was not what she had expected. Morgan and Iezzi, dressed in dungarees and t-shirts instead of armor, were watching Kane get suited up. Ana was surprised to see that this turned out to be not only a one-man task, but something a one-legged man could handle on his own as well. Somehow, she had expected a squire to be required, like a knight of old, but the Imperial Panzer Suits were considerably more versatile, opening at seams and closing around the wearer like a new metal skin.

She only caught the briefest glimpse of Kane before his suit sealed entirely, but he looked normal enough. His expression was fairly intense, but then it usually was. She pulled out her tablet and checked the readings again to find them completely dead.

"Chief?" she asked. "What happened to my biomonitor?"

"Took it off," he said through the speaker in his suit. "Where's Ed?"

Ana looked hesitantly at the other two men. Iezzi, still smelling of cloves and marker, shrugged and raised both eyebrows. "He's mad 'cause Morgan drew a dick on his head."

"I fucking did *not!*" Morgan shouted. "Iezzi did it, Chief! I had the shaving cream and I didn't even get to use it!"

"Secure that shit!" Kane growled. "Play time is over. How are Zimmerman and Anderson?"

Without the biomonitor Ana couldn't be certain, but she had a strong intuition that whatever had set Kane's blood pressure spiking was still a problem. "I treated Anderson for broken ribs and shrapnel and Zimmerman for a severed arm. They're both recovering in the aft crew quarters. Now listen: I had a biomonitor emergency on you not thirty seconds ago. Give me a few minutes to check you over, ok? Let's be safe."

Kane waved a hand in dismissal. "Gunther says I'm fine. Where are Caldwell and Martin?"

"Martin's in his rack," Morgan said. He gave Iezzi a questioning look, and Iezzi shrugged. "I ain't seen Caldwell since the fight."

Iezzi shrugged. "He might not have made it onboard."

For several long moments, Kane stood in ominous silence.

Ana was just about to try again when he spoke. "Morgan, start a search. Iezzi, hit the aft gear locker. I want a full inventory of our equipment."

Iezzi's face fell. "Seriously?"

"That's an *order*, Iezzi!" He pointed toward the door. "Move it, both of you!"

Ana stood in silence as the two marines departed. Kane, his face invisible behind his visor, stared down at her, and she felt a sudden chill. He could literally tear her limb from limb if that was what he had in mind, and there would be no Avalon as a fallback this time.

"What do you have in mind, Chief?" she asked.

"Work," he answered, and pushed past her to the door. As it slid open, he turned back and said, "You want some advice, doc? Lock this door and don't open it again until Ed tells you it's ok."

Ana stammered briefly. "What's going on?"

"Lock the door, doc. Do it now."

Ed's eyes could see well enough in the dark of the engine room, but he found the small flashlight he had borrowed from Bleys helped, nonetheless.

Captain Bleys would likely object to Ed being in his engine room, and while Ed would have obliged any requests to stay out, no such request had been made and likely wouldn't be unless Ed were foolish enough to be caught snooping.

The smuggler had quite an interesting setup. His disguises were very well done, and likely no one would have recognized the jump drives, save someone who had actually built them. The one on Bleys's ship was of fine quality and likely cost him a great deal, but oddly enough it was not connected, a fact they Ed found puzzling. Why would one have a jump drive that was not actually operational?

Ed filed the question away for later. This CPU could only handle a few thought threads at once, and right now another was of much higher priority. As a matter of fact, the disconnected jump drive was only the second most interesting thing in the engine room.

Even as Ed pushed thoughts of the jump drive aside, another train of thought intruded, this one an awareness of an entity calling itself Gunther trying to establish an encrypted communications channel from within the ship itself. Ed accepted Gunther's encryption keys and set up a secure voice channel.

"Kane," he said through his restored wireless connection. "I hope you're not angry with me."

"We have a problem," Kane answered. "The Pestilence is onboard, and you're the only person I know who can be trusted."

"What makes you certain the Pestilence is here with us?" Ed asked as he played his flashlight over a trail of blood that ran along the deck. The droplets seemed to terminate beneath a large section of ductwork.

"Iezzi is on the *Doro*," Kane answered.

Ed followed the droplets and looked beneath the ducts. "And why does that mean the Pestilence is aboard the ship?"

"Because Iezzi is *dead*. You killed him right out of the gate, blasted him into the pigpen with a rocket. I watched him go dark on my biomonitors."

Ed pulled at a loose panel beneath the duct, noting that it appeared to have been recently bent. It took more than human strength to bend back out again to expose the space behind it. The metal squealed in protest as he pulled. "Then I think we can assume you are not infected. The entity within Ana actually prevented her from reporting its presence, and I assume, were you infected, it would do the same with you. Are you protected?"

"I'm armored up and sealed against CBR. I don't know about anybody else, though."

"I would advise you to remain that way. I presume you haven't spoken to anyone else about this?"

"Negative. OPSEC is good."

"Keep it that way. You're missing a man, yes? Caldwell?"

"How did you know that?" Kane asked.

Ed ran the flashlight over the Panzer suit crammed into the space behind the panel. Blood and bits of flesh streaked the shattered visor and breastplate, but the name Caldwell was clearly visible beneath the gore.

"Because I believe I have just found him." Ed paused, then added, "What's left of him, at any rate."

Nolan Garrett is Cerberus. A government assassin, tasked with fixing the galaxy's darkest, ugliest problems.

GET INTERSTELLAR GUNRUNNER NOW!

When their mission fails, his begins.

GET EDGE OF VALOR TODAY!

"Aliens, agents, and espionage abound in this Cold War-era alternate history adventure... A wild ride!"—Dennis E. Taylor, bestselling author of *We Are Legion (We Are Bob)*

GET THE LUNA MISSILE CRISIS NOW!

Someone betrayed him. He'll probably die finding out who.

GET SUPREMACY'S SHADOW NOW!

For all our Sci-Fi books, visit our website.